The Alpha Prince
Kingdom of Askara, Book Three

By Victoria Sue

Copyright © 2022 by Victoria Sue

All rights reserved.

No part of this book may be reproduced in any form or by any electronic or mechanical means, including information storage and retrieval systems, without written permission from the author, except for the use of brief quotations in a book review.

Formatting by Tammy, Aspen Tree E.A.S.

Contents

Prologue	1
Chapter 1	5
Chapter 2	13
Chapter 3	20
Chapter 4	31
Chapter 5	39
Chapter 6	46
Chapter 7	67
Chapter 8	87
Chapter 9	94
Chapter 10	104
Chapter 11	115
Chapter 12	124
Chapter 13	131
Chapter 14	142
Chapter 15	151
Chapter 16	159
Chapter 17	167
Chapter 18	177
Chapter 19	187
Chapter 20	195
Chapter 21	204
Chapter 22	214
Epilogue	224
Also by Victoria Sue	229
About Victoria Sue	233

To Meredith:
Because you gave me what you believe in – Justice.

ASKARA

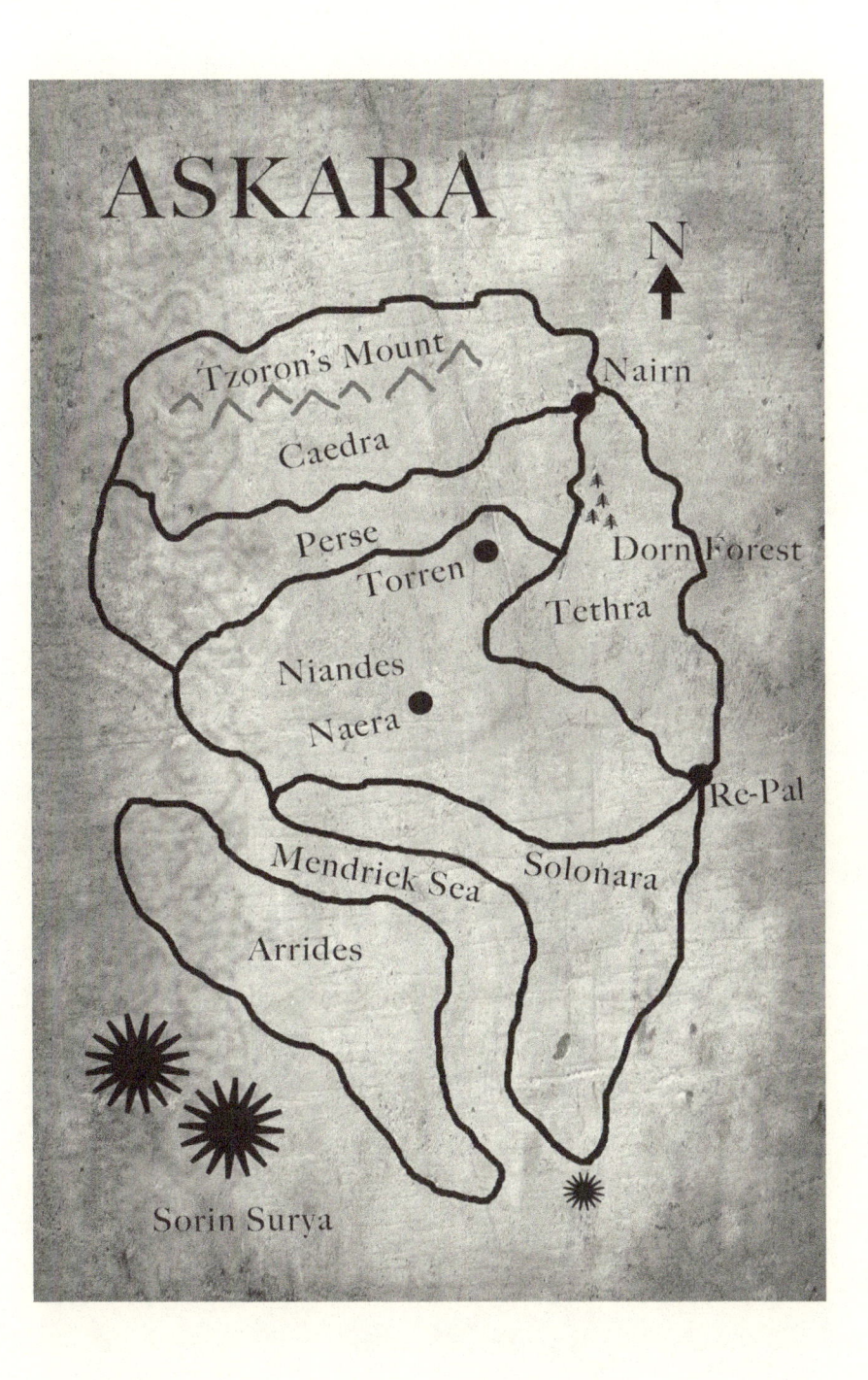

N ↑

- Tzoron's Mount
- Caedra
- Nairn
- Perse
- Torren
- Dorn Forest
- Tethra
- Niandes
- Naera
- Re-Pal
- Mendrick Sea
- Solonara
- Arrides
- Sorin Surya

Prologue

"It is time, Son."

Justice looked up. His mom stood at the entrance to the tent, a heartbroken expression on her face.

It was time. Time for him to say goodbye to his father, and to become the Alpha his people needed. He met his mother's sad brown eyes and for a second—a split second—panicked that he wasn't ready, that he needed more time...that he would never be even half the Alpha his father had been.

Then, just as the breeze rippled over the sands, he heard the whispers in his mind. Thoughts, feelings. Great sadness. But also, calm acceptance and trust. It was his pack. His father had always said he would hear them when he was ready. It was the mark of a true Alpha. Knowing they trusted him when he doubted himself gave him the courage to follow his mom inside.

His father lay on a pallet, his face pale. He lifted a shaky hand to Justice as he approached, and Justice had to press his lips together to stop a cry from erupting.

Justice sank down and clasped his father's frail hand. He had been bitten by an Ekali spider only two days ago, and while in a young wolf the shift would have been able to save his life, the venom of the spider was always fatal to an older one.

Justice pressed his father's hand to his lips and choked back a sob. "Father."

"Hush, Son," his father rasped with difficulty. "I haven't much time and I need you to listen carefully."

Justice nodded. *Anything.*

"Our people are dying. The wells are running dry, and Arrides no longer sustains us."

Justice squeezed his father's hand in agreement. He knew—and so did all their people. They had been forced to move their settlement too many times in the last year to chase their elusive water supplies.

"There is a legend of—" His father coughed and wheezed and for a minute Justice thought he would never be able to catch his breath again. He quickly helped his father take a sip from his water pouch and his father managed to gasp in some air.

"I showed you the caves."

He had. Justice didn't need the reminder. The Alpha had taken him there when he was twenty last year, as had his father before him and his father before that. He knew the secrets of his people.

"But there is something else."

"What?" Justice searched his father's deep amber eyes. His body was dying, but truth shone bright in them.

"When our people are at their most desperate the source will be revealed."

"The source of what?" Justice asked in confusion.

"And our people will be saved..." His father's voice grew weaker and his eyelids slid closed.

"What source?" Justice pressed. "A source of water?" They were getting desperate.

His father opened his eyes, but Justice could see the light in them fading. "I have searched all my life," his father rasped, "and failed. Now, Son, the task is yours."

The Alpha Prince

His father's eyes closed as he took a shallow breath. He never took another one.

Chapter One

Six years later

Cashel could hear the voices floating somewhere above the mist of pain but had no wish to open his eyes.

"Alpha, I am afraid your son's suitor was a little too... *enthusiastic.*"

The scuffling noises accompanying the voice of the healer dragged him higher into consciousness and he instinctively bit back the whimper. *Goddess*, it hurt.

"Are you saying my son doesn't have the *strength* to breed an Alpha?" came a voice Cashel knew all too well. If he had the ability to move he would have cowered instinctively.

"No, but Alpha, his neck is—"

The cut off retort and the choking noises were familiar. Someone had dared to say something Cashel's Alpha—Cashel's *father*—didn't like. Pain throbbed and pulsed. He could feel every bruise, every mark. He turned his head and gasped. Agony flared in his shoulder.

"Cashel?"

Had he not been lying down, the commanding tone would have instantly brought him to his knees. His heart beat frantically, stabbing his chest as if it were trying to pound its way to freedom. He drew on what little strength he had and attempted to open his eyes. To ignore the order would simply lead to more beatings.

"Alpha." Cashel's whisper was barely there. "I have failed you." There, if he said it first his father might not be as—

The slight tutting noise silenced him immediately. He opened his eyes and stared into the almost black eyes staring right back at him. Cashel nearly whimpered again. The fury on his father's face was obvious but for once it didn't engender more paralyzing fear. The overwhelming emotion he felt was sadness because his father wasn't angry that the Alpha-heir had brutalized him and nearly ripped him apart; he was simply angry that the gammas had had to interfere before the wolf got to penetrate him. Cashel wouldn't be impregnated and birth a pup. *An Alpha.* Because Cashel was a failure. Not only wasn't he the Alpha as first born he should have been, but to compound all else he was an *omega*.

"Heal him," his father decreed and swept past the cot he was lying on. With a nod to the healer he had nearly choked, he stepped out of the room, calling to the gammas as he left. The healer shuffled forward warily, and Cashel closed his eyes on the tears that threatened. *Heal me for what?* How many more times would he have to endure? How many days would he wake up in the infirmary before one of them actually killed him? His father promised much to the heir that could make him heavy with pup and many had tried. And each failure he had blamed on the heir publicly and Cashel behind closed doors.

"Cashel?"

Cashel opened his eyes again as Ramon spoke and gazed into the worry-filled brown eyes. "I'm sorry," he whispered again, meaning it this time.

"Hush," Ramon soothed. "Your father's temper is not your fault." Cashel watched in relief as Ramon crushed a small amount of white powder in a dish and poured it into a glass of water.

The Alpha Prince

"More," Cashel begged and Ramon looked up.

"I cannot, Cashel. Your body is not of the size it would need to be to take more, but your father has left with instructions you are to be able to travel tomorrow—"

"Travel?" Cashel interrupted in horror. "I doubt I will be even able to stand."

Cashel lived on the outskirts of Lapis-dar. His father had one of his many pack houses there—one he used to stay at if he was ever visiting Niandes, as Lapis-dar was closer to the border. It was now to all intents and purposes Cashel's prison. All the healers were there, and Cashel had gammas watching his every move. The only thing that kept him sane was his small collection of books.

Ramon smiled gently. "Take this and sleep." Ramon paused. "I would have asked him to let you shift before he left, but I didn't think—"

"No," Cashel interrupted. Shifting into his wolf may heal him instantly, but it wasn't worth the unmanageable pain the change would cause him. He hated his wolf. Hated it with every fiber in his being. "My throat," he rasped. He could imagine what his neck looked like. The heir had thought he could hold him down, and he could still feel the claws biting into it...as if Cashel was strong enough to fight. He was... *pathetic*.

Ramon sighed. "I can imagine how much it hurts, but this will help."

"Where am I going?" Cashel asked as Ramon stepped closer. The wolf wore the traditional gray robes of the healers with the deep gold emblem of Solonara woven into the left shoulder. The exact same as all the gammas wore.

"Tarik-dar."

"Tarik?" Cashel blinked in confusion. Tarik was nearly the size of a city. It had originally been the army base and was where they still trained. The parade grounds were on the massive expanse of dry earth that used to be where the silk cocoons grew, but the Nay'eth flies had infested them and they had been relocated, so now it housed the Alpha's palace. The city that had grown up around the palace and the barracks was huge, but Cashel hadn't been there since he was eight years old.

Ramon glanced at the closed door. "Tarik-*dar*," he emphasized and Cashel nearly rolled his eyes. Last year his father had renamed all the settlements on Solonara. Each name had to have the letters DAR added to it. He had read somewhere that a great Alpha had called his pack house after himself instead of the pack name, and Darius had thought it a splendid idea. It was pathetic until he had heard the first slave forget, and the slave had been nearly sliced in half by Darius's *Kataya* before the poor man had the chance to realize what he had done.

"Why Tarik?" Cashel asked.

"He wants you at the Alpha's compound for the games."

Cashel hated the games. They were originally a way for Darius's gammas to beat the hell out of each other, but they had grown more and more violent with each passing year. Cashel had not attended one since that same fateful day his father had finally admitted his son was never going to become the Alpha he wanted and turned to breeders to produce another pup. Cashel had been promised his own horse by his father, as all heirs on Solonara got their own colt to raise on their eighth birthday. A stallion that would lead them into battle at fifteen. His father was also obsessed with horses, and insisted on only the best. He had paid a lot of money for a breeding mare and they both eagerly awaited the birth. Cashel didn't leave the stable for hours when they noticed the mare was due to labor. His father arrived just as the foal had been born, except it hadn't been the colt they were expecting, but a beautiful mare. His father had lost his temper and immediately said the mare and foal would have to be sold. Cashel had done the unforgiveable and cried. Begged his father to be able to keep the mare, and his father had not only lost his temper with Cashel and hit him, hard, but he had taken a sword and plunged it in the foal.

Cashel had screamed and tried to pull the sword from the foal. He was used to his father's harsh words, but he had never seen such a wanton act of sheer cruelty. He had been soundly beaten by his father and had very quickly learned not to ever argue again. His first beating had seemed to unleash something terrifying in his father, and Cashel spent most of the next two years black and blue.

Another six years passed and his father had fourteen more children, all daughters, from nine different breeders. Cashel had never known his own mom as she had also been a breeder but had died when something had complicated his birth. Then had come the fateful day when Cashel had turned sixteen and had been summoned into his father's presence. That morning, he had entered the cavernous stone hall quietly but as he'd gazed in horror at the bloody floor he had nearly been sick. He could never stand to see anyone hurt or injured but this was a thousand times worse. A young woman lay in a pool of her own blood, her eyes wide open but unseeing. As the gammas went to hoist her up, Cashel would never forget what he saw next.

A baby girl. Clearly newborn, small and still, she lay on the cold stone floor still as death with the same sliced throat as her mother. The gamma picked it up and tossed the body onto that of its dead mother. Cashel took a shaky breath and had only a second to wonder why his mouth tasted so metallic. Then the floor moved and his world tilted abruptly.

When Cashel came to a few minutes later, he realized he had been beaten. And as if that wasn't bad enough, Darius had commanded him to shift for the first time. Omegas were unable to shift without their Alpha giving the command, and his father had never bothered before. Agony like nothing he had ever felt coursed through him as bones broke, some shortening, some elongating. Muscles tore and reshaped, and tendons snapped. He fainted a second time from the pain, only coming around in his human form as what seemed like gallons of water were poured over him. The gammas dragged him upright to hear the torrent of anger and abuse coming from his father. How he had failed him. How he should have died along with his useless mother. Then Darius had commanded the healers take him away and a whole new nightmare had begun.

He would love to say he had forgotten how many times he had been experimented on by yet another crackpot healer that had told his father he could fashion Cashel so he could give birth—but it would be a lie. He remembered every drug induced sleep, every sickening wakefulness, every fresh pain and scar as his insides were altered to be like a she-wolf. He had begged his father to end his torment but Darius had no intention of giving up the territory Alpha role to any other pack, and to stop that from happening he had to breed an Alpha-heir. There were some other smaller packs in Solonara, but every one of them had to swear fealty to Darius and they were barely allowed to govern themselves.

There were old stories. One healer had come from far away with a likeness of the original Alpha King and his omega. The omega had clearly been with pup, and after that his father had been obsessed that Cashel would deliver him one. So far, all Cashel had ever delivered was disappointment.

Ramon un-stoppered the flask he was holding and turned, looking uncomfortable. Cashel frowned. He had been so drowned in memories he had forgotten Ramon's words. "Why are the games so important this year?"

"The Alpha has opened the games up to all competitors."

"All," Cashel repeated woodenly, still unclear what any of it had to do with him.

Ramon sighed and with a firm hand cupped the back of Cashel's neck and lifted him slightly so he could drink the tonic. Cashel gulped it, eagerly welcoming the oblivion for even a short time. He swallowed. "Why has he decided I must go?"

"He has opened the games up to any Alpha-*worthy* competitor."

"What does that even mean?"

"It means that any wolf can enter the games. There will be individual tests of strength. Fights to the death. There will be a day where all the competitors are presented, six full days of fighting, and then on the seventh day the victor will mate you."

Cashel nearly stopped breathing, and it was only Ramon's soothing hand on his shoulder that kept him still. For two years his father had invited all suitable Alpha-heirs to try and impregnate Cashel. As each heir tried and failed, his father raised the bounty and it started becoming not only a test of virility but also a test of worthiness. Each wolf—egged on by his father—was increasingly violent with Cashel. The more dominant the wolf, the more likely he would birth an Alpha. It had nearly killed him last night as Torpeth had half-shifted in an attempt to show dominance and nearly ripped Cashel to shreds.

Ramon waited until his words registered. "He feels that only the strongest wolf will be able to succeed."

Tears pricked at Cashel's eyelids and he moved his head, gasping as fiery pain raked his shoulder. "What did he do?"

He gazed at Ramon knowing full well the old wolf knew what he meant.

"You have scarring," Ramon said flatly.

If Cashel had the strength he would have laughed. "You mean my scars have scars?"

"No, your neck. The heir was attempting the mating bite. It was only because Orindell and Bashell were present and pulled him off that you live." For a second Cashel wondered if that—his death—was the answer, but no—he wasn't there yet. Even after everything he still hoped.

"I still don't see why I have to be there." What did it matter? His father had chosen all his potential mates. Cashel's words slurred a little. He was beginning to feel the pull of the strong drug nearly instantly. Heat ran through his veins to soothe his body, and he longed to lie and simply drift. The pain was ebbing a little and he was tired, desperately tired. He yawned.

"Try and sleep, Cashel," Ramon instructed. "Concentrate on getting well."

So it can happen all over again. What was the point?

Chapter Two

"Don't stare. It encourages them."

Cashel jumped a little at the sound of his father's voice and turned quickly away from the carriage window. He immediately dropped his gaze dutifully at his Alpha's stare. After a second, when he knew his father's attention was back on the document he was reading, he went back to watching. They were currently riding through a village on the outskirts of the palace and it was heartbreaking. The poverty, the filth, the smell...the hopelessness of the humans who stopped to stare. If he had been born the Alpha-heir he was supposed to be, he would have found a way to stop his father's vile treatment of the humans, but being an omega didn't even give him the power over his own body, let alone that of any others.

They were in his father's carriage travelling to the games. Tarik-dar was about three hundred miles west of Lapis-dar. Cashel had barely recovered from his injuries of a few weeks ago and was now exhausted by the stress of being in Darius's presence, watching his every word in case he said something to cause anger. His father had been visiting one of his silk farms and he had collected Cashel on the way through.

"It will be a good turnout tomorrow," his father continued without looking at him, and Cashel's breathing quickened a little. Was he supposed to reply? Keep silent? Any wrong decision would immediately earn his father's displeasure and could quite easily escalate into a beating.

His father sighed and looked at Cashel. "Even if my choice of your mate has little to do with you, you could express gratitude I am going to the trouble of selecting the strongest wolf."

But not the kindest. Someone who would be just like his father. Constant discipline and constant criticism.

And then what about the pup? If he did manage to ever have one he wanted some say in how it would be brought up. Their world had enough monsters without him creating another one. Cashel murmured something indiscernible and his heart sank. It was futile. The pup would be given straight to the human wet nurses as he had. He would be lucky to ever see it again, and his heart ached with the helplessness and the futility of it all.

He heard a growl and glanced out of the window. The gammas were surrounding the carriage, some riding horses, some fully shifted wolves prowling ahead. Snarling and snapping at any unfortunate human that got near. Not that that was likely to happen. People scurried inside as they spied the procession. There was no human that dared linger or stare at the coach.

Cashel opened his mouth in a silent gasp as he saw a child shuffle by, carrying a bucket that was too heavy. But his shock wasn't from the weight. The little boy was no more than nine or ten, but the hands he grasped his burden with were clumsy because most of his fingers were missing. He was filthy. Thin, bare arms and legs, and the rags that hung from him were nothing against the chill of the early morning. He watched as the child struggled to keep the bucket steady and not lose any of the precious water he had dragged from the well.

It may be cold this early in the day, but the summer drought in Solonara was fierce. Water was more precious than gold.

He watched as the child suddenly stopped and lifted a surprised face to the sky at the same time as Cashel heard the tiny patter on the carriage roof. It was raining. Cashel gazed at the clouds that had formed so quickly. It was a common sight in Lapis, but very rare here.

"It's raining?" his father murmured and put down his papers in surprise as he too looked out of the window. But not at the little boy. The poor were invisible to his father.

Cashel just saw the little boy raise his arms to the sky in complete wonder before the carriage turned a corner and he was out of sight. There was nothing he could do to help any of these children, except dream of the day when Darius was no longer Alpha, and wonder if he would manage to survive that long to even see it.

He turned from the window quickly as he heard his father move. "I am hosting a banquet tonight for all competitors. I require you to be there and presentable."

Not by even the flicker of one eyelash did Cashel show his disappointment. He was still healing and even though his injuries had mended, Cashel was exhausted. Ramon had given him more tonic in the end and despite his father wanting him to travel the next day, that had to be delayed. Cashel was actually quite surprised his father hadn't made him shift—even if that was the last thing Cashel wanted; it wasn't like his father to tolerate any sort of delays. Without shifting, his long sleep was necessary to heal his injuries, but that meant he was unable to eat as he should and drink the special tonic he had to take for the rest of his life—ever since the healers had first started altering him.

Cashel snuck another look at his father because the Alpha was still busy with the documents his secretary had given him. No one dared to look at Darius in the eye. Cashel had known humans put to death for doing that, and no wolf would show such disrespect. His father was a huge man, like so many Alphas, and Cashel supposed he was deemed good looking to those who didn't see the contempt that curled his lip or the coldness that deadened his black eyes.

"How many competitors are there?" Cashel dared to ask.

"I had seven Alphas from Solonara and Niandes put forward their heirs or second sons." That made sense. Second sons would only ever be Alpha if something happened to their elder brother and that brother didn't have an heir of his own, while the heirs were those from small packs interested in a territorial leader's pack, and willing to renounce their own. "But as it is open to all challengers we are expecting many to present themselves tonight."

At the banquet, thought Cashel just as the carriage started to slow. He glanced to the side to see the red sands as they were called, where the silk worms had once been produced, and was now a barren wasteland that nothing ever grew on. He heard the order shouted for the gates to open.

The huge outdoor arena was in the center of what nearly amounted to an entire village itself. The gammas lived and trained in the barracks surrounding the arena but there were so many other workshops and slaves to cater to everything an army would need. Food, meat especially. And Darius owned the surrounding farms and slaughter houses. Leather for horses, clothes and furniture. Wood the workers used for everything from simple stools to barrels of ale. The smithies that fashioned the weapons. Then the ale itself. Darius owned a huge brewery near Varikdar and while Tethra supplied the wine, there were many other drinks the wolves favored. Then the human slaves to make sure everything worked exactly as the Alpha would wish. Thousands of them.

The carriage rolled to a stop and the door opened. "Alpha," the wolf intoned respectfully. Cashel wasn't addressed or even looked at, not that he wanted Gaven's eyes on him at all. The beta was Darius's wolf through and through, and had often been present when the latest healer had arrived at Lapis. Darius acknowledged his beta with a tip of his head and handed over the leather folder containing the documents he had been perusing in the carriage. The beta tucked it under his arm and stepped back to let his Alpha get out. Cashel watched as they both stepped away, neither wolf even looking in his direction.

"Cashel?" An older wolf wearing healer robes stepped forward to the open door. "If you would come with me, please. The Alpha wants you prepared for this evening."

Cashel hid the sigh, knowing any other wolf who was the son of the Alpha would never be addressed by his first name, and obediently stepped out of the carriage and looked around as many people hurried past. Surya shone brightly even though for Solonara it was a cool day. He knew what amounted to a cool day in Solonara was the equivalent to the height of summer in the northern territories. Not that he would ever get to find out.

Sorin shone weakly to the left. The sun never as bright or as warm as her sister, and at nearly midday the two suns had already separated. The noise hit him first. The bustle of shopkeepers in the busy market barely a few feet away from the building he was being shown. Then the smells. He inhaled the aroma of freshly baked bread, and the spicy lamb paste that was often smothered on top. He couldn't remember the last time he tasted that. He couldn't remember the last time he had been hungry at all.

"Cashel," the wolf repeated, clearly not in favor of Cashel gazing at the heavens. Cashel ducked his head immediately and cursed silently. The wolf would never dare lay a finger on him as his father's son, but it was too heavily ingrained in Cashel not to obey every order of the Alpha no matter who spoke it.

Cashel followed the wolf to the nearest stone building, ignoring the stares of both gammas and slaves alike. They probably wondered who he was – no, of course they knew. The whole games were because he was such a failure. He had hoped Ramon might accompany him, but his father wouldn't allow it after Ramon had thought to question Darius, even a little. There seemed to be hundreds of people looking, some even coming close enough to bar his way. The fact that they were even attempting to without any fear of reprisal was humiliating.

Cashel kept his head down and stepped inside the building the wolf had vanished into. Cashel walked up the first flight of steps and turned the corner to be faced with another. Heavy footsteps from above made him tip his head back and he quickly pressed himself near to the wall as a group of ten huge gammas ran down them. None of them stopping, none of them even acknowledging him. If he had been his father, they would have waited respectfully.

But he wasn't.

Cashel drew a few breaths in as he got to the top. He was a little dizzy from the exertion, still weak from the injury and blood loss. He knew it would take his body three or four more days before he was back to full strength.

He followed the wolf into a medical bay. Cashel stiffened in alarm. "Why am I here?"

"Merely an adjoining room, Cashel. In case we need it later," the wolf explained rather ominously and gestured to a closed door. "Your rooms are in there. There is food and drink already prepared, and pleasure-slaves ready to bathe and prepare you."

Pleasure-slaves? How Cashel kept in the shiver of revulsion was beyond him. This had been his father's latest idea—using pleasure-slaves to encourage his body to be more receptive before the Alpha-heir bedded him. It had been an embarrassment. The girls had been convinced it had been them getting him hard when in fact he was thinking of the swordsmith he had seen talking to one of the gammas that morning. He had been gorgeous. Smooth pale skin and deep brown eyes. A couple of inches taller than Cashel, if that. Slim, toned body. Not the huge monsters that usually made up the ranks of the gammas or the heirs. He didn't think that wolf would have been able to hurt him. Cashel paused as he realized what he had said. *Able* to hurt him? Was that how bad it had gotten? That he thought in terms of who was going to hurt him, not that anyone might not want to in the first place?

He took the proffered glass from the healer containing his tonic. The daily strengthening herbs and meat extract he had to take because his own stomach was no longer able to tolerate the real thing. He drank it down automatically as the closed door opened and two female slaves entered.

"He has to rest for an hour, then be fed and bathed. You have your instructions." The wolf waved the slaves off. Cashel set the glass down and glanced at the wolf who had dismissed him. He didn't even know his name.

"My prince?"

The small pixie smiled invitingly and held out a hand. *Prince?* Cashel took it gratefully and with some amusement. The wolf had shown him no respect but this little sweetheart was treating him like royalty. It was going to be a strange day.

Chapter Three

"**Y**ou could have slit his throat and no one would have stopped you."

Justice didn't respond to Armand's shocked whisper. He was too stunned by what he had just witnessed. The Alpha-heir had accompanied Darius and Darius had just abandoned his son in the open street with not a single gamma to protect him. The wolf who had spoken to him had scolded him like a child and the gammas had noticed Darius's behavior—some blocking Cashel's path deliberately to taunt him.

"He's certainly an easy target," Zane murmured quietly. Zane nodded towards the doors Cashel had disappeared into.

Justice turned to Zane as he felt the ripple of his wolf just below his skin. He took a deep breath. What the hell was wrong with his animal? They had shifted and run in the early hours as they had camped just outside the city, one of them staying with the horses.

He felt a warm breath on the nape of his neck and turned to idly scratch under his stallion Kashir's ear, just where he liked it the most. Kashir had taken a step towards him; even though he was free, the stallion wouldn't move from Justice's side. The two horses that they had bought in Salem for Zack and Armand had to be tethered.

"It's odd," Justice allowed at last, feeling some response was needed.

Armand glanced at him. "I believe the word is fortuitous, Alpha."

Is it? Justice couldn't help feeling mildly offended for the wolf. He knew Cashel was an omega by all accounts, which was the reason for the games. He was submissive in a lot of respects, but only to his Alpha, not everyone else. The heir had looked *terrified*...although why that was bothering Justice was completely beyond him. The heir would soon be dead along with his no-good father. Maybe he was doing him a favor. He certainly hadn't looked happy.

Cashel opened his eyes groggily. Where was he? He blinked heavy eyelids and focused on silk drapes. *Drapes?* He swallowed down a dry throat and turned his head to the side hoping for a glass of water.

"My prince?" Cashel blinked his eyes and looked to the side. The young girl he remembered from earlier was kneeling by the bed, head bowed. She was holding a goblet that Cashel hoped contained water. He sat up and had to clutch the sheet he was lying on while the room spun. He swallowed sickly and nearly growled in frustration. The tonic had obviously contained something to make him sleep. He glanced down, realizing he was naked, and his face heated as he said a silent prayer that she had not been the one to undress him.

"Water?" he croaked, and the girl nodded eagerly. Cashel extended his hand and she stood in a graceful fluid movement. He took the cup and sniffed cautiously.

"It is simply water, my prince." Cashel looked up at the sound of another voice. Another human female, but older. As he registered the fine lines at the side of her eyes and the gray streaks in the dark brown hair pulled tightly back off her face, he would have hazarded a guess that she was maybe twenty years older than him. He could be wrong though, and she was certainly still a stunningly beautiful woman. The young girl with the water was fourteen—fifteen, at most—he supposed. Cashel shrugged and tipped the goblet to his lips. It would make no sense sedating him as he knew he had to prepare for tonight. The cool water flowed down his throat but he stopped drinking very quickly. Even water made him sick if he drank it too fast.

"Do you feel rested?" The question startled Cashel and he was at a loss to reply. Why would she even care?

"Better, thank you."

"We have food all prepared, my prince." She continued stepping forward and Cashel saw she was holding a robe. He opened his mouth to ask why she was calling him *Prince* and then snapped it shut just as quickly. His father. It must be an order from his father. Why, he had no idea, but he certainly couldn't ask someone who was simply following orders. She shielded him as he stood warily and tugged the silk robe around him, shivering slightly.

"You are cold?" Her eyebrows lifted in surprise, and before Cashel could move a step she pulled the throw from the bed and draped it around his shoulders. Cashel opened his mouth to thank her again, but she carried on. "I will instruct the slaves to make sure there are fires lit while you are here."

"Thank you...?"

"Helena," she smiled.

"Thank you, Helena," Cashel repeated.

"Would you prefer to eat or bathe first, my prince?"

Cashel felt grubby from the carriage ride, and even though he resented the choice of whether to sleep or not being taken from him, the rest had helped. "Bathe, please."

Helena bowed again and clapped her hands once. The door opened and a stream of young girls hurried in. Cashel tried not to roll his eyes. He didn't mind them being there—privacy was something he had lost a long time ago—but he would bathe himself no matter what order his father had given.

Cashel allowed himself to be pulled into the next room and smiled as he saw the huge bathing pool. Fragrant steam rose from its inviting water and steps led down into it.

He turned to thank Helena once again only to quickly glance away as she disrobed. "No," he said quickly. "Please stop."

Helena stopped in astonishment just as she was about to step out of her dress. She flushed and quickly pulled it back up. "Of course, my prince. Perhaps Bella or Sara would be more to your taste?" The young girl and what seemed like an even younger one obediently stepped forward. "Bella is very skilled in massage," she added. Cashel felt sick. That children were offered up as pleasure-slaves without any thought was wrong.

"I would prefer to bathe myself, Helena," Cashel explained. "It has been a long day and I wish to gather my thoughts in preparation for tonight." Cashel trotted out the excuse as confidently as he could.

She paused and then bowed gracefully, beckoning everyone to leave. At the last second she gave Cashel an assessing look, but turned and closed the door before he could wonder what it meant.

Cashel groaned as, after disrobing, he took the first step into the warm water. It really was fabulous, even though he had no idea what it represented. He had seen the opulent rooms in his father's pack house as a child. The bathing room there was twice as big and his father owned many pleasure-slaves, all female. He had never even asked Cashel if he preferred the company of males or females. It wouldn't have mattered anyway because it had to be a male to impregnate him.

Maybe that was why his father had sent the female pleasure-slaves. He was assuming Cashel would be more relaxed and receptive with them. His father had never allowed Cashel any special treatment before. He lived in a plain room in the back of the pack house, and read as many books as he could get his hands on. He had been taught to read but nothing else. All his other knowledge had been self-taught after his father had washed his hands of him when his omega nature started to surface. He had been happy though. He had friends amongst the slaves and some of the lowliest gammas so long as he was never anywhere his father was.

"My prince."

Cashel started from his memories and looked to the door. Helena stood with a man. He was tall but human, thank goodness. Young, lightly muscled. His chest was bare and Cashel's mouth suddenly felt dry as he stared at the rings pierced through each nipple. The silver gleamed starkly against the black of the man's skin, and was quite breathtaking. He had shaved black hair tight to his scalp, and the deepest green eyes Cashel had ever seen. He clasped his hands tight so he wouldn't fidget. Helena smiled. "Would Axel be more suitable to help you dress, my prince?"

Cashel was speechless. How had she known? His disgust at Bella and Sara had been because of their age, not simply because they were female. He contemplated Helena slowly. Her dark brown hair was tied neatly in a knot at the back of her head, and her deep brown eyes were framed by big thick lashes. She was stunning, and for a human slave she had a grace about her that was surprising. He also had an inkling she understood his objection to the girls' ages, and had a feeling she didn't miss much. He stood as if making a decision and Helena stepped back bowing her head, as Axel stepped forward with a huge robe. Within seconds he was wrapped up and being guided to a chair. Axel stepped to the side quietly as three young serving girls all hurried forward. One holding a skin of wine which she poured into a goblet before Cashel had the chance to decline. Two holding amazing platters of sliced meat – chicken, beef, spiced lamb. Cashel's mouth watered. He had been given such simple fare for so long. Years in seclusion forgotten about, and then only what his stomach could tolerate.

His stomach growled a little and he gazed longingly at the lamb. It had been his favorite meat as a young child but he hadn't eaten it for years. He picked up some bread and the special wafer-thin flat pieces specially made for scooping up the lamb mixture and other spicy pastes loved in Solonara, then took a napkin. The girl waited obediently while he dipped the bread in the lamb and scooped a little up.

The flavors burst on his tongue and he couldn't help the moan of sheer delight. He closed his eyes. The flat bread was crunchy but not hard to chew. He swallowed carefully and waited a few seconds, eating slowly as he had been taught. As he opened his eyes he saw Helena looking at him almost puzzled. Her face slid into a polite mask.

"Some wine, my prince?"

Why not? The healers had always cautioned him against alcohol but surely one glass wasn't going to hurt? Cashel was almost giddy at his treatment. He still thought the term prince was a little excessive but then his father had always fancied himself royalty, so he guessed it made some kind of warped sense. Cashel took the goblet and sipped. He immediately wrinkled his nose at the dry taste and looked down. It was white and quite bitter. Helena gestured to the serving girl to bring a different skin, and a glass of what Cashel could see as red was poured into another goblet and offered over.

"Thank you," he said quietly and reached for the goblet. "What is your name?"

The young girl offering the wine started at the question and looked up in shock. Her hand jerked just as Cashel clasped the wine and some spilled onto his fingers. Immediately the young girl fell prostrate to the floor, her face pressed into the stone. Helena drew a hissed breath in.

"My apologies—" Helena hurried to speak.

"Nonsense." Cashel smiled and wiped his hand on his robe. "It was my fault." He looked at the girl still with her face pressed to the floor. He could see her shoulders shaking. "Please get up." He glanced enquiringly at Helena, who was staring at him like he had two heads.

"Orelle."

"Orelle," Cashel repeated and looked at the small girl who cautiously raised her head. He smiled again and took a sip of the wine. *Wow*. He just managed not to cough as the liquid seemed to burn his throat.

"It is one of the Alpha's favorites," Helena rushed to explain. "But we have many more if that is not to your taste."

Cashel took another sip but this time he could taste the faint spice and realized the wine was warmed, which surprised him. Now he'd gotten over his initial shock, Cashel thought it was actually quite pleasant and sipped slowly. His stomach seemed to be tolerating it anyway. He finished the bread and the lamb but regretfully declined the rest. Axel filled his glass, which Cashel seemed to have emptied. "My prince, if you are finished, Axel would help you ready yourself and I will lay out some clothing choices for you."

Cashel nodded and stood, passing the goblet to Axel who extended his hand for it.

Two hours later Cashel was simply floating. He had had scented oil massaged into his skin. Shaved, and his long dark brown hair brushed until it had shone, and then patiently woven into small braids and beaded. All the time Axel had kept his goblet full and Cashel, completely unused to such treatment, had let it carry him away. He had even struggled to stand still while he emptied his bladder before he had lain down on the padded table.

"My prince, if you could roll on your back?"

Axel had thoroughly massaged every part of his back and ass until lying on his front was becoming not just uncomfortable but downright painful. Cashel almost giggled. He couldn't remember the last time he had even woken up with an erection—certainly not since the healers had gotten their hands on him—and he certainly had never had anyone else's hands on his cock except his own. None of the wolves attempting to mate and impregnate him ever thought about Cashel's own pleasure.

He moved gingerly, Axel holding the towel to cover him, then starting on his front. Cashel was helpless to bite back the moan as

Axel's deft fingers brushed over his nipples, and his cock throbbed. A second later Cashel opened his eyes, startled, as he felt Axel's warm lips close over the hardening nub. "Axel," he gasped but Axel ignored him and Cashel felt him reaching under the towel. *Goddess.* The first brush of Axel's lubed finger drew a mixed groan and cry from Cashel the likes of which he had never heard from his own throat. Cashel's mind swam from both the unexpected pleasure and, he was sure, the wine—because he had lost count of how many times Axel had refilled his goblet. Cashel's lips parted, feeling the tingling in his spine and his balls draw up tight to his body. "Axel," he repeated helplessly. He was going to come. Axel's talented fingers slipped into his hole and back out.

Sudden pressure on his cock staved off his orgasm and Cashel felt an almost painful tightening around it and something cold against his entrance.

He jerked as suddenly his ass was breached by something much bigger than fingers. "What are you doing?" He tried to lift up but large hands clamped him to the bed. *Gammas.* Two of them, effortlessly holding him down. His ass burned and his cock hurt. He had been hard to the point of nearly exploding but—he peered down. A brown leather ring lay nestled at the base of his cock with straps disappearing and fastened to what was currently in his ass.

"Stop being such a baby."

It was Gaven. The beta-commander had entered the room quietly. The sneer on his face was as obvious as Helena's discomfort as she stood next to him. Cashel closed his eyes as he felt the heat rush to his face. The ring was tightened to the point of discomfort.

"What are you doing?" Cashel ground out, determined the tears pricking at his eyelids would not fall and round off his humiliation.

"As your Alpha decrees," Gaven replied succinctly. "He has been advised the mating may be more successful if you are suitably prepared." Cashel's eyes popped open.

"In seven days," he almost screeched. He was to be kept like this for the seven days the games would last?

Gaven didn't bother with a reply. "You are required in the great hall immediately." The beta turned on the heel of his leather boots, but paused as Helena quietly bowed in front of him.

"Perhaps his slave could take it off after the presentation?"

Cashel was stunned. For a slave to question an order was unheard of, but Gaven stared at Helena for barely a second, grunted in acquiescence and stalked out of the room.

Cashel swallowed down both his surprise and his shame. One of the gammas simply bent down and lifted him up and onto his feet. Cashel swayed and the other gamma clutched his arm. Axel held out the robe and Cashel looked at his dark green eyes brimming with apology. It wasn't his fault. Axel had been following orders the same as he had been doing. Resentment flared through him and he tightened his grip on the gamma's arm. The only time he had felt pleasure. The only time he had felt the soothing touch of another human for years, and it had been ruined.

He ignored the robe and held out his hand. "The wine," he ordered. He even left off the *please* which he would never do.

Axel blinked his eyes in surprise but quickly passed it over. Cashel tipped the entire contents down his throat and felt quite triumphant when he handed the empty goblet back without choking. His father wanted to show him off. The elaborate preparation wasn't for Cashel's benefit despite what Gaven might have said. He knew his Alpha. Darius didn't care about anyone else whatsoever and he was merely being pimped out as some prize. He turned and took a step towards the bed where his clothes had been left out and stopped, just biting down on a groan before it escaped. The thing in his ass pressed in when he moved. Cashel was rock hard but the added stimulation was incredible.

One of the gammas snickered. "Del," the other one warned, and put his arm around Cashel's waist. Cashel stared in surprise. A *gamma* was being considerate? They all hated him. No, they all *ignored* him. Gaven, he was sure, found him a tiresome nuisance and encouraged all the other wolves to treat him with derision, and always called him by his first name. If he had been born an Alpha, none of them would dare because his father would have never allowed it. But Gaven had the ear of the Alpha, and they just copied him.

"Walk slowly, my prince," the gamma murmured, and Cashel studied him for a second. He had never seen him before so he must never have worked at any of the other pack houses. His grey hair was shorn tight to his head, and his brown eyes regarded him steadily.

"Thank you," Cashel murmured and gave over a lot of his weight, but even so, every step was torture as they reached the bed. Cashel knew many would find such stimulation pleasurable and he would have done so if it had been intended in that manner. But it was simply another way of control. He knew whatever was in his ass would keep him hard. The ring would keep him from coming. He held his hand out to Axel and Axel passed him more wine.

The gamma holding him up cautioned, "My prince—"

"Cashel." The sound came out slurred and his lips were going numb. He just wished his ass was too.

"Cashel," the gamma acquiesced. "My name is Hale. You are drinking one of the strongest wines Tethra makes. You are expected to walk into the banquet and stay awake for the presentation of the competitors," he added dryly.

Cashel grinned, appreciating the sarcasm. "If I have to wear this, I need something to dull how it feels or I won't be able to walk anywhere."

Hale sighed. "Then please sip water as well?"

Cashel snorted out a laugh. It was an excellent suggestion but his cock wasn't going to make any attempt to empty his bladder easy when it was pointing the wrong way.

Hale chuckled in sympathy and stood holding him while Axel quickly dressed him. Cashel just let Axel lift whichever of his limbs he needed until Cashel was dressed in long white colored silk flowing pants. A red sash was tied to his waist—his father's colors—and he looked expectantly at the bed for a shirt or a tunic. Axel stood back looking pleased.

"My shirt?" Cashel asked.

"This is all you are commanded to wear, my prince," Axel replied respectfully. Cashel sighed. He would freeze. "Then make sure the wine is warm because I'm going to need it."

Chapter Four

At least he was sitting down now. He had dutifully stood next to his father while the other Alphas from Solonara had all presented themselves, and he would have been blind not to miss the stares. He had thought his pants would cover him, but he soon realized the gossamer thin silk was see-through. His trussed-up cock was on full view for everyone to see. There had been two Alpha-heirs and five second sons. There had also been a beta-commander now that the challenge had been opened up. Cashel had been too fuzzy to take notice of many names, but he remembered the beta-commander Malcolm from Alpha Tarrant's pack. The beta was huge. Had to be at least fifty, and Cashel didn't think the wolf's enormous belly would mean he could have gotten anywhere near Cashel to impregnate him. His favorite was Bryan. The second son from a pack close to the border with Tethra. Of them all he seemed the kindest, but he was also the quietest and Cashel doubted he would be able to beat Malcolm in any sort of fight.

Cashel desperately wanted to close his eyes. He should have heeded Hale's words, and even though he had dutifully sipped water he had drunk far too much wine. Axel and Hale had helped him to the bathroom before the presentations had started and the wine had sloshed sickly in his belly. Hale had even dared risk his Alpha's wrath and requested if he could get him a shirt because he had been shivering on and off for some time. Darius had denied it of course. Axel had taken his cock ring off twice so far as the presentations had seemed endless and Cashel had nearly whimpered in relief. The last time, Hale had stopped Axel putting it back on, and even the threat of Darius's wrath hadn't seemed to faze the gamma.

Now Cashel was simply exhausted. His eyes kept drooping shut and Axel kept discreetly nudging him when they didn't immediately open.

A strident voice had him focusing on the line in front of his father. He had lost count of the number of wolves who had stepped forward to take part in the games. The presentations seemed to have been going on for hours, but at least he didn't feel cold anymore. Just numb.

"Cashel." He looked at the man who stood in front of his father and blinked in resignation. It was Vijay. A beta from Lapis who had ruled the little village like he was the Alpha King himself. He should not be surprised to find he was a competitor. His father hadn't objected when Vijay had used his first name either.

"Vijay," he acknowledged and the big man leered. How Cashel kept his revulsion in check he had no idea. The humans were in fear of him, but not because he was a wolf; Vijay Reyelle was a totally different kind of predator. Blackmail was a favorite, or threats. He would promise the murder or rape of a daughter or a mother or a sister until whichever young boy he fancied came to him on his knees, and then usually stayed that way. He ruled the gammas absolutely and for some reason was trusted by both Gaven and his father, which meant that Cashel or anyone else was helpless to interfere.

Cashel used to sneak out occasionally and visit the smith in the village. He still adored horses and he found it soothing to hide and watch the gammas bringing them in to have their hooves trimmed and shaped. One such day, just over two years ago, old Cazick had been summoned to see a lame horse, and there was just Jatel, his apprentice, working on some swords. Vijay had brought his horse in to the smith. He had immediately decided he would have Jatel, and threatened the boy that he would accuse his elder brother of conspiring against the Alpha and see his throat slit if Jatel did not come willingly to his bed that night. Cashel had heard every word and stepped out of his hiding place. Vijay hadn't been afraid. Cashel had no power over him, but Cashel knew he was what the beta really wanted.

That night was the only time he had ever had something to thank Gaven for. Vijay's hands were on his ass, his fingers cruelly biting into his skin, and the beta's rancid breath puffing over his skin as he undressed him. Cashel closed his eyes, knowing it was the only thing he could do to protect his friend. He heard a slight sound and looked up to see Jatel advancing on them both and brandishing the small knife the smith kept for trimming the hooves with. The sound of a footfall made Vijay turn around. At the same time, a cry went up from the gammas at the gates—alerting an arrival. Jatel just had a chance to duck behind a pile of straw before he was seen. Vijay never got his cock sucked, since Gaven wanted him to return to Tarik with him.

It was the last time he ever saw Jatel because Gaven had brought with him the healers his father had found, and Cashel never left his room after that. And up to this day it had been the last time he had ever seen Vijay. The beta's eyes narrowed and his eyes travelled up and down Cashel's body. He felt sick, and in that moment knew if Vijay won, he would rather die than spend even one single night in a room with that man. Cashel swallowed and lowered his eyes. He couldn't bear to look at him.

"Alpha." A deep voice boomed out and echoed in the cavernous room. Cashel jerked his head up. It was the last of the competitors, thank the goddess. Cashel widened his eyes as he took in the wolf who stood respectfully in front of his father. It wasn't just the man's voice that gave him pause, though. He was Alpha-big. Large muscles rippled along his legs as he walked in breeches that fit him like a second skin. Cashel shivered involuntary as he gazed at his powerful arms, what they must feel like to have them wrapped...

Cashel put a break on his thoughts. He didn't have any reason to suppose this Alpha wasn't as cruel and unfeeling as all the rest, and a smoky voice wasn't an indication of anything except that Cashel should know better. He wondered where this Alpha was from because, while he wore a loose shirt similar to most of the gammas, there was no sash to indicate his pack colors.

"Your pack?" Gaven intoned loudly. The beta was acting as a master of ceremonies but all replies were addressed to the Alpha.

"Justice," the deep voice resonated loudly, and the beta made a note of it as he had done all the others.

As Cashel stared he saw the wolf turn his head to look at Cashel. They had all gazed at him. Some with barely concealed disgust and some with obvious appreciation of Cashel's semi-nude body on display. Cashel shivered. The deep amber eyes looked at him like he was prey.

His father frowned. "I am not familiar with your pack name. I am assuming you are from the far north? Caedra perhaps?"

Cashel saw the slight shake of the wolf's head as he turned back to address Darius "Actually, my pack is the furthest south."

His father scoffed. "I know every pack in my territory."

"Of course, Alpha," Justice agreed solemnly. "But Solonara merely extends to the Mendrik sea. My pack governs the whole of Arrides."

The gasps that rose around the room were accompanied by the sounds of swords being unsheathed, but his father narrowed his eyes. "Are you expecting me to recognize your claim as territorial Alpha," he sneered, "of a *penal* colony?"

Justice never reacted and that in itself was impressive. How the huge wolf stayed still was beyond Cashel. He knew how proud the Alphas were, and to have someone—especially another Alpha—insult him so must have been unbearable, but Justice appeared unshaken.

Only his eyes changed, their amber depths darkening. He simply turned his head so all could see his mark. The A was clearly readable on his skin, showing his Alpha status. Darius grunted, seeming unconvinced.

"The validity of my claim is surely an issue for another day," Justice continued smoothly, "as I was under the impression that this was an open tournament, and the requirements were superior strength and ability, not pedigree?"

Cashel gaped. He didn't think anyone had ever dared question his father... and lived.

Darius's gaze turned sardonic. "You wish to breed my son?"

Cashel nearly groaned out loud. It was one thing everyone knowing why they were here, it was another thing entirely acknowledging it openly. Cashel's breath caught in his throat as he waited like every other person in the great hall for Justice's reply. The amber eyes flicked to him and settled. Justice seemed to take a long slow breath but Cashel was incapable of doing the same. Even as his lungs burned all he could see was the strong stubble covered jaw, full pink lips curled as if the man found something amusing, and those eyes...

"It would be an honor." The wolf bowed low, his gravelly voice seeming to bathe Cashel in heat. Cashel tried to clear his throat. He heard the servants rush to replenish goblets, conversations restart, his father turn to Gaven and whisper quietly, but it was as if they were happening somewhere else. "My prince?" The deep throaty voice settled over Cashel's skin almost like a caress and he shivered, completely unable to drag his eyes from Justice's gaze. His lips parted —he desperately sought a reply, anything that wouldn't make him sound like an idiot—but just at that moment the slaves appeared with the Hash'da.

Cashel felt every drop of blood drain from his face as the sickly-sweet smell of the bloody animal hearts washed over him. It was a traditional delicacy taken by the wolves before battle. The high amounts of rich animal blood were supposed to give the wolves strength and help them be victorious. In years gone by it had been the hearts of their enemies, in the days when the packs warred amongst each other. He remembered skipping over that particular chapter in the book he had been reading.

Cashel averted his face desperately and tried to breathe through his mouth but his stomach was churning sickly and he clamped his lips shut. He looked around for Axel or Hale, but Hale was talking to another gamma and Axel had stepped over to the table to refill his water goblet.

"My prince?" the wolf repeated again and Cashel had a second to see the glower cross the wolf's features at Cashel's seeming inability to acknowledge him, before he clamped a hand over his mouth and leapt to his feet, rushing from the table to the closest door which luckily led to the garden. He managed to make it as far as the trees before his stomach finally rebelled and he vomited what seemed to be everything he had ingested for the last few days.

Cashel fell to his knees, retching. He took a few harsh gasps in and retched some more. He was going to die and if the wine didn't finish him off he would do it himself. If someone had turned up with a sword right at that moment he would have happily run himself through. So long as he could keep his eyes shut. And of course, the thought of his own blood being spilled made him vomit again. He leaned over, his arms wrapped around his middle, sharp cramps pulling at his insides.

"Cashel?"

Cashel startled a little at the voice and the warm hand on his shoulder. It wasn't Hale or Axel, so he cautiously opened an eye. Then he closed it again immediately.

Why? Why him? Of all people to witness his humiliation it had to be the one Alpha his traitorous body had responded to.

"No," he whimpered.

"No, you're not Cashel?" The rich deep voice rumbled again, this time laced with a little humor.

"It's not funny," he snapped miserably with what seemed to be the last of his energy and he slumped forward.

"Of course not," the wolf—Justice—replied solemnly. "Would you like some water?"

Cashel peered up into the same golden eyes he had first seen only a few moments ago and wondered again about the unusual name. He was going to nod his head but thought better of it. It didn't seem necessary as he was offering him a small leather pouch for him to drink from. It seemed to have been fastened to his belt, but Cashel was too wrung out to wonder what Justice was doing carrying water around when it was plentiful in the compound. His hands shook so violently he nearly dropped it before Justice covered Cashel's hands with his and held it steady.

"Just a little," Justice cautioned.

Cashel took a few sips and then spat it out. He took a few more and swallowed it cautiously, waiting to see if his stomach objected. He heard the sounds of shouting and recognized Hale's voice, knew he'd been missed. He glanced up at Justice, shivering uncontrollably. Justice frowned but immediately pulled his shirt out from his breeches and up and over his head. Cashel had a second to appreciate deep bronzed skin before softness engulfed him as the shirt was pulled over his head. It was huge on him of course, but warm and soft and Cashel clutched at it gratefully.

"Cashel?" Hale ran over, followed by Axel. "My prince, are you well?" Hale glanced at the other wolf.

Cashel nodded and tried to stand but his legs refused to cooperate. Justice simply placed one arm around his waist and gently lifted him to his feet. Cashel swayed and the wolf tightened his grip. Cashel swallowed. "Thank you—"

"Justice."

Cashel tried to pretend he had never heard the name, as the golden eyes glittered with anger, as if he was daring Cashel to question his word.

Cashel blinked stupidly, his brain foggy. It was easier to feign ignorance and he wasn't out to impress anyone. Maybe pretending he had forgotten their earlier meeting would ease his shame at their current one. "Is that what you are or what you are called?"

The stern mouth widened into a smile. "Good question, little prince."

Little? Cashel should have been offended but he felt too wretched to care.

Hale cleared his throat hesitantly. "Alpha?"

The man looked at Hale but Cashel, even muzzy as he still was, knew it was ridiculous to doubt, whatever his father had said. You could practically feel the Alpha pheromones bouncing off the trees. He giggled weakly, and both Hale and the wolf...*Justice* stared down at him. His knees wobbled and he leaned further into the wolf's side. Justice's eyebrow lifted but instead of taking a step away from Cashel, who didn't seem to be able to stand upright no matter how much he tried, he bent and hooked an arm under Cashel's legs and swung him gently into his arms. Cashel's lips parted on a token protest but Justice tilted him into his chest and shushed him gently. "Perhaps it would be expedient if you could lead the way to the prince's chambers?"

"My apologies, Alpha," Hale replied. "Perhaps you would allow me to carry him?"

Cashel felt the wolf shake his head. "He is no burden."

Cashel would have puddled at the words if he wasn't already firmly ensconced in the warmest cocoon he had ever been in. His mind drifted as they started walking, and he breathed in lungsful of the rich woodsy scent either from the wolf that was carrying him, or the shirt he was wrapped in. He smelled wonderful and Cashel was relaxed and nearly asleep until he heard Hale question him again, but his mind was too foggy to work out the words. Cashel felt the second shrug from Justice and sighed a little becoming almost boneless. He felt the warmth of clean breath on his skin as Justice leaned down to hush him once more.

Chapter Five

Sleep hadn't come easily, despite his long day. Justice and Hale had delivered him to the healer that seemed to be on permanent duty outside his rooms, and that had dragged him into consciousness. The disapproval was evident in the healer's voice when Hale tried to explain Cashel may have had some of the strong Tethra wines the territory was famous for. Feeling like a child, he had wanted to curl up somewhere away from the looks and had tried to get out of Justice's arms but the wolf had been too strong. Even the healer had deferred to the Alpha when he simply asked where Cashel's bed was and Justice had gently laid him down on it. He had hushed the healer when the man's voice became strident and full of derision—and bade him go and get some water, Axel a cold compress for his head, and warm blankets for the bed.

Cashel hadn't even realized his head was throbbing until he felt the cool cloth cover his eyes and he sighed in relief. "Thank you," Cashel had whispered.

"You are entirely welcome, little prince."

Cashel hadn't minded the *little* comment then.

He had woken three times, convinced each one he was going to vomit once more but Axel had been there every time with small sips of water and the tonic the healer had insisted he take. He was just lying quietly, listening to Axel's soft snores—he had bade the young man to lie down on top of the giant bed, feeling guilty he had been up tending him—when Helena quietly let herself into the room. Not for the first time he wondered why he didn't merit the privacy of at least a knock but he thought that was a human tradition. Slaves weren't expected to be heard, so they would never dream of waking a sleeping wolf to enter somewhere they were supposed to go.

"My prince?" Helena smiled and Cashel studied her, suddenly wondering if he had seen her before yesterday. She reminded him of someone, or possibly he had seen her years ago when he had last been to the compound. She placed the glass of tonic down on the bedside table and Cashel sighed. He was heartily sick of the stuff. He sat up, squinting when the drapes were pulled aside letting in the morning sun.

"Good morning, Helena," Cashel replied and obediently picked up the glass.

"How are you?"

Cashel glanced at Helena knowing full well she would have been told of his embarrassment last night but there seemed no judgement or ridicule in her words. "I'll live," he quipped. She smiled as Axel grunted and opened a bleary eye. As soon as he focused, he shot out of bed and started stammering an apology.

Cashel interrupted. "You waited on me all through the night and I am very grateful. I told you to sleep there in case I needed any more assistance. Why don't you go get bathed and changed while I drink this?"

Helena nodded as if in agreement and Axel hurried from the room.

There was a knock at the door and Hale stepped in. "Good morning, Cashel."

Cashel pinked a little but there seemed to be no censure from

Hale either, and he relaxed. "The Alpha has requested you join him for breakfast."

Cashel almost inhaled the tonic and nearly dropped the glass he was sipping from. Hale and Helena rushed over to rescue the glass as Cashel choked and gasped for breath. Hale smacked him on the back and Cashel put his hand up for mercy. It was like being thumped by a bear.

"My father wants me to go for breakfast?" he squeaked.

Hale nodded solemnly, but his brown eyes twinkled. Cashel sighed and swung his legs out of bed. Helena pointed to the outfit on the chaise and then left with an admonishment to drink as much water as he could. Cashel watched her leave the room in confusion and glanced at Hale to ask how long she had worked here, but the words died in his throat as he took in the gamma's expression. The only word that fit what he saw was longing. Hale gazed at the closing door behind Helena as if his whole life had just walked out. He blinked and turned to look at Cashel as if realizing only for the first time he was staring at a closed door.

Cashel stood and stretched. He was naked but now Helena had left, so he didn't care. He heard a sigh from Hale. "You need some meat on them bones."

Cashel accepted the robe Hale passed him, his mind full with another problem. Was Hale mated? Was Helena? She was a human slave and therefore forbidden to mate a wolf, but maybe they met in secret? But then Hale didn't look like he was protecting a secret. He just looked completely heartsick.

Cashel sighed, putting the problem out of his mind and turning to the other most obvious concern. "Why has my father asked me for breakfast?"

Hale frowned, looking puzzled. "You don't normally break your fast together?"

Cashel snorted. "The last time I ate in his presence before last night was on my eighth birthday."

Hale's jaw dropped. "I don't get to share much with my son or my two daughters since they mated. One's in Tethra, but the other two are close and would be upset if I didn't see them at least every week."

"But you are not an Alpha whose only son is an abomination," Cashel said lightly and stepped into the ornate pool, wondering how it was full and warm already when no one had come into the bathroom.

"It's fed from springs under the compound, and heated by fire," Hale explained, guessing correctly at Cashel's thoughts. "The other rooms have pools but they are cool, and have to be heated by hand. It was one of the reasons why the Alpha moved his pack house here."

Cashel nodded, wishing he hadn't said what he had to Hale. It was hardly the gamma's fault his father despised him. He shivered slightly and sat down in the warm water.

"Axel will shave you when he gets back, or I can help."

Cashel turned to the gamma. "I can shave myself. I don't need to be waited on."

"I might not be too careful anyway." Hale sat and held up his enormous hands.

Cashel's eyes crinkled in humor. "And you're a bodyguard, not a bodyslave."

Hale grunted. His grin was wide though. "Bodyguard, huh? I got a promotion?"

Cashel flushed. "I'm sorry." He had assumed that was why Hale was there—and because none of the gammas from home came with them. He had been pleased they hadn't. They were all either rough and mocked him, or ignored him completely.

"Well, all I know is my beta-commander bade me stay with you while you are here."

"Gaven?" But Cashel didn't really need the nod confirming the name. Next to his father, Gaven was usually in charge. For all the years he could remember, Gaven had been by his father's side. In fact, he had seen more of Gaven in the last two years than Darius. His father only ever saw the healers for their reports.

"And being an omega is a rare thing. You should be proud."

Cashel glanced back at Hale. The wolf was gathering the shaving implements together. "Proud?" he repeated incredulously.

Hale paused holding a wicked looking razor. "Yes, have you gotten any of your gifts yet?"

"Gifts? Why would I get presents?" Then he laughed. "You mean *abilities*? I'm a simple grower," Cashel shrugged.

Hale frowned. "I didn't think there was anything simple about getting crops to grow in harsh places."

"Maybe I would have more gifts if I was a female," Cashel shrugged, wanting the subject closed and quickly.

"Hmm, I dunno," Hale said. "My friend worked for an Alpha whose second son was an omega. Got mated to an Alpha in Caedra, or maybe Tethra I think. He's an apothecary. Can heal the human workers easily."

"My father wouldn't heal any humans. He simply replaces them," Cashel said flatly.

"Anyway, she says the original omega way back when he mated the Alpha King had some scary good abilities. They were supposed to able to read each other's mind, and he was definitely a man. Everyone knows that."

Cashel dipped his head. Oh, he knew. Every scar on his belly was because of Oliver. Cashel shrugged and tried to downplay it. "Being a grower is hardly of any use here."

"How old are you?"

"Eighteen." As if that had anything to do with anything.

Hale nodded. "Maybe you're not old enough, but I know a lot of northern packs would count themselves blessed to have you."

Cashel began to soap his arms and began to breathe, as Hale seemed to have closed the subject. His father had sent priests to question him for years and they had pronounced him a grower. He could make plants bloom in any weather, and crops grow with alacrity. His father had been disgusted. He had enough human slaves to work his fields and had no need for his son to do that. He didn't know what else Cashel could do and Cashel had no intention of ever letting his father discover it.

The door to the bathing chamber opened and Axel stepped in. Hale nodded and said he would be outside to accompany Cashel when he was ready. Axel immediately stripped off his tunic and Cashel held a hand up. He liked Axel. He really liked him, but he would far rather have him as a friend than a pleasure-slave. Axel's green eyes widened but he paused. "My prince?"

"Cashel," Cashel instructed. "Pass me the robe please." He stood up and wrapped the drying robe around himself. Axel bent and dried his feet before Cashel could tell him not to do that either. Axel gestured to the chair in front of the mirror. Cashel sat and let Axel start to shave him. His own hands weren't steady with the thought of meeting his father.

"Do you have family?"

Axel smiled. "I still live with my mom. She's a seamstress in the compound and my elder brother is apprenticed to the stonemason."

"That's a skilled job. You must be proud of them." Cashel closed his eyes, not wanting to watch the knife near his skin. "Your father?"

Cashel opened his eyes at the silence.

Axel rinsed the knife. "He worked in the quarry and there was a landslide. My father and my uncle along with the others were trapped and died." Axel looked at Cashel, his green eyes luminous with grief and resignation.

Cashel swallowed. "The Idris quarry?" Axel nodded. "I'm so sorry." The Idris disaster had happened about seven months ago. There had been a huge landslide and everyone had been buried. And what did his father do? Instead of ordering more slaves and his gammas to try and dig the men free and check for survivors he had just ordered that area closed off and said he was unwilling to lose any more men in a fruitless search. It had been callous and even some of the gammas had offered to search, but they could not when Darius had forbidden it. There were guards posted and the families of the humans were banned from the area as the wolves said it might cause more slides. Over a hundred men were buried and forgotten about.

Some said there were stories of the earth moving for quite some time after the landslide. His father used it as an excuse to demonstrate the ground was still dangerous, but there were whispers that some of the victims may have not died straight away, and the earth shifted as they tried to claw their way back.

Axel returned to shaving Cashel's face. After a few quiet minutes, he finished and cleared his throat. Cashel stood and dropped the robe, knowing what was expected of him. No body hair whatsoever. Cashel had undertaken this humiliating ritual since his father had decided Cashel would breed an heir. He wasn't sure whether he was trying to make him look female or more palatable for the mating. As usual he just had to do as he was told. He was relieved the blade Axel used with such careful precision was smaller but he still held his breath while his balls and ass were scraped free of hair. He didn't let it out until Axel lowered to his legs.

"There." Axel stood straight, obviously pleased with himself.

"Thank you," Cashel said. "What are your usual duties here?"

Axel wrinkled his nose. "Anything I'm told."

"How would you like to stay with me? I'll be completely honest—I have no idea where I may be required to live, only that it will be in the territory."

Axel's face lit up. "Really?"

Cashel chuckled and nodded. He allowed Axel—brimming with enthusiasm—to help him into his silk breeches, shirt and sash in his father's colors. He was ready. He just had no idea why his father wanted him.

Chapter Six

Justice stood by the window as soon as Sorin's first rays bathed the sky. He had barely slept, and not just because of the noise from the powerful storm that had swept the skies last night. Not that he wasn't used to rising immediately as the suns shone over the desert, but there was a bigger problem that had prevented him getting any rest.

Cashel. The prince he had come to kill was his mate. They had all agreed the heir was to die—as well as his father, on the assumption they were both just as bad—but now what did he do? His wolf had told him they were mates as soon as they had touched; and the animal's distress at leaving him in his own bed—and not immediately claiming him—had nearly driven him mad. His wolf was an Alpha as much as he himself was, and they usually worked in harmony until Justice had made himself leave Cashel last night. The thought of Cashel being anywhere he wasn't had nearly brought on a shift last night. Even now, Justice's skin was tight as it stretched to contain and leash his animal's power.

He hated the cluttered room and suddenly longed for the wide open plains from home where a wolf and a man could breathe in harmony. He also disliked sleeping anywhere his stallion Kashir wasn't. He supposed he could understand horses not being allowed in the bedrooms—a bare smile graced his lips—and even though Zane had promised to stay with his horse, it still seemed wrong. In the desert horses were only second in importance to water, and Kashir had saved his life more times than he could count.

He gazed at the courtyard below, already busy. There seemed to be some sort of market being set up and Justice watched in interest as a cart containing what looked like beer was pulled into place. He stiffened suddenly, his sharp ears picking up the footsteps and the door latch lift but before whoever was attempting to walk in could even open it, he whirled and lifted his Kataya. The blade was never out of his sight, and only not on him because he was currently naked. The serving girl that entered his room looked up, promptly shrieked and dropped the full jug of water she was carrying which smashed noisily onto the stone floor. Two gammas came running in, swords drawn. "Might I suggest," Justice said evenly, lowering his blade, "you warn all house servants to knock before entering my chamber."

The gammas nodded nervously and practically carried the shaking woman out of the room. In another few seconds two more servants were back with a mop to clean the water and more hot water so Justice could bathe. He actually longed for a bath. He had had two since they had crossed the sea, and still marveled that water was so plentiful it could be wasted on such an extravagance.

What was Cashel doing right now? Was he also bathing? Was he taking soap and gliding it over—

A snarl echoed in his head as the animal inside him attempted to get free. Justice closed his eyes and took some deep breaths. He couldn't claim his prince before the games were ended and he sent a signal to the nine ships moored out of sight waiting for it. And then it would still take three days to travel from Salem.

He was just pulling his breeches on when Zane and Armand

knocked and entered the room. They promptly collapsed onto the chairs by a small desk, and helped themselves to the bowl of fruit.

Armand looked around at the small but opulent room and whistled slowly.

Zane snorted. "He hates it," he pronounced and took a huge bite out of an apple.

Armand's eyebrows rose up. "You hate it?" The disbelief was apparent in his voice.

Justice shrugged. "It's a little cloying." There was just so much in the room that was completely unnecessary, and even in the middle of the night when the temperatures in the desert dropped dangerously below freezing, he had never slept with so many covers on a bed in his life. Decorative pottery and books seemed to litter every surface. In fact, when he had been shown the room he had questioned the gamma, thinking he had been directed somewhere already occupied.

Zane's voice dropped. "What is it?" Zane was regarding him steadily. He knew Justice wasn't as calm and unruffled as he usually seemed, even if no one else could tell. "Did you meet the omega?"

Armand scoffed but he kept his voice low. "From what I heard in the kitchen last night, I wasn't expecting our Alpha to be in his own bed this morning."

"Damn, Justice." Zane's eyes widened. "That's fast even for you."

Justice ignored the teasing. "He was sick."

Armand shrugged. "It matters not, seeing as he's going to be dead soon anyway."

Before Justice realized what he was doing, his claws were around Armand's throat. Armand immediately went limp in his grasp and, rasping for breath, tilted his head to expose it a little more. It was a tremendous show of true loyalty and absolute submission.

They could all smell the blood as it ran down Armand's neck. Justice's nostrils flared and he took a breath, his anger barely receding enough for him to relax his grip. Another breath and he took a step back and dropped his arm, the claws retracting. "You will not touch him. *Ever.*"

Armand immediately sank to his knees. "Gravest apologies, my Alpha. Please know I would never insult your mate, and I pledge my life to protecting his as well as your own."

"He is your mate," Zane said. It wasn't a question. Justice's response could be taken for nothing else.

Justice blew out a long breath as his wolf was back under his control. He nodded, accepting the apology and the declaration. He might regret this reaction against one of his closest friends, but he would not apologize for it. It would demean them both.

Justice walked to the window and took a deep breath, trying to calm down. He could smell the fragrant Juno bushes and their small white flowers that reminded him of his mother when he had been young. She had managed to grow one in a small pot and his father had allowed her to keep it even though the only things usually granted water were what kept them alive. The flowers were prolific here, of course, and he would make sure any of his people that wanted would have a garden redolent with them.

He had things to do first, of course.

"How do you wish to proceed?" Zane asked carefully.

Justice understood the question and how this changed their plans. He was disgusted by the show of his mate last night and didn't understand how his father could have done what he did. Children were a gift on Arrides, and there was not one that wasn't fiercely loved and protected. "The plan still stands with obviously the caveat of claiming my mate as soon as the games are completed and our warriors are ready to attack."

He understood the look of disbelief Zane and Armand both had. It was unheard of for an Alpha to wait to claim his mate. The ritual courting between his people was superseded by the need for an Alpha to find his mate. Simply because any that tried to prevent it risked being mauled and killed by a very angry Alpha wolf. Justice didn't know if he had the strength to wait for the games to finish before he claimed Cashel. "I may have to take one day at a time. I may have to move things up, even."

"Alpha," Zane started, which made Justice pause. Zane had called him Justice since they were old enough to talk. Calling him Alpha meant he was including the pack in whatever he was going to say. It was Zane's none too subtle way of reminding him of his responsibilities. "I understand you wish to give your wolves time to get here, but we have to think of the safety of your mate and the health of the pack. Another six days is too long."

Justice knew what he meant. The phrase "the health of the pack" really meant the health of the Alpha. The two were intertwined at such a basic level, one couldn't be happy and prosper without the other. The pack needed Justice to claim Cashel.

"Then we need to send word to Salem," Justice agreed and immediately felt lighter because the decision had been taken. He had to get through three days, if that.

"I also needed to report that Kashir has already caused some interest," Armand said. Justice nodded. The huge white stallion would draw some looks but he wasn't the only fine horse in the place. Darius, he knew, was an avid horse breeder.

Justice stood. He needed to do something to keep himself occupied. "I have been invited to breakfast by the Alpha. I have no idea who will be there. I don't doubt for one second it will be an intimate meal, though."

"It isn't for all competitors," Armand answered with confidence. "Just the heirs or second sons. That's seven of them plus you."

"And who did you have to fuck for that information?" Zane baited him.

Armand waggled his eyebrows. "Oh, the information was freely given. The fucking was to say thank you for it."

Zane rolled his eyes and glanced back at Justice. "The knock-out rounds start at eleven. Heirs or second sons don't have to take part today. Was there any problem last night?"

"With my Alpha status? No, but I think questions may come this morning."

"And you still think saying you are from Arrides won't get you arrested?" Zane asked.

"I won't hide who I am," Justice said flatly. "There is no law that says I don't have a legitimate right to return."

Zane was silent, but Justice understood why. A thousand years ago the first Alpha of his line was never supposed to survive, much less be able to impregnate a female. In those days, the wolves only ever left their prisoners at the beach. They cared not what happened to them after, assuming death or madness and death would quickly follow. A small indigenous human population lived there in secret, terrified of the wolves finding out they even existed. One day, a young girl had found one of the outcast wolves collapsed on the sand and couldn't let him die. She had nursed him back to health and they had fallen in love. That wolf had secretly watched as other wolves were banished to the desert, then he rescued them too. Over a thousand years passed and though the original human and wolf populations were all gone, the memories of their ancestors endured.

Justice had committed no crime; he just wasn't supposed to exist.

There had been wolves sentenced to banishment over the years that Justice knew deserved it. Their true nature usually showed itself early on and the wolves then dealt with it swiftly and deadly. Everyone was given one chance, but one only. Their secret and their freedom were too important to risk.

Justice had presided at the *taduir*—or council meeting—six years ago, shortly after the death of his father—when the subject of their increasing population rose again. Many years ago, the elders had imposed a ban of one child per couple. They had not the resources to provide for more, and while Arrides was huge, a big population was unsustainable, fresh water being the scarcest resource. The wells that were dug had to be very deep and the biggest one had just dried up.

At the time, his mother's best friend's son and his mate had just given birth to twins. Twins were so rare they were unheard of, but the law was clear, and one pup had to die. It wasn't even that one was a girl and one a boy. Females were as valued as males on Arrides and worked just as hard. It was the fact that there were two. The elders insisted that either the parents had to choose or the gammas would be sent to take whichever one they grabbed first. Another couple had even offered to raise one, but the elders argued they may want to have their own someday as they were newly mated, and if the law was broken once it set a dangerous precedent.

Justice had listened to the arguments all around him. If the law was upheld, Justice knew he would have no choice but to kill one of the babies. His father had always said the first job of an Alpha was to protect his wolves, and to do that a baby must die.

Justice had heard enough and just as the decision was reached he rose to speak.

Justice spoke for some time. He had friends—sons and daughters of many of the elders' present—and they were all agreed. They didn't want to live their lives in secret anymore. They had committed no crime and were ready to petition the King for their release. The elders were all stunned, especially as Justice's arguments were all thought out and he named the support he had, which included someone from every family present. He was also cautious. The elders were impressed he was not suggesting a rushed mass exodus without thought or preparation and suggested they send more scouts. Justice and his friends had been landing in secret in the fishing town of Salem-dar for months and no humans or wolves had cared that there was one more boat amongst hundreds.

In the end, the elders had no choice. Justice was Alpha. It was undisputable that he heard his pack, even if he didn't reach the traditional age of maturity for another five years. He had indulged the elders for long enough. They had a choice. Either they relinquished their idea of control, or he was prepared to fight any challenger they put forward to the death. The elders had quickly ceded to his authority. There was no one foolish enough to challenge Justice.

Justice stood determinedly and pushed his memories aside. The past belonged just there. It was the immediate future he needed to concentrate on. "It will not bode well if I am late."

Zane and Armand stood up, and Zane leaned closer, speaking even more quietly. "Did you make contact with her?" They both waited for Justice's reply.

Justice shook his head solemnly, though he wished he had made contact. It had been far too long.

Armand and Zane glanced at each other and then back at him. "If we hear anything we will of course tell you straight away."

Justice nodded, but pushed the thought away. Keeping their secret would save his people, and he would not lose sight of his goal, no matter how things had just shifted personally for him. They agreed to meet later by the stables. Kashir would need exercising as he hated confinement as much as his master, and in the six years since Justice had bonded with him, he had never allowed another rider on his back.

Justice walked out into the courtyard. The compound housing the army and Darius's pack house was the largest place he had ever seen. It seemed bigger even than Salem. The settlements on Arrides were very small, and placed according to a water source. He ducked his head, stepped around the stall holders that seemed to be doing a brisk trade, and walked over to the huge stone building where the registrations had taken place last night. He spied the small garden to the side and the trees he had finally caught Cashel at. Skin and bone. He could still feel the ribs on the young man as he had clutched him tight. First to hold him while he had been sick, and then when he had carried him because he was unable to walk. Justice couldn't help the small smile. The omega had gotten drunk—something, according to Hale his bodyguard, he never did. It was almost a rite of passage where Justice was from, but Cashel seemed to have picked a strange time to do it.

And timing was everything. Justice knew that better than anyone. The reports from Solonara were frightening. It was clear that the territory wouldn't be the safe haven for his people that they had hoped. He was convinced it was the mysterious source of their survival that his father had spoken of as he had died, but Justice and his friends soon had to change their plans. That meant taking the territory by force if they had to. It had taken another five years of planning, training, and building huge ships, but they were ready, and then they had gotten the message from their contact about the games. It was the perfect diversion. At no other time could Justice gain unquestioned entry to Darius's inner circle.

Justice showed the special token identifying him as a competitor he had been given last night to the gammas guarding the door and he was immediately granted access to the same hall he had seen last night. There were two tables arranged in a T formation. The competitors were all expected to sit on the downward table and, he assumed, the Alpha and his betas sitting across the top. Justice quietly took his place, nodding in acknowledgement at the other heirs already present. He counted the available seats quickly. There were but fifteen seats in total including that of the Alpha. He wondered why he had been included, unless it was that his Alpha status had gone unchallenged, which Justice doubted.

The door at the back opened and two gammas immediately appeared and stood at either side. Darius swept inside and all the competitors stood and bowed. Gaven, his beta, was immediately behind him, as was the clerk who had noted all of the competitors' names last night. The last person through the door had Justice's heart hammering as if it were preparing to leave his chest. It was Cashel. The fact that he was awake was surprising. The fact that he was able to walk even more astonishing. Justice's wolf tensed. Cashel was so pale his skin was nearly white, which was some feat in the heat of Solonara. His eyes were downcast until someone directed him where to sit, but Justice remembered their blue intensity from last night, even as unfocused as they had been. At least he was clothed this time.

He had watched all the competitors present themselves to Darius last night. The ones who glanced at the omega barely concealed their

The Alpha Prince

disgust and not one of them—save him and one other—had made any attempt to meet their supposed future mate.

The prize was the territory and the wealth that came with it. Bedding the omega was simply a chore that had to be endured to get what they wanted. Justice narrowed his eyes watching the serving girls as they rushed to bring the food out. People were eating and chatting. The noise grew exponentially in the room as the Alpha started to address the competitors individually. Cashel never moved. He wasn't spoken to by either his father or anyone else. Unable to watch and not be nearer any longer, Justice stood and walked over to where the omega was aimlessly pushing a small amount of food around his plate and making no attempt to eat any of it. "Not hungry?"

Cashel jumped and looked up in alarm. Justice took a step back. The fear on Cashel's face was palpable. Dark shadows ringed his blue eyes. His left cheek was swollen, and the discolored marks were evident on his arms as his sleeves slid up. He had neither bruise when Justice had put him to bed last night. "Who did that?" Justice growled.

Justice was quickly aware of the beta coming to stand by his side. "Alpha? My lord would like to talk to you." Justice glanced at Gaven and forced his anger down, obediently inclining his head. *Lord?* Was that what the territory Alphas called themselves, or just this one? He took a last glance at Cashel, but his head was firmly lowered once again, so Justice turned and followed Gaven back to where Darius was watching him.

"I am told you have a fine stallion," Darius said. "You merely need to name your price and I will include him in my breeding program."

Justice bowed. "I am honored, my lord, but we already have a mare chosen for him to service when the games are finished."

"You seem enamored of my son," Darius said, changing topic abruptly. The surprise in his voice, while not obvious, was heard.

Justice wondered if Darius was even aware how insulting he was being to his own child.

"Isn't it why we are all here?" Justice replied smoothly. "The honor of mating your son," he pressed.

Darius's eyes narrowed. It was clear he wasn't about to take Justice's words at face value. "And having your pack formally acknowledged has, I suppose, nothing whatsoever to do with it?"

It was Justice's turn to incline his head as if the point had been fairly won. "Indeed, Alpha. My pack, although small, is eager to serve you in Solonara in whatever way possible."

Darius's eyes narrowed once again. "So, you are not claiming the territory of Arrides?"

"Who would ever want to claim endless sand and little water? My wolves wish to be granted the right to stay here and serve their territory Alpha in whatever way they can."

"How many of you are there?"

"Ten," Justice lied, which he hated having to do. "I have two men with me and the others are waiting permission before they land."

"You have a boat?" Darius asked.

Justice badly wanted to say no, of course they had all swum the four hundred or so miles across the Mendrik sea, but knew the sarcasm would merely earn him the sharp end of a sword. "A small one, Alpha." He infused his voice with regret.

"It is certainly not something we were ever expecting," Darius admitted. "As far as I know only male wolves have been sent to Arrides."

"I was told some she-wolves were smuggled out many years ago, my lord," Justice said quickly. They knew from their illicit trips to Salem that it was completely impossible for wolves to scent their hybrid status and Justice still didn't know why. They had learned that hybrids were illegal and if found were immediately slaughtered. Their wolves, however, just smelled like other wolves. "But breeding, as you know, is problematic and the desert supports very little."

"Evidently so, as your pack is merely ten." Darius waved his hand

and turned to his clerk. "The competitor is allowed but his status is not. Remove him from the list of Alpha-heirs and second sons. He has to compete with everyone else." Darius turned back. "You had better go prepare. I believe the first round starts in under two hours." Justice bowed. He had never expected any favors anyway. "And for your sake I hope you are successful," Darius added. "If you fail to qualify I will send gammas to put to death all those you have brought with you, and your stallion will be mine."

Justice heard the tiny gasp from Cashel but he doubted anyone else did. So, his omega had a soft heart. Justice's face ached with the effort not to smile.

He headed to the stables. The first test was horse skill which was why they had risked bringing Kashir. There was no test of horse skill he could fail with Kashir. Werewolves sometimes had trouble riding horses. The animal often spooked when it sensed the internal wolf and many wolves gave up trying to master them. Solonara was different in that any wolf that served in the army had no choice but to learn to ride. He knew the same applied to Niandes, and of all the territories they were the two with the largest armies. He also knew that the humans were rebelling. Niandes and Tethra had particular problems with the rebels. Caedra to a lesser extent as half the territory was covered by the Tzoron mountains. Perse was a simple farming community and there were few people to rebel. He had no quarrel with the humans and as soon as he was territory Alpha he would meet with their leaders.

Either way, Solonara was the territory he had to defeat first, but he wasn't greedy. If the other territories left them alone he wasn't interested in them or their petty battles. He had promised his wolves a home many years ago and nothing would dissuade him.

Not even sparkling blue eyes.

Justice groaned. He needed to try and push Cashel to the back of his mind so he could concentrate. Of course, it didn't help that Cashel was delicious. When he had held the small body last night he wanted nothing but to claim him, but sick and in those circumstances were not the time to take his mate. *His mate.* Something warm settled his insides at those words. He had always assumed his mate would be female, but he cared not, really. In fact, casual sex in the desert happened more so with men, as in the desert females were unwilling to risk their precious one and only chance of a pup with anyone but a life mate. Not that as Alpha he didn't have many offers. He was simply too focused on his goal to be distracted. Cashel not being able to have a pup wasn't a problem. He could just use a breeder. The problem was, as the thought entered his head, Justice's wolf rebelled. He knew just how he felt, even though he didn't see any other way around it. His pup would be the start of a new future. His name—after all—wasn't merely a coincidence.

He was well aware of the position Darius was taking with his son. Darius refused to accept that a man simply didn't have the insides to create and nurture a pup, and he was basing his information on a questionable legend thousands of years old.

Pups were so precious on Arrides with the one-pup rule, the very thing that had started Justice on his journey. For instance, he knew other Alpha-heirs often had a *Luna-Madre*—or moon mother—but on Arrides pups were such a gift they were swaddled next to their mom's body for the first ten days and never parted. Thereafter wherever she went so did the pup until the age of five when the father would share the role. Years ago, his mother's best friend had been murdered. Another she-wolf, Sierra, had just lost her third pup, born in silent death and not with a lusty cry. No desert air had ever filled those tiny lungs and neither sun would shine on a tiny smile. In grief and madness Sierra had wanted what all other mothers had and so Sierra had drugged another pregnant she-wolf and cut the pup out of its mother's belly. The pup had been Zane. It was a miracle he had lived at all, but his mother hadn't been as lucky. Even when his cries had brought nearly all their camp running and the gammas had easily overpowered Sierra, it had been too late for Zane's mom. A year later when Justice had been born his mom had named him as a gift to their people, and thereafter his mom had raised him to deliver the plan she had decided on when her friend had died.

And no blue eyes, no matter how they shone, would alter a course in the making for every one of Justice's twenty-six years. His mother had been unaware of the legend his father had spoken of, but that wasn't in the end why he was here. His people were dying, and as awful as it sounded, he had more faith in his sword than in his dying father's last words.

"Justice." He looked up at Zane holding Kashir, and his breath caught a little. The stallion was magnificent. Pure white with a simple black *defir* strapped to his back. No wolves on Arrides needed either a saddle or stirrups, and no bit would ever saw at Kashir's tender mouth. They simply had a soft woven strap surrounding his muzzle and up and over his ears that allowed reins. The defir was another strap that fitted similar to a saddle but was merely for securing extra water and weapons if needed.

Justice had ridden with his father long before he could walk. They were taught that a horse's submission could only ever be freely given, and not taken. At the age of eighteen all wolves were taken to the Patir hills where the wild horses roamed. They were given two days to convince a horse to partner with a wolf. If they failed they would never become a warrior, but take on subservient tasks for the pack. All Justice's warriors had their own horses, but Kashir was the only one that had accompanied him, Zane, and Armand. They had purchased two horses for the other two wolves to ride when they had landed in Salem-dar. Kashir brought enough attention himself, and it wasn't prudent to have betas also riding what looked like such rare animals. It would bring too much attention and have people questioning where the animals had come from. Darius had already noticed him judging from the offer to breed from him.

Their story was that they had bought Kashir when they had landed.

Justice took the woven reins from Zane and allowed Kashir to headbutt him once in greeting. Any more would be disrespectful.

Likewise, Justice didn't slap the stallion on his neck as he had seen so many other riders do, but gently offered his hand to Kashir's muzzle to sniff and then stroked the stallion's nose as it dipped obediently.

Zane offered his hands for Justice to help him mount but it was unnecessary as Justice leapt onto Kashir's back. His wolf making the movement seamless and fluid. Armand came to stand beside Justice and whispered. "I have heard today is not as simple as simply riding Kashir. Be warned, my Alpha."

Justice nodded and with a light squeeze of his legs showed Kashir where he was to go. "Zane, I am allowed a groom. Stay close."

Zane nodded but his eyebrow quirked in sardonic humor. Between them both, Zane, if anything was an even more gifted a rider than Justice. He was a *Shaman-le*. On Arrides it was said that Zane's father could talk to the horses. Knew instantly if one was sick, or in foal, and Zane was the same. His own horse—Luna—was a mare. Unusual as most of the warriors naturally rode huge stallions, but Zane and his mare had bonded instantly, and he hadn't had to go to the Patir hills to find her. She had simply appeared one morning on the outskirts of their camp and had refused anyone near her except Zane. She was as brave as Kashir and allowed only Kashir of all the stallions to get close. When things were settled it was the hope of both of them that Luna would carry Kashir's foal.

Justice followed the other competitors to the parade ring. He guessed around thirty other riders were present but he was surprised there weren't actually more. There was a huge gamma directing riders, and much to his disgust there seemed to be some sort of wolf obstacle course to ride through. All competitors had to ride through a throng of noisy humans, shouting, swearing, banging metal blades on the backs of pans. When the first fully-shifted wolf jumped out at the horses, that was when they lost the first five. Then there were another two because another wolf came up behind the line.

Kashir never so much as twitched an ear. He was steady because Justice was steady. The stallion knew only to be alarmed when Justice was, and the only thing that had ever threatened them was coming upon a nest of rattlesnakes. Even then Justice had only been afraid for Kashir. The snakes were deadly, but Kashir had stood obediently still as the snakes had slithered over his hooves. It had nearly killed Justice to remain calm when he wanted to give the signal for Kashir to run, but they had both walked away successfully from the threat.

On the next pass, they lost another six horses when some idiot started letting off firecrackers. Mini explosives designed for simple celebrations—and to be honest, no rider that couldn't control his horse around one of them was worth the title of Alpha. Justice wouldn't have even accepted him or her as a warrior. Not that there were any female competitors here today. He knew Askara had very strange views on women that the men on Arrides didn't share. Women were a gift from the goddesses. Not only did they ensure the survival of their race with every pup, but Xyanna, one of his warriors currently in charge of a ship, would take out the heart of any man who dared to say she wasn't capable of it, and do it with flair. None of his warriors would ever be stupid enough to challenge her.

By the time they had completed a third circuit, Justice was bored, but the competitors had been whittled to seventeen. He glanced over at the empty dais that had been set up presumably for the Alpha to watch the competitors, and was surprised to see it wasn't empty anymore. There were three figures, and he recognized the broad expanse of the gamma, Hale, straight away. Did that mean the other two were Cashel and his servant?

Justice stared. They were too far away for him to make out and the servant was holding some sort of shade over his master's head. Justice looked to his side. The competitors were taking a five minute rest while the gammas set the next test up. With an unseen command, he bade Kashir to walk towards the dais. He saw Hale move his hand towards his knife in warning, and he silently congratulated the gamma. He would kill anyone that thought to lay a hand on his mate, and was glad someone else thought so too. Kashir walked up to the base of the platform and the servant moved slightly so Cashel came into view. Justice bowed his head. "My prince," he murmured. Cashel seemed incapable of a reply but his blue eyes didn't dip to the floor this time. They remained on Justice and Kashir.

Cashel cleared his throat. "What's his name?"

Justice was taken aback. He was used to being asked after Kashir – but usually what his price was, not what he was called. They had met many horse dealers on their journey from Salem offering to buy him, and one or two that had thought to even help themselves. Justice and Zane had soon changed their minds. They had even let one of them live.

"Kashir," Justice answered.

Cashel's blue eyes softened. "He is beautiful."

"Do you ride, my prince?" Justice asked respectfully.

Cashel shook his head regretfully. "Not anymore."

The shout went up from the gammas wanting to restart the competition, stalling any further questions. Justice made to turn, but then stopped. "Would you cheer for us?"

Cashel smiled, and Justice caught his breath. *Wow*. Why had he not seen how stunning Cashel was before? He had merely seen what he was, not *who* he was, and the bruises had distracted him earlier. His blue eyes shone under thick brown lashes that framed them beautifully. The small, slightly upturned nose, and the wide full lips that made Justice want to touch them with his own. Kashir started a little, picking up on Justice's own shock at the direction his thoughts were going in.

"Of course," Cashel replied, and Justice turned Kashir back. His mate was beautiful, not that it mattered.

"Riders dismount."

Justice quickly dismounted, giving over Kashir to Zane, then stood attentively, wondering if they were going to battle hand to hand. Then his eyes narrowed as six horses were led into an enclosed ring.

A gamma stood to face the competitors. "There are six horses and seventeen competitors remaining. The winners will be the ones to successfully mount and ride one horse a full circuit of the ring. The horses may only be ridden once."

And that was it? No further instructions? Justice thought quickly. This could go one of two ways. The fastest, most agile wolf could leap atop the nearest horse and try and outrun the others, or it would turn into a battle to simply slay any competition. The servants turned and each of them rubbed something—a leaf?—in his hand and then offered it to the horse to smell. It took the first horse barely five seconds before it went mad, rearing and bucking. Justice dived for the ring as soon as the cry went up and the servants rushed out before they were caught with flying hooves. Whatever the horses had been given was sending them wild and Justice was furious. Competition almost forgotten at the cruelty on display. He had heard horses scream before in agony as a sword had ripped through them, and once when a rattlesnake had bitten a mare. It wasn't something he wanted to hear again, and he leapt over the high fence into the madness before him. Three of the wolves didn't even attempt the ring. Two were hit and killed instantly by flying hooves, and another three or four were crushed as two of the horses rolled to try and rid themselves of the wolves that had thought to jump on top of them.

Thunder rumbled overhead, but Justice didn't look upwards as some of the others did. He didn't dare take his eyes from the scene in front of him. He had seen the reaction and knew whatever had been given to the horses was causing some sort of hallucinations in them. He turned at another agonized cry, this time human, and saw a black gelding bite down almost through a wolf's leg as he had tried to get near him. Everything in Justice screamed at him how wrong it was to mount animals that were in such pain. From the corner of his eye he saw Armand and Zane watching in complete horror. Armand's arm on his friend. He knew how much it would be killing Zane not to enter the ring, but he wouldn't leave Kashir. The competition would also be forfeit if Zane interfered, and too many were depending on Justice to stay in the competition until his men got here, and to do that he had to win.

He just hadn't expected this.

Justice whirled as he sensed the movement to his left, and his Kataya was buried in the other wolf before he could run his own sword through Justice. So that was how it was going to be. He sidestepped quickly as another horse fell to the floor writhing, and was too late to stop another wolf from striking one on the head. He recognized the wolf as one who had spoken to Cashel right before he did last night. The horse stumbled but remained on its feet and the shock was enough so the wolf could jump on its back.

Two horses lay on the ground heaving breaths but making no attempt to rise. Four competitors were battling with each other and two yanking on the bridles in an attempt to make them get on their feet. The one who had hit the horse completed his circuit and just managed to jump free as the horse collapsed under him. The crowd cheered, but Justice wanted to take his own knife to the man who carelessly stepped around the animal and never looked back.

He had a second to register hot breath and whirled to face a black mare. Her eyes were wild and hot ragged breaths poured out of both nostrils. Her flanks heaved in terror and her head swung looking for escape. Justice turned back suddenly, meeting the sword with his own knife, and another competitor dropped to his feet.

He looked up and saw that he now faced three. The wolves looked as mad as the horse behind him. All holding their knives, one licking bloodstained lips and all looking like the animals they were half shifted into.

One focused on the mare and balled his fist. Justice knew they had seen the last competitor do exactly the same and there was absolutely no way he was going to allow anyone to hit the mare behind him. The crowd cheered again as two other wolves successfully completed the circuits and rode from the ring. The two horses on the ground had never gotten up at all. That left Justice, three more competitors and the black mare behind him. His hand went to his knife just as one wolf fully shifted and pounced at Justice. Justice felt teeth sink into his arm and his knife drop before he got his other arm around the wolf's neck and squeezed. He let the wolf go as soon as it went limp and whirled around just as one man stabbed the other. That left the two of them. Justice was facing the mare that was breathing a little quieter but swaying on her feet. She looked as if she was going to go down, and Justice needed this to be over quickly. If she went to the ground, he wasn't convinced he could get her to her feet a second time. The other wolf took a step to the mare, holding the knife in front of him.

"I don't want to kill you," Justice said, "but I am stronger and faster. Walk away." The other man's lips twisted and he nodded to Justice's arm, which was bleeding profusely, then gleefully waved his knife in front of Justice.

"You have no weapon."

Justice sighed, then, whirling in the move his father had taught him, he pulled the small dagger he kept hidden in the sash at his waist and threw it. The dagger embedded itself between the man's eyes and he was dead before he hit the floor.

But Justice had no chance to register he had killed once again, as the mare went down to one knee as her fore legs wobbled. Justice stepped straight up to the mare and caught her bridle, crooning softly in the language of his people. He told her how brave she was, how beautiful, and if she stood once more for him, how he would set her free and she would never be disrespected ever again. He gently pulled on her head and gazed into her brown eyes. She was covered in sweat, but as he talked her ears twitched and she took notice. With a shuddering breath, she heaved to her feet and stood, blowing out air with her head hung down.

"As keira mar, sanjeli?" Justice asked the question softly. *"Will you carry me, princess?"* The mare heaved another breath and stood still. Justice swallowed and as carefully and as gently as he could, he quickly mounted. She took a cautious step, then another as the crowds started cheering. She even managed a slight head toss, which made Justice smile. He was convinced it was the equivalent of her sticking her tongue out at the audience. He hardly dared breathe as she completed the circuit and he immediately dismounted as soon as he cleared the gate. The crowd went wild, shouting and feet stamping. Armand hurried over and Justice leaned close and whispered. "Buy the mare. I care not how much she costs."

Armand nodded his understanding and Justice gave the mare a last stroke on her muzzle before he allowed the reins to be taken from him. He glanced at the stands automatically, and the dais, but they were empty.

Chapter Seven

The four successful wolves from the first round—both betas, a gamma, and Justice—were invited to a celebratory banquet that night along with the Alpha-heirs and second sons who had yet to fight. Justice had shifted as soon as Armand had arrived back with the mare and they had both seen she was stabled next to Kashir. She didn't have a name, so Justice had named her Sanjeli like the princess he had called her. Zane had pronounced she was reasonably fit for an old lady—she was at least fifteen—but her knees were giving her some trouble. She was also hungry and he didn't think she liked humans. Zane had said that with a chuckle as she had head butted him, and they had all laughed.

When Armand had finally said Justice needed to shift to heal his arm, he realized he had felt a little light headed. He was also starving, but would hunt no animals without permission. The scrawny cow he would have finished as a light snack may have been providing enough milk to keep the human family from starving. Even if he had the right as a wolf in Solonara to take any animal from a human as he had been told, it didn't mean it was the right thing to do.

He shifted back, then retired to his rooms and asked for a bath and a meal. He was offered—but declined—a pleasure-slave to help him bathe. Pleasure-slaves weren't something he had ever enjoyed before on Arrides because they didn't exist. They didn't exist in Salem either—or they did, but you had to pay for them. If there had been such a woman or a man here he would have been tempted, but he would not take someone who was being forced, even if ultimately it wasn't him doing the forcing.

Armand and Zane came to his room to share the meal. Zane was grinning. Kashir had refused to settle until the partition between the horses was removed. Then he had stood over her while Sanjeli had lain down and gone to sleep. Justice was impressed, but Kashir was a fierce protector, and having decided Sanjeli was one of his mares, Kashir wouldn't let anyone lay a hand on her in anger ever again.

"She's covered in cuts and scars," Zane explained as he tore through an entire cooked chicken with obvious delight. "But Kashir came a little too close the first time and she bit the end of his muzzle."

Justice grinned. His stallion would have to learn to treat the lady with more respect.

"What's happening tomorrow?" Armand asked. "They gonna drug some other poor creatures?"

"We find out tonight. There will be some announcement after the banquet." Justice was itching to just get the whole thing over with.

Zane glanced at him mischievously. "Your mate saw you win."

Justice gave up pretending to feign indifference. "When I looked, he was gone."

"Actually, I think he got into trouble. If that's possible for a so-called prince," Armand added.

"Meaning?"

"And why is that?" Armand interrupted before Justice had the chance to answer. "Darius isn't the king, why on earth would he call his son a prince?"

"Actually, I know," Zane said. "I was talking to some of the other grooms before you started and apparently it's a new title. He can't be given the title of Alpha-heir because he's not an Alpha, so Darius came up with this."

"And," Armand continued, "apparently in Solonara it's offensive for anyone to call an Alpha's male sons by their first name, but so not apparently with Cashel. The beta-commander calls him by his name and his wolves copy."

Fury turned Justice's vision red. He would slit every throat that dared to offer an insult.

"How do you know?" Zane asked.

"The beta-commander turned up before the horses were given the leaves to talk to Cashel. I was closer to the stands." Armand blushed slightly. "The girl I spent last night with was one of his servers."

"What happened?" Justice asked sharply. He hadn't liked Gaven one little bit, and there was still the issue of Cashel's bruises.

"The beta told Cashel he was making a spectacle of himself," Armand replied and scowled.

"Because he had spoken to me?" Justice's breath caught. He hadn't meant to cause Cashel any problems.

Armand shook his head. "No. Apparently he was too far away at first and after you left he wanted the prince a little closer to the competitors so they moved nearer to the ring. The spectacle was because the prince got upset at the treatment of the horses."

Justice tightened his jaw before he said something he may regret. He was five seconds away from storming out to find Gaven and slicing the beta open with his Kataya. Not that he thought for one second he would fool Zane, who was watching him intently. "What did he do?"

"He summoned the beta to try and stop the competition."

"He did?" That even surprised Justice.

Armand squirmed a little. "Valerie told me—"

"Valerie?" Zane interrupted.

He grinned. "My date for tonight."

Justice snorted. "Date" was such a human expression. They had first heard it at the docks.

"Apparently your prince has been sick."

Justice lifted an eyebrow at Armand. The tone was bordering on being disrespectful to Cashel. He had already challenged Armand once about it though, and between the three of them they never observed any titles. It wasn't Armand's fault Justice was feeling over-protective of Cashel. "How so?"

"Valerie's aunt works in another of Darius's pack houses in the village of Lapis or Lapis-*dar* as they're all supposed to be called now. They have a lot of healers there all for the prince."

"What's wrong with him?" Zane interrupted.

Armand shrugged. "I don't know exactly. She's gonna tell me more tonight, but she thinks it's got something to do with him being an omega."

Justice stood up abruptly. His wolf was pacing inside him and the restlessness of his animal was making his skin crawl.

"Can I help?" Zane asked, but Justice shook his head. It was simply his wolf demanding he be with his mate. Justice knew exactly how he felt. Armand and Zane stood. "We're going to check on the horses, but one of us will be near the great hall tonight as well. Probably Armand as he has an in with the kitchen staff," Zane said dryly.

Justice agreed to meet them both for breakfast unless any problems arose and they both left. He got dressed slowly, trying to calm his wolf. His wolf wanted to race over and claim his prince, soothe every hurt, protect him... and yeah, fuck him until he couldn't stand. He knew it, his wolf knew it. How had it got to this? That the love and responsibility he had for his people were clashing with his need to mate. It should be in sync. Justice blew out another agonizing breath. What if he had to choose?

Justice stood in the entrance waiting his turn to be announced. The top table was half full already. The Alpha was already there. Cashel wasn't there that he could see, and he didn't know whether to be relieved or disappointed. Justice stepped forward and glanced to the side, but the ringing in his ears drowned out what was being said as his jaw dropped.

Cashel *was* there. He was on a *pedestal*—for want of a better term—displayed as if he was some prize. He was also completely naked and trussed up in some sort of strap that encased his semi-erect cock. His head was bowed but Justice could see the slight tremble of his bottom lip. Nearly masked by the shaking of the rest of his limbs either because he was ashamed or because he was freezing. The great hall was cool now that the suns had set and Cashel had nothing—including any natural body fat—to keep him warm.

Justice felt his nails sinking into his palms as his claws came out. The pain was welcome though. He needed something, anything, to stop his wolf from shifting and either slaughtering as many here as he could, or simply picking Cashel up and running with him. Justice blew a breath out and tried to calm. Neither option would help either of them, but his animal was fairly screaming to be allowed out. He needed to be clever.

"Justice."

The Alpha's voice boomed out and everyone fell silent. Darius waved at an empty seat on the end of the top table. "Congratulations. All winners today are entitled to a small boon of their choosing. Horses, some jewelry." He waved his hand expansively.

Justice smiled and bowed in acknowledgement. His wolf, sensing his decision, calmed immediately. "You are very kind and I am honored. My one wish is that I may be allowed to have Prince Cashel sit next to me while we enjoy your hospitality."

Justice wanted so badly to laugh at the look of utter astonishment that passed over Darius's face but he turned his head to the side as Gaven stepped close and nodded at whatever instruction he was given. In a few seconds there had been another place setting and a chair set on the end of the table. Justice bowed low again and walked to the end as a servant helped Cashel down from the pedestal and to his seat next to Justice. Conversation restarted and the servants rushed to offer food and wine. Justice took a deep breath. There was something that smelled incredibly good that he couldn't put a name to. Darius must have excellent cooks.

"You brought me luck today," Justice said as the servants backed away.

Justice felt Cashel stiffen and he turned to fully look at him. He blinked as he took in the set of Cashel's jaw and the way his luminous eyes flashed. What had he said? Was he angry to be sitting down? Had Justice caused him more embarrassment? He had seemed pleased when Justice had spoken to him before the horse challenge. Justice took a swallow of wine to cover up the fact he was at a total loss.

"I must congratulate you."

Justice turned over the words Cashel seemed to wring reluctantly from his lips. He *must* congratulate him. Not that he *wished* to congratulate him, but as if he was obligated. A thought filtered into Justice's head, and he remembered what Armand had told him about Cashel trying to stop the competition. "Do you know what the horses were given?"

Cashel raised his eyes and looked at Justice for the first time since he had entered the hall. "Shrome leaves, but I am sure you are aware of that."

Shrome leaves? "I have never heard of them, but were such a plant to exist on Arrides I would wipe it from existence."

"It doesn't have the same effect on wolves." Cashel sounded like he was disappointed. Justice searched his face. The blue eyes he had seen sparkle and had wanted to drown in were dull and flat. It was him. Cashel was disappointed in him.

"It is disgusting," Justice replied emphatically. "Our horses are our family in the desert. We depend upon them for our very survival. Sanjeli will never be put through that ever again."

Cashel looked confused. "Sanjeli?"

"The mare that gave me permission to ride her from the ring."

Cashel tilted his head. "Gave you permission?" he repeated dryly as if Justice was deluded. "Wait," he said, interrupting as Justice was going to answer. "How did you know the name of the horse?"

"I named her Sanjeli after I bought her. Sanjeli means—"

"Princess," Cashel finished.

It was Justice's turn to be surprised. "You know the language of Arrides?"

"I have studied *Askaran*." Cashel glanced around to make sure no one was listening. "Sanjeli is Askaran for princess. Why did you buy the horse?"

Justice took another swallow, trying to sort out the details in his head. What was *Askaran*? As far as he knew all the territories spoke in the common tongue, so he assumed that was Askaran even though he had never referred to it as such. He didn't know there was a separate language on Askara. It had not been something they had ever come across in Salem. "Askaran? But everyone seems to speak the common tongue."

Cashel smiled. "Askaran is an ancient language spoken by our ancestors. As we share the same ancestors, it is not surprising Arrides thinks of it as their own. It's fascinating, really."

Justice was silent as Cashel went from shy and timid to enthusiastic in the blink of an eye. So, his little prince was a historian? "I bought the mare because she carried me from the ring and earned me my chance for tomorrow." Cashel's blue eyes searched his own as if for a trace of deception. "She is ensconced in the stable with her protector."

Cashel's lips widened on an amused smile. "Kashir," he said, catching Justice's meaning.

"When we have finished perhaps you would like to meet him properly? At the same time you can check I am not abusing either of them." A flush stained Cashel's neck and he immediately dipped his head. Justice cursed. He hadn't meant to cause him any discomfort, or criticize. "Kashir is vain enough to love every chance he gets to be admired, and I am sure Sanjeli is desperate for a kind touch."

A flash of sadness passed over Cashel's face as he lifted it, and Justice ached with the effort of keeping his arms still. All wolves craved touch, and he had an inkling a kind touch wasn't something Cashel was used to. "I would love for you to meet the horses," Justice pressed.

Cashel nodded and sipped his water. The dinner was slow and arduous. Cashel shivered intermittently, and after offering his tunic once and being turned down with an alarmed expression, Justice didn't press again. Over the course of the next hour Cashel sat closer and closer to Justice. Justice didn't think Cashel was even aware of it, but it was as if Cashel was seeking his heat out. Justice pressed his thigh as close to Cashel's as possible and inhaled the gorgeous scent from earlier. Cashel must be wearing some sort of body oil that was the best thing Justice had ever smelled in his life. Justice badly wanted to take Cashel's hands in his to warm them as his fingers seemed blue. It would have helped if the prince had eaten more than but a few mouthfuls of soup. Justice hoped Armand may have some more information for him when they met at breakfast because he wanted to know why Cashel barely ate when he was already so thin. He also didn't understand the still livid bruises on Cashel's arms. He had learned when they had landed in Salem that omegas were unable to shift without their Alpha's permission, but that didn't make sense. Surely Darius would want his son healthy and happy. If for no other reason than at least to entice the competitors. His wolf was content though. The nearer Cashel was, the more his wolf was settled. It was something else Justice would have to think about later.

In another few minutes, a servant brought Cashel a separate goblet containing a thick, syrupy liquid. Justice inhaled unobtrusively. It smelled like meat, which was odd. Why wasn't he eating the real thing? Cashel had pushed a piece of chicken around while Justice had eaten two whole ones. He had refused the steak also, and he shuddered as he drank what looked like a vile concoction.

The banquet was breaking up. Pleasure-slaves were literally draped over nearly every wolf, and Justice had already waved two away much to Cashel's badly concealed astonishment.

The Alpha stood and took his leave, accompanied by three young girls. Cashel watched as Gaven followed him. Cashel's servant appeared at his side and Cashel stood.

"Will you do me the honor of visiting Kashir?" It looked like Cashel was about to leave, and Justice saw him wince as if standing caused him pain. Then Justice remembered what Cashel had on. Fuck, the man must be in agony. "Perhaps after you retire for a little while? I can wait," he added hopefully. He could see the indecision on Cashel's face.

Cashel bowed his head. "I will meet you at the stables in an hour."

Justice beamed. Ridiculously happy, and the shy smile he got in return would make every minute he had to wait worth it.

"Justice?" Armand stepped forward as Cashel left with his servant. "Do you need me any more tonight?"

Justice glanced behind Armand, at the serving girl who stood smiling shyly. She was beautiful. Long auburn hair swept up. Her huge hazel eyes watched Armand with something akin to adoration, and a smattering of freckles completed the stunning picture. "Be careful," Justice cautioned. She didn't look like a pleasure-slave. There was no powder used to hide tired lines, or a well-worn or mistreated body.

Armand followed Justice's stare, and Justice was surprised when instead of a smart reply, he got an obedient nod.

Justice walked to the stables and let himself in. They were barely a few minutes' walk away. The complex was huge, but there was a smaller area for visiting horses. He didn't like that it was completely unguarded at night though, and Zane and Armand were taking turns watching over Kashir and now Sanjeli. The Alpha's own horses were in a separate block.

He saw a shadow peel itself away from the wall, but he had

smelled Zane before he had seen him. "We are having visitors in a little while."

It was dark enough that he couldn't see the quirk of Zane's eyebrow, but he could imagine it. "Ones you have invited?"

Justice nodded and opened the door. He lit the sconce surrounded by the metal that protected the flammable straw from any stray sparks. He walked past two empty stalls and three with horses occupying them until he got to the end that Zane and Armand had altered to make one. Sanjeli lifted her head but didn't get to her feet. Kashir snickered softly. He held his hand out and Kashir took the apple Justice withdrew from his pocket. Justice let himself into the stall then bent and offered another to Sanjeli, which she took delicately. "Has she been on her feet?" He hoped it was trust that kept her lying down and not sickness or pain.

"The Shrome leaves have a sedative effect after the initial mania," Zane replied, and bent to gently stroke her neck. "I am mixing a poultice for her near foreleg." He pointed. "You can see the swelling."

"Are the leaves something you have heard of?"

Zane nodded. "They are not indigenous to Arrides but are mentioned in my father's texts."

Justice nodded. Zane's father had meticulously noted every ailment and treatment he had ever come across. His interest had been in horses, but he took notes of anything that might affect the wolves and the humans as well.

They both heard the massive doors open and looked towards the dim light. Justice stood.

"My prince." He bowed.

Cashel moved forward and Justice saw the slave had accompanied him but not Hale. He frowned. "Where is your protection?"

He saw Cashel and the young man exchange amused glances. "We slipped out, and please call me Cashel." Cashel came further forward, his eyes lighting up when he saw Kashir. "Oh my, he is even more stunning close up."

Justice was having problems articulating around his quickly

drying tongue, and realized it was because his mouth was hanging open. He snapped it shut. He daren't glance at Zane.

Zane stepped forward and bowed. "My prince."

Cashel smiled. "Cashel," he repeated, a little more insistent.

Zane looked beyond Cashel at the other young man. "My name is Zane."

Cashel drew the hesitant servant further forward. "This is Axel."

Justice would have to be deaf to have missed the hurried indrawn breath from his friend as Axel took the offered hand. He gazed at the man. He was older, he thought, than Cashel. Dark brown hair and quite startling green eyes that deepened nearly to black as he stared dumbstruck at Zane. His hand completely covered in Zane's large one. "Axel," Zane repeated slowly, carefully, as if relishing every letter. Justice wanted to roll his eyes. But then he knew the same dumbstruck expression had been on his own face barely minutes ago.

Justice cleared his throat and Zane ushered both Cashel and Axel into the stall. Kashir immediately stepped forward. Justice was sure there was not so much as one shy bone in his stallion's body. Cashel held his hand out before Justice thought to offer a suggestion, and Kashir mouthed his fingers, snorting in disgust when they were empty. Then Cashel laughed and Justice forgot anything he was about to say. The deep throaty chuckle was nothing like he was expecting. If he had to guess it would have been something approaching a girlish giggle, not an earthy sound that set heat rushing through his veins.

"My apologies, *warrior of the desert*. I keep no apples in my room, but I will make sure my hands are not empty when I see you again." Justice shouldn't have been surprised that Cashel knew Kashir was a direct translation of the word warrior on Arrides, or that the full term included the phrase *of the desert*. The fact that he referenced a future visit filled Justice's heart with a strange emotion. Very soon they would never be apart. Cashel glanced down at Sanjeli. "Will I cause her distress if I go closer?"

Justice immediately lifted a hand to bar Cashel's path. He didn't want Sanjeli to take Cashel as a threat and hurt him, even by accident.

"No," Zane interrupted, shaking his head a little and dropping Axel's hand. "She takes him as no threat, Justice." Justice dropped his arm. Cashel slowly stepped closer and fell gracefully to his knees.

"I have lived here all my life and this is the first time I have ever seen the stables," Axel said, wonder in his voice.

"I was just going to get some water for them," Zane replied.

"Oh, can I help?" Axel said eagerly.

Zane smiled and handed him an empty bucket. "I spotted a small room the grooms must use. There is a small enclosed stove for warming water, and I believe some tea," he added hopefully. Justice nearly laughed. The boy had no idea what Zane was offering or the significance. Sharing tea was a ritual nearly as old as the sands themselves. Zane had basically just asked Axel if he was interested in him. The tea would be followed by another invitation, possibly as simple as a walk. If Axel accepted, it was the precursor to their families discussing the terms of a life union—something so simple on Arrides but not something that would ever be allowed in Solonara. At least not yet.

Their voices faded as the two men stepped outside. Justice turned back to Cashel who was gently stroking Sanjeli's neck. Kashir stood on guard over both of them but he looked like he was going to sleep.

"You should be careful going anywhere without your bodyguard," Justice scolded.

Cashel shrugged. "I forget I have one here."

"But, surely it is something you have had to get used to all your life?" Cashel was a territorial Alpha-heir, and an omega. Not that Justice had worked out the significance of that yet. He knew omegas were highly revered and sought after but he had no idea if there had ever been any first-born sons with omega abilities. He would have to ask their contact.

"I have never had a personal bodyguard until my father

appointed Hale two days ago," Cashel said and stood up. He looked longingly at both horses.

"Have you ever ridden?" Justice asked, leaving the question of why he had never had a bodyguard alone. It was not something that mattered anymore as Justice would protect him now.

Cashel shook his head. "Not since I was a child."

"Because you are an omega?" Justice pressed and then immediately realized he had said the wrong thing again when Cashel stiffened and his head came up defiantly.

"Being an omega does not make me incapable. I was forbidden by my father." Cashel took a step to the stall door and Justice blocked him.

"Forgive me. I never thought to suggest otherwise." Cashel was shivering again, even though he was better clothed, the cape he wore wasn't thick enough to warm him, and Solonara was similar to Arrides in that the temperatures dropped quite dramatically at night due to the clear skies. Justice immediately took off his own jacket and draped it around Cashel's shoulders before he could protest. "I simply meant," Justice continued, "that omegas are precious to Askara, and should be protected as the gift they are."

"Precious?" Cashel repeated, the scorn dripping from his lips. "I have a bodyguard here so my father can control me without actually locking me away." Cashel must have immediately regretted his outburst because he ducked his head and hunched inwards, pulling Justice's jacket tight.

Justice very carefully hooked his finger under Cashel's chin and gently raised it until Cashel's blue eyes were focused on his. "I cannot agree with your father's reasoning, but when you are mine no army would ever be enough to protect you. I will never let you out of my sight. We will ride together in the day, and every night you will sleep safe in my arms."

Cashel's lips parted as if he were about to talk but Justice silenced them with his own. The sound that came from Justice's throat as they touched was nothing he had ever made before, and then they were kissing. Justice's arms wrapped around Cashel to pull him forward, nearly lifting him off his feet, and then Cashel wrenched himself backwards and scrambled away, putting his back to the stall partition.

"I am sorry," Justice offered but Cashel was shaking. "What is it?" Cashel shook his head and wrapped his arms around his middle. Justice hunched down and simply waited until Cashel's breathing slowed.

He had scared him. "Would you like me to escort you back or summon your servant?"

Cashel looked up and took a settling breath. "It wasn't you. I am simply wary of Alphas."

Justice took another breath. Wary of Alphas? He was untouched? Possibly, but that was rare in a wolf, almost unheard of. "You have no need to fear me," Justice explained. "It is better that I have the experience to make your first time worth—"

Cashel's derisive snort shut Justice up fast. "I am not some untried boy," he whispered. "Quite the opposite, in fact." Justice moved forward slowly. He wanted to be closer but he didn't want Cashel any more scared than he had been. He turned around with his back to the same wall as Cashel. Kashir sighed and relaxed, sleeping on his feet. "You must know the purpose of the games."

Justice nodded. "To have the honor of mating you." He said it in case Cashel was unsure of his intentions.

Cashel's lips pulled up in mockery of the earlier smile. "Not exactly, though, is it? The actual purpose is to get me heavy with pup."

Justice shrugged. As his original intention was to end Cashel's life along with his father's, he had never given a single thought to the possibility of Cashel having a pup. To be honest he thought the idea was some sort of huge hoax perpetrated by Darius to keep being a territorial Alpha, although from the information they had been given there was no other wolf in the entire territory that would dare challenge him for the role.

"You should know many have tried and been unsuccessful."

Justice's mouth fell open, and for a second he thought the howl he had heard his own wolf make in protest had come from outside. *Many have tried?* Fuck, what had his father made him go through?

Justice thought for a moment. "You don't know me. You have little reason to trust me, but if you didn't you would not have come here tonight." Cashel glanced at him. Justice could see the indecision all over his face, and the longing. Cashel was exhausted. Whatever his father had put him through, he could recognize someone at the end of his tether, and Cashel was certainly there. He also had a wolf in there, somewhere. It must be buried deep in his mind, as Justice hadn't sensed it at all. In fact, it hadn't occurred to him that he should have, but now that he did think about it, it was odd that his wolf didn't seem strong enough to protect him at all. It was certainly unable to regulate his body temperature, which was strange. And it didn't seem to be sensing Justice as his mate either, which was frankly baffling. Wolves knew instantly, even if their humans took a little catching up. A wolf's connection to their mate was instant.

His had been.

Cashel was also nearly touching him without realizing it. But that was an Alpha thing. He was used to random pack members turning up ostensibly just to pass the time of day. He had seen it with his father so many times and had asked him why. "Because they need my touch, Son," his father had explained. "The Alpha isn't just here to give orders and expect instant obedience. I am a touchstone. They need me in their lives to center it. We wield a power that is almost a living thing. All the pack members are naturally drawn to it and want to please their Alpha." Justice had said that sounded great. Zane was a pain in his ass and he couldn't wait for the day he could order him around. His father had roared with laughter, but then had asked him a question. "And what if Zane got hurt or injured doing what you had ordered him to do?" Justice had squirmed. He didn't like that idea.

"But he's my friend, really," he had supposed.

"And Neil?" Justice had immediately glowered. He hated Neil

with a passion. Neil was three years older than him and tried to make him feel stupid every chance he got. He opened his mouth to give an angry retort and imagined Neil hurting because Justice had taken his horse or denied him food. Alphas had the right to do that; he knew they did. But Neil looked after his little sister that had been bitten by a snake last year. They had had to cut off her foot to stop the poison spreading because she had been too young to shift and his father had not been there to compel her. Another wolf had cut off the foot because Neil's dad had sickened and died when Neil was barely six. Thinking about all that didn't make Justice want to take anything from him at all. It was hardly surprising Neil was always in a bad mood.

"Exactly," his father had said as if Justice had spoken all that out loud. "Never forget an Alpha is basically the head of a very large family. You need to keep that family safe and happy. A good Alpha eats first to keep himself strong, but he makes sure the kill is enough to feed everyone so no one goes without."

Justice sighed. His father had been a very wise man. He would have known what to say to Cashel.

"And what happens if you never get heavy with a pup?"

Cashel jerked as if Justice had stabbed him. His round eyes filled with a hopelessness Justice couldn't stand, and with a low noise in the back of his throat he pulled Cashel over to sit on his knee and bent him forward into his chest. The tears had already started and Cashel sobbed. He clutched at the front of Justice's shirt and he shook with grief. Justice just held him close and hushed him for the second time in two nights. All the pain and fear came pouring out with hesitant anguished words. How he had been so scared. How the last heir had half-shifted and tore into him. How he had no choice but to do what his father asked and how much he was trapped.

"No," Justice promised as the storm of tears finally abated. "I swear to you—" Justice stopped. He was just about to say that Cashel was his mate and he would be wherever Justice was for the rest of his life, but... *that makes me exactly like Darius.* Cashel had no choice.

Had never had any choice. Going from being forced to mate because his father made him, to being forced to mate because of Justice's wolf's need was the same thing. The human part of Cashel had no say in either and if Justice dominated him and took his choice from him, it made him no better than Darius. Cashel would resent him, if not at the beginning when he was grateful to be protected, then at the end when he was trapped by his own body again. Even as everything in him screamed to say the exact opposite of what he was about to, he gritted his teeth and said the words anyway. "I promise when this is over and I am Alpha you will be free to do whatever you want and live wherever you like."

Cashel raised tear-swollen, shocked eyes. "You would do that?"

Justice nodded. The hope that shone in Cashel suddenly made him feel ten feet tall even as he hated promising the exact opposite of what he needed. "On my honor. I know you have no reason to believe —" But Justice's words were cut off as Cashel fastened hungry lips over his own. Justice froze. *No.* He wrenched Cashel from his arms. "The offer is freely given," he growled. "I do not need payment."

Cashel leaned against him as if boneless and Justice was unable to keep him at arm's length. Cashel snuggled in close and lifted his head so it was under Justice's chin. He could feel the warm breath from Cashel. "I have only ever had people take from me but twice you have held me, first while I was sick, and second while I cried all over you. You haven't judged either time. If I stood and walked away now you would let me."

He would, but it was likely Zane and Armand would have to hold him down. He would do anything to see his mate whole. "I don't know the Alphas you have met, but none of them have the honor to call themselves such."

"Would you do something for me?"

Justice tightened his grip but then unclenched his fingers before he panicked Cashel. "If it is in my power to give."

"Would you kiss me but stop should I need you to?"

Justice gazed at Cashel in complete torment. He had no idea

what he was asking, but Justice would run himself through with a sword before he would deny his request. He nodded, hoping Cashel didn't need him to articulate it.

Cashel pushed up and hesitated before pressing a chaste kiss on Justice's firmly closed lips. Justice growled and Cashel's eyes widened. Justice smiled ruefully. "I'm sorry. Please ignore my wolf. I have no trouble controlling him." Cashel nodded and tried again, but this time moved his lips over Justice's.

Justice closed his eyes in desperation and mentally started reciting the funeral rites of his people. He heard the sigh from Cashel and opened them. The sadness was evident in the downward turn of his mouth.

"What is it? Did I scare you?" He had held himself rigid. How he hadn't moved when Cashel did was beyond him.

Cashel let out a little sigh again. "I know I'm not very attractive compared to the she-wolves. I—"

"Who told you such an outrageous lie?" Justice demanded. Cashel's shy smile made him all warm inside. "You are breathtaking," he repeated in case Cashel didn't understand what he was saying. "And I don't just mean the gorgeous package on the outside," he added. "I mean you also have a good heart." He nodded his chin towards Sanjeli's head. She had moved so her head was touching Cashel's foot. "Horses are excellent judges of character."

"I can still be a good person and you not find me pleasing," Cashel argued.

Justice shook his head. "It is torture to stay still and not lay you down and kiss the length of your naked body, but I would sooner die than have you afraid of me." *And he had made a promise.*

Cashel's breath hitched and Justice saw his pupils dilate as his words registered. "Show me," Cashel whispered.

Justice obediently bent his head, swiping his tongue at the seam of Cashel's lips which parted instantly to allow him entrance. The gorgeous smell from Cashel wove around them both, and Justice's cock throbbed and pulsed as his heart hammered in his chest.

Justice's wolf snarled and snapped inside him, urging Justice on, but he kept him tightly locked away. One gentle kiss simply melded into another and another until Cashel wrenched his head free simply to breathe. Justice buried his head into Cashel's neck and licked and sucked the delicate skin. He pressed into Cashel and Cashel groaned. The sound, long and low, was full of want and need. "Want you," Justice ground out desperately and tried to ease back, worried his control wasn't as absolute of his own body as it was of his wolf. He had a second to doubt what he was doing. To worry he had lost his mind. To fear for his people and that of Solonara, and then Cashel licked his pink swollen lips and extended his arms up.

"I want you too." It was all the invitation Justice needed and every other thought left his brain. In seconds, he had his breeches off and Cashel sat up and wrenched his shirt off. Justice traced a finger over every scar and every bruise. Never again. No one would ever so much as harm a hair on his head. Justice would kill any that thought to even look at what was his. Justice bent his head, unable to resist another kiss, and Cashel arched in response as Justice's fingers slid lower and under his clothes. Justice wished they weren't in a stable. That they were somewhere warm so he could strip Cashel down and worship his naked body. Cashel arched again off the straw as Justice slid his hands under the loose breeches Cashel wore and finally closed his fingers around Cashel's thickening length. The cry from Cashel was delicious but Justice silenced it with his lips lest it would bring Zane back.

There were many things Justice wanted to do. He wanted to suck and lave Cashel to completion with his mouth. He wanted to bathe him, and slick him with the rich Agarva lotion to make his skin soft and feel cared for. He wanted to lay him down on soft clean furs, wrap him in silk sheets, kiss every inch of his beautiful pale skin, but every gasp and mewl from Cashel's throat was thundering Justice down a quickening path he had no brakes for. He wanted to be inside Cashel. He needed to be inside him like he needed air to breathe and his heart would stop its rapid crescendo if he was unable.

The outside door opening shocked them both and Justice groaned even as he inhaled a scent he hadn't smelled for five long years. Cashel moved quickly, alarmed at the noise, and scrabbled for his clothes, righting them with a few tugs. They both saw the figure move quickly, and then lower her hood. Cashel gaped in astonishment. Justice, of course, did not.

Helena stepped forward. "My prince, you have been missed. The healer went to check on you and I invented a story about you being with Bella and asking not to be disturbed, but I think he will check again soon."

"How did you know I was here?" Cashel asked as he accepted the cloak Helena removed and wrapped himself up to hide his face.

"Hale is outside keeping watch and will escort you safely back. He followed your scent." But Justice knew it was no coincidence she was here. "Please go quickly, my prince," Helena begged and with a quick glance at Justice, Cashel hurried from the stable. They both waited a beat until the stables were empty.

Helena extended her arms and Justice walked straight into them.

"Mom," he choked out and clutched her tight.

Chapter Eight

Justice blinked and sat up immediately. He had fallen asleep in the stables after his mom had left. They had barely exchanged a dozen hurried words as she couldn't be caught with him. He wondered if Cashel was awake and didn't like the thought of him waking up alone. The answering howl in his mind told him his wolf didn't like it either. Justice stared unseeing, going over in his mind what had been said. He had promised Cashel could leave, and then Cashel had kissed him. He had writhed in pleasure, suddenly seeming confident. Justice had nearly driven himself insane trying to please him, but not possess him. To give of himself but not take anything back. Could he do that? Let him go but ensure his safety?

Justice absently stepped up to Kashir and rested his head on Kashir's neck. The stallion never moved but Justice knew Kashir was very well aware Justice would never hurt him. Was that what it was? Had he given Cashel the confidence for *an experiment*? Could he find the courage to kiss so hungrily because he didn't worry Justice was making demands?

That he would let him go?

Justice was reeling. In three days he had gone from arriving to kill a prince, to finding out they were mates, to realizing they might never be together.

He peered towards the stable doors and saw the dim light showing it was nearing dawn. He groaned and Kashir snorted softly at him, then walked to the opposite corner and stood with Sanjeli. Where was Zane?

Justice got to his feet. He quickly let himself out of the stall and walked to the little room where Zane had gone. He pushed open the door and Zane blinked an eye open from where he was huddled in a bedroll.

Axel sat up and groaned.

Cold washed through Justice and he lunged for the young slave. "What are you doing here?" He thundered. Zane was up in a second and put himself firmly between Justice and the man he had slept with.

"What's wrong?"

"You risk us all by him being here," he nearly spat the words but knew it was a ridiculous thing to say. No one would care if a wolf bedded a human slave. He was simply jealous because Zane had slept next to a warm body and he had not. Justice whirled to leave, but Zane's hand on his shoulder slowed him. Axel scrambled to his feet, stammering apologies.

"Justice, it isn't Axel's fault you cannot have your mate." The door slammed behind Axel's retreating back. Justice sighed.

"I promised to let him go," Justice whispered.

"What?" It was Zane's turn to stare at Justice. "You mean he *isn't* your mate?"

Justice blew out a long breath as two grooms walked in and began their morning tasks. They ignored both him and Zane, and Justice pulled Zane outside so they wouldn't be heard. "He doesn't feel the pull and I didn't bite him. We were interrupted."

Zane's eyebrows lifted. "By?" He drew the word out mischievously.

"Our contact." Justice would never risk acknowledging his mom until it was safe to do so.

It had been over five years ago. Three full moons after his father had died he had woken to find her dressed and in his tent.

He had sat up, alarmed that there was something wrong. "Mom?"

Helena had smiled her beautiful smile and knelt down, taking his hand in both of hers and pulling it up to cup her cheek. "My Alpha."

Justice had waited. She had called him by his title for a reason.

"I am travelling to Solonara."

"You are *what*?" He had jumped up, alarmed. But she had gentled him as only mothers do.

"We need accurate information. There are only a few of us gifted with a hawk." They used the birds to send messages, and his mother was exceptional with them. It was she who had taught Armand.

"Exactly, which is why Seth will go."

She had smiled again. "Mara is with pup. Seth's place is with her," she admonished gently.

"And your place is with me," Justice stressed.

She shook her head. "My place as Enfantata—"

She hesitated. Enfantata was the title given to the Alpha's mother. It was a term of great respect. An Enfantata often helped with the teaching of the younger ones. That they learned respect and the ways of the pack.

Justice stood quickly, ready for any objection.

"My place," she resumed, "is to support my son and protect the pack. I can gain access to the pack house as a servant."

"No," Justice had choked the word out. "I absolutely forbid it." But his mom had simply looked amused. It was his right as her Alpha to say that, but he knew as her son he had no such power.

"Come, walk with me to the beach." She held her hand out. "What did you decide to do about finding the source your father spoke of?"

Justice searched her gaze in frustration. "A source of what?"

Helena smiled. "I don't know, but I loved your father. He would not speak of something unimportant."

Justice had capitulated, knowing she was right. There was no one else better qualified. She was as equally skilled with a needle and thread as much as a knife. Could protect herself if necessary and didn't suffer fools, but everyone adored her. For the first time in years Justice had wanted to cry. Erdal stood quietly on the sands with his small boat waiting to take her and her two small bags. Justice passed her some coins he had gotten on his last trip. They had no need of them here.

She shook her head. "If I am found with a lot of money it would take too much explaining." She gestured to the pack in the boat. "I have plenty of food, and will send word of my arrival very soon." Justice's eyes had slid to the light cage and sure enough both his mother's mated pair of hawks were in there.

Justice had spent the next day on the beach waiting for one of the birds. Two days later he had been rewarded with a note saying his mom had gotten a job in a tavern, but in a week she had secured space to travel towards Tarik. Justice had winced imagining what she was doing. His wolf had howled at the thought of her in any danger, but in just over ten days she had gotten a job as a maid in some rich merchant's house. Two years after that she had started working for Darius and another three saw her become his trusted housekeeper in charge of everything except the security. They could never have planned anything without her. It was unlikely they would have even found out about the games in time.

Zane squeezed Justice's shoulder, offering comfort, and drew him back to the present. "I cannot smell him on you," he said, "which is surprising. I wonder if it has anything to do with him being an omega. I must admit to being puzzled he has no discernable scent."

Justice's laugh was filled with sheer incredulity. "Then there is something wrong with your wolf's nose, my friend, because I could smell his gorgeous scent before I even knew what it was."

"Think." Zane's voice dropped. "No one has ever been able to tell we are what they call hybrids either. We put that down to the humans on Arrides being a different breed to the rest of Askara, but that makes little sense. You may be able to smell Cashel, but trust me when I say no one else can."

"You can't?" It didn't make sense but Justice hadn't the time to devote to puzzling it out. When they had first landed in Salem all those years ago, the stench of fish in the whole port was enough to mask any scent, and then they had gradually realized that no one seemed able to tell the difference. Maybe the reason Zane couldn't smell Cashel was similar, although he knew every scent of a wolf was unique to his or her mate.

Zane walked with Justice back towards his room. "I am assuming our plans have changed?" Justice growled but didn't answer until they were both in his room away from wolves' ears. Armand arrived within a few seconds.

"Something interesting happened last night," Armand said as he walked in.

Zane snorted and ignored the dark look Justice sent him.

"Someone unsuccessfully tried to bribe Valerie's younger brother who is a stable hand. They must have noticed me with her."

"Bribe him to do what?"

"Plant a bottle of pepper chaff in our belongings." Only the stable hands had access to the saddles and the bags, whereas the belongings in their rooms were open to all the house slaves.

"Pepper chaff?" Justice repeated. "Whatever for?" Pepper chaff was a short-acting stimulant, but only the same as about three strong cups of coffee or even the Ceylan tea he used to brew on Arrides.

"Really?" Zane said, interested. Justice and Armand both looked at him waiting for the explanation. He carried on. "Pepper chaff can in large enough doses counteract Shrome leaves, but the effect on the body is often fatal. It may be used in an emergency." He glanced pointedly at Justice. "If, say, someone needed to calm an animal but didn't care about its future wellbeing..."

"You think someone cheated yesterday?" Justice immediately understood.

"No," Zane said flatly. "I think this is worse. I think someone wanted it to look as if competitors cheated. If they had succeeded in planting the pepper chaff on you and it had been found, it would have resulted in death. The rules as read out yesterday were very clear."

Armand whistled. "Someone obviously doesn't want you to win."

"Where are our saddles now?"

"Being guarded by Tamarl, Valerie's brother," Armand smiled. "He is completely obsessed with Orest, and I have promised to teach him how to catch and tame a hawk of his own."

They all ate. Justice pushed his food around aimlessly. Where was Cashel? Was he safe? Was he thinking about him? Why didn't he seem to recognize him as his mate? The questions were driving him insane.

"He's heartsick," Zane explained as Armand watched him askance. Armand nearly threw himself back in the chair which creaked alarmingly and put his hand over his chest.

"As am I," he declared.

Justice smiled for the first time since he had woken up but he noticed Zane didn't.

"What's the plan?" Zane asked.

"We need to send the message to our people," Justice decided. "As agreed."

Armand nodded. His beloved Orest would take the message straight to their scouts in Salem waiting for the order to advance. Fires would be lit in an agreed place to bring the boats in.

"So, three days early?" Zane nodded. It would take his army at least four days to land and get to the capital.

"You are still going to take the territory by force?" Armand interrupted.

Justice nodded, but he couldn't wait for the competition to end as had been the previous plan. "I don't trust Darius, or what he might do. If the ships land tonight we can take the city in three days. I just need the chance to get Cashel to safety because as soon as Darius knows the ships have landed I don't know what he will do." He looked at Zane and Armand. "If you wish to secure someone they must be at the stables before dawn." They both nodded in understanding. Justice had a feeling they would be taking three people.

Chapter Nine

When you are mine...

Justice had been so sure, but Cashel had ignored his wolf for so long the animal had retreated so far down he wasn't sure how to ever call it back. The one time he had shifted had been such agony he never ever wanted to go through that again, so he firmly ignored every tentative brush the animal inside made upon his mind. Over time it had become fainter and fainter until he had stopped being able to sense it at all.

And now he had no way of telling if Justice was his mate or not. He had no friends to speak of—none since he was old enough to even care about such things as mates.

Justice had been so gentle with him last night. He was strong, solid, dependable, but Cashel didn't want a crutch. He wanted a love borne of mutual respect and friendship. He understood the genetic call of his body—and his animal, if it even still existed inside him— but he didn't want to exchange one prison for another. Justice may keep him safe but he yearned for more. And while he was desperately attracted to him, Cashel feared it was simply a natural response to Justice making him feel safe and wanted. And then Justice had said he would let him go, which had dumbfounded Cashel. He had known Justice was telling him they were mates without using the word. Alphas were the epitome of possession, which meant only one of two things: Justice was trying to make him think they were mates and making false promises, or he had held himself back for some reason known only to him. Was he just saying what he thought Cashel wanted to hear? Or was he being gentle because he understood how afraid Cashel was of Alphas?

Cashel hadn't slept when he returned. Having to leave Justice had been the hardest thing he had ever done in his entire life, but with all these doubts running through his mind he was almost glad they had been interrupted. And really, if Justice had been sincere, he wouldn't have been able to let Cashel go. The competition rules that Gaven had insisted upon and read out were absolute. Anyone caught cheating would be immediately put to death, and he was sure that fraternizing with him—or even worse, them being caught in bed—would be exactly that. No. Somehow, he had to get through the next five days until Justice was victorious as the man was sure he would be. Then—he hoped—they would have the rest of their lives to sort everything out.

He was bathed and dressed before a shamefaced Axel let himself into his room quietly, but Hale immediately followed so they didn't get a chance to talk. Cashel didn't dare so much as breathe as Hale came close, in case he smelled Justice on him, but the wolf couldn't have noticed anything. He stood obediently in his collar waiting for Axel to put the cock ring on, but Hale shook his head when the boy picked it up from the square of linen it was wrapped in.

"I received no specific instructions on how you were to be prepared today, so leave it off." Cashel chewed his lip. He didn't want Hale getting into trouble.

"Are you sure?"

Hale nodded. "And we have been summoned to appear quickly."

"But the games don't start for at least another hour," Cashel protested.

"To the great hall. I don't know what's going on, but Gaven's angry about something." Cashel stumbled back as his knees nearly gave out. It was Justice, it had to be. *Sorin's heart*. Please don't let him have said something to Gaven or his father.

Hale caught him and looked him up and down. "Are you well?" Axel came close to his other side, his eyes big and round.

Cashel drew in a breath and Hale's voice softened. "I dare not ignore an instruction, but I will make sure you are comfortable wherever we are to watch the games from." He looked at Axel. "Stay close to your prince today. If anyone questions it, say you have orders from me."

Axel nodded and clasped Cashel's arm as Hale let his other one go. Cashel had no choice but to follow, dread weighing down every step. They slipped into the hall silently, a mere few seconds before his father and what seemed to be thirty guards. Gaven stepped forward and requested the competitors be brought in. Cashel's eyes were riveted on Justice as he stepped forward with the others, and of course Justice's eyes immediately focused on him.

He could breathe. Worry seemed to trickle away as the amber eyes burned with confidence, and something else Cashel could not —*dare not*—put a name to.

"Challengers, I have grievous news." Gaven stepped forward and the four winners including Justice were immediately surrounded. "Because some competitors seemed to subdue their mounts with ease yesterday, we have had a complaint." Gaven looked around the assembled onlookers. "Of cheating."

There was a gasp from the hall. Wolves were a proud race and to be accused of cheating was akin to being accused of treason. Darius stepped forward. "I want the winning competitors from yesterday to step forward and agree to submit to having their belongings searched."

Malcolm, the first wolf to successfully ride from the ring yesterday, stepped forward, protesting his indignation, but he was ignored. The locked boxes containing the saddle bags were brought forward and emptied one by one. Justice never even glanced at his own. He acted unafraid and simply disinterested as if the whole farce had nothing whatsoever to do with him.

Each box was searched until Gaven held up a small brown packet somewhat triumphantly and Malcolm the beta blanched when he saw it. "It isn't mine, Alpha. I swear," he begged and dropped to his knees in front of Darius.

Darius tilted his head to the side as if considering the plea, but a second after he lifted his hand, a gamma stepped behind the wolf and simply slit his throat. Cashel jumped, as did a lot of those assembled. It had happened so fast, not even the wolf on his knees had a chance to see the blade. Complete silence reined as the beta shifted into his wolf—an automatic reaction to save his life—but the gamma behind him was faster and this time the blade plunged in the animal's chest and stopped its heart. He shifted back to human immediately and lay bleeding out on the floor. Cashel closed his eyes at the horrific sight but the next sound from Gaven had him opening them in terror.

"Justice, step forward." Gaven's low order was almost an insult. Justice was an Alpha. It was obvious in every line of the wolf's body, from the mark on his neck to the sheer confidence that exuded from him. Gaven was simply a beta-commander, and should Justice win, he would become his Alpha. It seemed odd the beta would be so careless and simply refer to him by his given name.

Cashel had seen the look on Gaven's face last night when his father had granted Justice the boon. Furious hadn't even come close, which had made him pause. He'd always thought that Gaven despised him, that he was a pathetic creature that brought shame to his father's name. But now he wasn't so sure. Oh, he was convinced Gaven still despised him, but he wondered if he had higher ambitions than being a beta commander. What if Gaven wanted the coveted Alpha role? But Gaven hadn't entered the competition so it didn't make sense.

The slaves quickly searched Justice's belongings and Justice never once took his eyes from Darius. He showed not one morsel of fear—and neither did he react when the slaves didn't find anything. Gaven scowled. "Search again," he bit out but Darius held up a hand to stop them. Without saying anything, Gaven inclined his head and ordered the next competitor to be searched. There was no more found. Cashel blew a shaky breath out and felt the last of his anxiety drain out of him. Axel took his arm. Cashel felt sick. The adrenaline and fear coursing through him made him lightheaded and shaky now it had gone. He had had nothing to eat or drink except a few sips of water, as his stomach had been twisted in knots all night.

"Please accept my apologies," Darius continued. "There are refreshments being set out and the games will start in an hour." He turned around and marched out, followed by Gaven and his guards. Cashel sank to the nearest seat when his legs refused to keep him upright anymore.

"Are you well, my prince?"

Cashel looked to see Justice flanked by Zane and Armand watching him carefully, but even if he hadn't, after last night he knew that voice better than his own. He opened his mouth but no words came out. Or none he could speak anyway. He couldn't beg to be kissed, or even simply to be held in the same strong arms as last night.

"I had a restless night," he murmured, and smiled shyly. Justice's answering grin was nearly blinding.

"Will you watch the games today?"

Cashel nodded. His father had been very clear he was to be present.

"Then perhaps you would do me the honor of wearing my token?"

Cashel stared at the small flower Justice held out. It was a sprig from a Juno bush. They were common all over Solonara, but as he stared at Justice he had a feeling they had a greater significance to him.

"I would be honored." He nodded to Axel to take the flower. If Justice was upset that he hadn't touched him he didn't show it, but

Cashel didn't trust himself. The way Cashel felt, one touch and he would have flung himself into Justice's outstretched arms.

"Perhaps you would allow me to get you some refreshments?"

Cashel tilted his head to look at Justice just as a servant appeared with his tonic. It would be so nice to share a simple meal and his belly rumbled as if it was agreeing. "Maybe when you have finished today?"

"Of course." Justice bowed and Cashel watched as the three men walked from the hall. He heard the sigh from beside him and glanced at Axel who looked as heartsick as he was, but bit back any comment. Zane was a wolf. Axel a human slave. They could never be together, and Cashel had no power to change that.

Cashel sipped his tonic, finishing in time as the gammas arrived to escort them to their seats. Cashel smothered a groan as he saw there was a group of seats arranged on a dais next to the parade ring. Judging from the guards already present he was to be with his father, and as if he had wished it Darius, Gaven, and the rest of his retinue walked to the stand. Darius eyed Cashel. "You look far too pale," he snapped in irritation. Cashel dipped his head meekly and took his seat as indicated three down from where his father sat. There was nowhere for Axel to be anywhere near him. Even Hale was a good ten feet away, which, judging by his scowl, he didn't like.

Darius rubbed his hands and accepted a goblet of wine when offered. He had a table brought and helped himself to the nuts and sweetmeats as arranged. Cashel hid a deep sigh and focused on the ring. Justice was one of the first ones out. Seated astride Kashir, he made all the other wolves seem less somehow. Cashel heard his father murmur to Gaven. "Did you find out where that horse came from?"

Gaven shook his head. "I am told the wolf bought the animal in Salem."

Darius growled. "Then find the breeder and remind him that I should always have first choice of any animal he has."

"If he loses Alpha, the animal would be yours anyway," Gaven replied silkily. Cashel's heart sped up.

"Mmm," Darius pondered. "I can make it a condition of acknowledging his pack."

Gaven bristled. "He's trouble. I would never turn my back around him. His ancestors are murderers and thieves."

Darius smiled but Cashel couldn't decide whether he was agreeing with Gaven or not. He shrugged. "It matters not. Horses go missing." Darius looked pointedly at Gaven, and Cashel held his breath. Did Darius believe no one could hear him, or was he so confident he simply didn't care, knowing he would never be challenged? Gaven bowed and slid away but Cashel watched him talking quietly to one of his gammas. The gamma nodded and disappeared. Cashel knew they were up to something and he wanted to warn Justice but he knew he wouldn't be allowed to leave.

The gamma stood in the middle of the ring, lifted his sword asking for quiet, and the crowd hushed. "The first challenge will be hand to hand. Each competitor will try and unseat the other by whatever means necessary. The fight will continue until one competitor surrenders. If neither do then the fight will continue to the death."

Cashel couldn't help his gasp, and Darius looked in irritation at the noise. But...to the *death*? Cashel's heart that was already beating fast nearly stopped. The first two competitors nudged their horses forward. Cashel relaxed a little when Justice left the arena with the others. Cashel barely noticed the first fight, too intent on working out how to talk to Axel without anyone hearing him.

The crowd roared and Cashel turned to the fight. He hissed in a hurried breath. Both warriors were dismounted. One was limping and clutching his side. The other circling, brandishing his sword. Light on his feet he darted one way and then the next. It was obvious the injured wolf couldn't move half as quickly, and Cashel held his breath. Then the injured wolf lowered his sword and turned towards the Alpha with his head bowed indicating his surrender.

The other wolf also sheathed his sword and turned towards Darius as the crowd cheered him. Cashel looked at both horses, uninjured. He sighed in relief and dutifully clapped for the victor along with everyone else. Servants stepped forward to bring Darius more wine and Cashel turned to Axel. The man stepped forward quickly with some water for Cashel.

"Come now, Cashel. This is a celebration." Darius beckoned to the same slave with the wine and pointed to Cashel's goblet. Axel stood back, unsure of what he was supposed to do.

"Please congratulate the winner for me, and enquire after *all* the horses." He looked pointedly at Axel.

"Really, Cashel," Darius interrupted. "What is this sudden fascination with the animals?"

Cashel paled a little. Gaven must have told his father he had tried to stop the competition yesterday. The beta had a smug expression on his face, of course he had.

"I merely appreciate warriors in all forms, Alpha," Cashel answered and shot another look at Axel. He made a shooing motion with his hand in dismissal, something he never did, and Axel turned obediently and walked away. Cashel bit his lip. He hadn't managed any warning, and had no idea whether Axel would even pass on his message to any riders except the two that had just fought. Without thinking, and because he was thirsty, Cashel lifted the goblet to his mouth and took a gulp. He managed to not choke but the wine was awful. Well, he was sure it was in fact one of the best Tethra produced but it was one of the strong reds his father favored. Cashel had no intention of drinking any more. The memories of his shame in the garden in front of Justice were too fresh.

A few minutes later another two competitors arrived and the games continued. Gaven beckoned over Hale and told him to return to other duties as Cashel was going to remain with them. Hale shot Cashel an apologetic look as he disappeared, but he could not disobey a direct order from his beta-commander.

No one died. That was the best way to sum up the next four hours. There were still fifteen competitors and the morning seemed to drag on forever as one by one all the competitors eventually surrendered to a winning opponent. Some of the fights were long. Cashel was sure they were technically skilled but knew his father and his cronies were getting bored both by the conversation that had erupted all around him, and by the quantity they were drinking. A slave stepped forward to offer Cashel more wine even though he had had none since the first sip.

"Some water, please," Cashel almost whispered, convinced his father wasn't listening.

"No." The growl from his father was so loud all chatter in the stand stopped immediately. He glanced at the servant. "Bring him some wine." He leaned forward and Cashel swallowed nervously. "No son of mine sips water like some girl."

Cashel lowered his eyes quickly and obediently sipped from the fresh goblet that was produced. He could have cried in relief when the next two competitors came into the arena. Cashel didn't drink any more wine, but he daren't ask for any more water. The suns beat down mercilessly, and even though the dais had a linen cover, there was no breeze to bring any relief from the climbing heat. Within an hour Cashel's head hammered with every clash of swords, and his mouth was dry. All his healers had been very clear. Because his stomach could hold so little, he was to take small amounts of fluid very often. His father had read the reports from his healers, but maybe he just simply didn't care. His lack of sleep was making him incredibly tired and at one point the roar from the crowd made him startle and open his eyes, not remembering he had even closed them.

After the next two challengers finished, his father stood and announced a break for the midday meal, except the meal in Solonara wasn't usually in the middle of the day, but in the early afternoon when the sun was at its hottest, since everyone who could stayed inside. The stores were always closed for two hours and many people even slept if they could. Cashel nearly laughed at Darius's announcement because as far as he could see, the Alpha hadn't stopped eating or drinking since he had sat down. Darius completely ignored Cashel as he swept past, but Cashel didn't mind. He would just sit and wait until they came back. He wasn't even thirsty now, and he definitely wasn't hungry.

"My prince?" Cashel raised heavy eyes and squinted at Axel. "Do you need to retire?"

Cashel shook his head, bemused. He was quite content to wait here. He felt like he could doze safely away from his father's sight. Axel frowned. "I will go get you some water," he pronounced and almost ran. Cashel wanted to reassure him he wasn't thirsty, but Axel disappeared too fast. Cashel gazed at the empty arena and saw the gammas positioned to guard the entrance to the stands where he sat. He closed his eyes against his aching head and slumped in the seat.

Chapter Ten

The morning had been endless. As far as Justice could tell, the competitors had been quite evenly matched, and they had all shown some self-preservation instinct and surrendered before they were slain. None of them were in a hurry to repeat the sight of the wolf being slaughtered that morning. Justice stood with the others as the Alpha and his retinue swept into the room and the slaves then immediately began serving food and drink.

After five hours of waiting interspersed with gently exercising Kashir, Justice was irritable. Some food would help, though. Justice's heart sank as Cashel's chair remained empty. He had hoped Cashel would have been as eager to see him again as he was desperate to see Cashel. His wolf was restless, and Justice sympathized. It was going to be a long day and there were still four competitors left to fight, including him.

"Alpha?"

Justice looked up as the slave spoke. It was Axel. He frowned. Axel held a platter of meat, but Justice had no idea why he was in here when he should be with Cashel.

"Justice," Axel whispered.

Justice went completely still. Axel had surprised him by calling him Alpha, which Darius had technically said he wasn't, but the slave was risking the sharp end of a sword by addressing him by his first name. Justice stood, every hair on his neck upright. His wolf was growling. Axel turned and walked from the room without a word, putting the platter down as he neared the door. Justice followed him outside.

"What is it?" Justice asked as soon as they were clear. He knew Axel had deliberately set out to get his attention.

"My prince is still in the stands. I tried to get him to move, but he won't."

Justice blew out a long breath and his heart slowed. "He is probably sick of having to listen to his father," Justice replied with a little sarcasm, his irritation at the long day showing.

"No." Axel put his hand on Justice's arm and Justice stiffened.

"What is it?" A slave would never dare touch a wolf unless asked.

"He has been out there for nearly six hours and was allowed no water. He was instructed to drink wine."

Justice smirked. So, the little prince was going to get hammered again, was he? Justice didn't blame him. The wine would have tempted Justice if he still didn't have to fight this afternoon.

"No, you don't understand." Axel sounded frantic. "Cashel wouldn't drink it. He has had nothing. He is behaving oddly and I'm worried he will make himself sick. Gaven sent Hale to do other duties."

"You mean he's out there on his own?" Justice's voice rose incredulously.

Axel nodded. "The gammas are guarding the stands but I'm worried. He has to have certain drinks, especially water."

Justice was already walking quickly as Axel continued trying to explain. "Why does he have that dreadful tonic all the time?"

"I don't know exactly." Axel was having to run to keep up with Justice's massive strides. "He said his own healer wasn't allowed to come here. All I know is he eats really small amounts as often as he can." Justice swore when he saw even the gammas that had been guarding the entrance to the stands had gone. "He has scars."

Justice nodded. He had seen some of them last night. "Why doesn't he shift?"

"He is forbidden."

Justice didn't reply to that. He knew the strange rules forced upon she-wolves, and he supposed—as the only omegas he knew apart from Cashel were female—those rules applied to the omegas themselves.

He jumped up the stands. He could see Cashel slumped in a chair under the silk awning where he had sat yesterday. "Cashel?" Justice reached him. At first glance he looked asleep, but when he didn't answer Justice placed a hand on his head and pinched the skin on his arm between his thumb and finger. The skin was slow to spring back. Without a word Justice bent down and picked him up, heart thudding. Cashel was hot, burning, and his head lolled back on Justice's arm as if he was unaware he had been picked up. He had seen this in the desert so many times, especially with the kids. Dehydration could sneak up on them without warning and go from a simple headache to death in a few hours. He clutched Cashel to him and started running. "Get Zane from the stables, tell him to meet us at my rooms, and tell him what's wrong."

In the heat of the day, the streets were empty. He didn't meet one person as he ran. Zane caught up with him as he burst through the door to his rooms. "Sun sickness," he snapped and Zane simply nodded and opened the door to the bathing room.

Justice didn't even pause. Still carrying Cashel, he stepped down into the tepid water until he was waist deep. Zane stepped in behind him and started to strip Cashel while Justice held him. Justice sat down, immersing both of them up to their necks.

"Let his head fall back," Zane instructed and unclasped the collar from Cashel's neck. He threw it towards Axel. "Bring me a jug."

While Justice held Cashel, Zane poured the cool water over his hair. Justice knew what he was doing. The greatest heat loss from a body was through the head, and Cashel needed cooling and fast. Justice could have cried when Cashel's dry, cracked lips moved. Zane beamed and waded to the edge to ask Axel to pass him some water for Cashel to drink.

Zane passed Justice the goblet and Justice murmured, gently holding the goblet to Cashel's lips. Cashel swallowed a little and Justice took what seemed like the first breath since he had seen Axel. Cashel's eyelids fluttered.

"You're safe. I have you," Justice said. "Just rest," he added. Cashel moaned pitifully. Justice knew his head would feel like it was being cleaved in two. After another few seconds Cashel took a sip of water and blinked his eyes trying to focus on Justice. He parted his lips as if he was going to try and say something but Justice held the goblet to them instead. Cashel swallowed and his eyes drifted shut again.

Zane pressed his hand to the back of Cashel's neck. "He is cooler. I think you got him in time." He looked over at where Axel stood anxiously. "What is in that tonic he drinks?"

Justice smiled. He should have known Zane would have noticed.

"The cooks grind fresh meat, mixed with a little fat and blood."

Zane shot a puzzled glance at Justice, then back at Axel. "Why doesn't he just eat fresh meat?"

"He is also forbidden to shift," Justice added for Zane's benefit when Axel shook his head apologetically, indicating he didn't know.

"That's common," Zane answered. "Well, not the forbidden part, but I understand she-wolves have been forbidden from shifting for so long, it has nearly been bred out of them. They are incapable unless commanded by their Alpha. Omegas—more commonly female—are the same."

"By his Alpha?" mused Justice, and the look Zane shot him flashed the same understanding. Even though he hadn't bitten Cashel to mark him as his mate, he was willing to bet his own Alpha status was enough to compel Cashel to shift. Shifting would cure his headache instantly, to say nothing of whatever else was wrong with him. "Is he cool enough to get out?"

Zane nodded and took a huge drying cloth from the pile. Zane held out his arms and Justice couldn't help the soft growl that escaped his lips. Cashel was naked. Zane arched an eyebrow and the brown eyes crinkled with humor. Justice huffed, ignoring the smile and stood, passing Cashel to Zane. He stepped from the water, stripped from his wet clothes and picked another drying cloth to wrap around his waist. Zane immediately passed Cashel back to him and Justice strode into the bedroom. Axel had drawn the curtains so the room was dim. The overhead bamboo fans worked on a weight and pulley system. Once Axel had set it off, it was balanced so it wouldn't slow for hours. Justice sat on the bed and shook Cashel's arm.

"I don't want you to be frightened, but I need you to shift into your wolf."

Cashel tried to struggle ineffectually. "No. N-no, please. P-please. I am forbidden." He stammered his pleas in such a rush to get his words out and his eyes filled with tears.

Justice pressed him close and hushed him. Zane frowned, but pulling on fresh clothes belonging to Justice, he guided Axel out and closed the door behind him.

Justice wiped the wet hair from Cashel's brow, and then the tears that spilled onto his cheek. "I'm not going to do anything you don't want, but I think I can compel you to find your wolf." More tears fell.

"I don't have a wolf," he whispered. "I haven't felt him in years."

Justice pressed a kiss to Cashel's forehead. Of course Cashel had a wolf, but then why had shifting caused him pain? He would give anything right now for his mom to be here so he could ask her advice.

Justice bent and kissed Cashel's mouth gently. "I will never make you do anything you don't want to unless it is to save your life. You are too precious to me to risk, but I know you are in pain, and exhausted. You can barely stand. Shifting would cure all that."

Cashel shook his head frantically as his breaths sped up and

Justice hushed him again until he quieted. "You need to sleep and I need to go and fight. I will send Axel back in, and Zane will stay to make sure you are safe." Cashel gazed back, his eyes shimmering, but he smiled in relief. Justice's breath caught because, sick and in pain as he was, Cashel still had the ability to make his heart stop every time he flashed him one of his beautiful smiles. Was that why Cashel didn't act as though Justice was his mate? Was his wolf so cowed Cashel didn't even feel it anymore?

"I have to be present at the games." Cashel murmured.

Justice didn't argue. Cashel had to realize this himself. Justice slid off the bed to make room for Cashel to get off and stand. Cashel put a hand to his head and moved slowly. It took every bit of self-restraint Justice had not to help him, or command him be still. Cashel's hands shook and his face was parchment gray. Justice could barely look, but he had to admire the determination he had. Justice had once suffered sun sickness as a boy. He hadn't been able to move for twelve hours without his head feeling like it was going to explode, and he had been fit and healthy to start with. Cashel reached the edge of the bed and with a determined glance swung his legs over the edge and stood. Justice had a second to see Cashel's eyes roll into the back of his head before he caught him. He laid Cashel down gently and stood back. Justice closed his eyes and felt his own Alpha wolf, coalesced the strength and the power and opened his eyes to stare at an unconscious Cashel. "Omega," he growled. "Present to your Alpha."

Cashel blurred and Justice had a second of satisfaction as a small, pure white wolf now lay on the bed. He knew Cashel would be special. He sat and carefully lifted Cashel's head onto his lap, running his hands through his soft fur, and talking comfortingly while he waited for him to stir. "I knew you would be beautiful," he murmured. Cashel moved his head and blinked slowly. Justice needed him to shift back before he was fully aware and had the chance to panic. Now he had done it once, it would be much easier the second time. They would work on it together. None of his wolves ever needed his permission to shift, and their females shifted at will.

He stroked the length of Cashel's sides. "Cashel, heed your Alpha." In another second, Cashel shifted back to human and was blinking in confusion. Justice smoothed his braids and bent to kiss his head.

"W-what happened?"

Justice smiled. "Your wolf just acknowledged me as your Alpha."

"M-my wolf?" Cashel seemed to be in a complete daze. Justice nodded and stroked Cashel down his back.

"Your change was as fluid as mine. It didn't seem to cause you any pain. How long is it since the last time you shifted?"

Cashel swallowed and Justice reached over for the water and held it while he took a sip. "I have only shifted once when I was sixteen and my father commanded me to. It was the most excruciating thing I have ever felt." He shivered and Justice slid him onto his lap and held him close. "You are so warm," Cashel gasped.

"I don't understand why you were prevented from shifting. Even first shifts among my people don't hurt. They are confusing and often abrupt, but don't cause pain. Is that why you were forbidden? Because your father thought it would hurt you?"

Cashel snorted derisively. "My father has never shied from causing me any pain. But he never explained why I was forbidden to shift and I never asked. I was just so relieved not to go through that again. I learned not to disobey him very quickly." Justice remembered the bruises he had seen and knew what Cashel was saying to him. "It is likely it hurt because you were forced to deny your wolf for so long. Wolves are simple creatures. Your father forcing you to deny your wolf would have caused it to turn away from Darius as an Alpha. It hurt because Darius would have had to exert a lot of force to make you shift."

He rocked Cashel gently in his arms, unwilling to let him go. Everything in him screamed he had to stay to protect him. There should be no way a shift should cause pain, and Justice wondered if Cashel was making the connection that the shift that Justice compelled hadn't hurt. That Cashel's wolf recognized Justice as his Alpha.

"What is that incredible smell?" Cashel murmured. Justice gazed at him in consternation. Cashel's face was flushed. His eyes, even as gorgeous as they were, seemed huge and unfocused. He looked like he had eaten some of the blue capped mushrooms that grew in certain areas of the Patir hills. Maybe it was the lingering effects of the sun sickness. They needed to go.

"Promise me you will take water." He carefully deposited Cashel on the bed, stood, and passed him the small water pouch he normally carried at his waist. "Take this. If you do not draw attention by calling for Axel I don't think anyone will notice." Cashel took the pouch and sat up.

"I feel a lot better."

Justice clamped down another order. "Just please be careful."

Cashel licked his lips. "You have to go?"

Justice wanted nothing more than to stay. "So do you," he said regretfully.

"How many are still to fight?"

"Four including me."

Cashel nodded. "At least it will be a lot faster. I won't be outside as long."

There was that.

"We both need to go before we are missed," Justice urged. "If I am not there they may forfeit my bout." They had come too far for him to lose now. Not that the competition would stop the coming battle, but he was afraid if he lost he may be removed from the city. If that happened he wouldn't be able to protect Cashel, and he couldn't allow that. He couldn't ever allow that.

Justice sighed, leaned forward and cupped Cashel's cheek. He immediately noticed Cashel's pupils dilate even further. "We will talk about everything tonight."

He saw the swallow run the length of Cashel's throat and was beset by a sudden urge to follow the movement with his tongue. He growled but that made Cashel smile, so he huffed and strode to the door.

"Be safe," Cashel called after him. Justice paused, and the smile that tilted his lips also warmed his heart.

"We have another problem," Zane greeted him with outside, as Axel walked past them both and went inside.

"I want you to stay here," Justice replied as Zane fell into step beside him.

"Agreed," Zane paused. "Armand is with Kashir." The tone in Zane's voice made Justice pause and look up.

"What is it?"

"Axel was sent with a message from Cashel earlier. He was instructed to enquire after all the horses."

"All of them?" Justice repeated.

"I think it's some sort of warning. Do you want me to come and find you after I ask Cashel?"

Justice shook his head. "We both knew Kashir would draw attention. He is to be guarded at any time he isn't with me."

"There are only three of us," Zane pointed out.

"It's enough. As soon as the fights are over today Cashel won't ever be out of my sight until we are done. The ships will dock tonight and I expect Darius to have warning of them by dawn which means the games will be suspended anyway. We leave tonight after the games are done and go meet our wolves. That gives you and Armand a chance to gather together those you want to protect."

Zane nodded and Justice turned and carried on back to the stables. He ran in and relieved Armand immediately. Armand had to go and see if Orest had returned with any message. Around him all the grooms were saddling the horses in preparation for the afternoon. Not just for the competitors, but for the gammas that circled the arena. Justice didn't care that he had to prepare Kashir himself. In the desert the responsibility of your horse was never given to anyone else, and besides, Kashir just wore the simple Kefir and not the heavy saddles that the others wore. Sanjeli crowded close as if she was

The Alpha Prince

curious and Justice stroked her muzzle quickly in greeting, to which she snorted in disgust and returned to her hay. He eyed her as he tightened the strap under Kashir. She looked better already. It was obvious Armand had groomed Kashir to within an inch of his life, and Sanjeli looked like she had had similar treatment. He heard his name called out by one of the gammas at the entrance and gathered Kashir's reins to lead him out.

It was time.

The competition was a knockout. The wolves had been fighting in groups of four. Names were drawn of two pairs, including Justice's own. The winner from the first fight would then fight the winner from the second. It meant that Justice—as he had no doubt whatsoever he would be victorious in his fight—would have to fight again immediately afterwards. He shrugged to himself. He didn't envisage either fight to cause him difficulty.

Cashel was back to sitting under the awning and had a table with a goblet on it in front of him. Justice watched him pick it up a few times when his father or Gaven glanced over, but he never actually drank from it. *Tonight.* Tonight, he would finally hold Cashel in his arms; and as much as he wanted to worship every inch of his gorgeous body they needed to talk.

An unmistakable squeal from a horse in pain chilled the blood in Justice's veins and he watched in horror as one of the horses crumpled under its rider, Darden, a second son from a pack on the east coast of Solonara. The huge arc of blood spray through the air indicating his neck had been cut. Gammas ran onto the arena but the rider still mounted whirled his horse around and charged at the second man while he was still scrabbling to get off his dead horse. Justice swore. It was Vijay, one of the riders who had copied Malcolm and struck the horse. In the heat of battle any advantage could and must be used but he hated the second rider deliberately killing the first horse to give him that. He never asked nor made any attempt to allow the surrender of the first man—just sliced with his sword as the rider stood up. He never got the chance to even reach for his own sword before his head was cleaved from his body.

There was a gasp from the crowd, but then the victor raised his arms and his sword in triumph and the audience cheered. Justice looked at Cashel, the horror and distress apparent on his face even from here. Darius and Gaven were clapping and Vijay stepped forward to the Alpha, obviously wanting further acknowledgement. From where he stood, he couldn't hear what was said, but Vijay said something to Darius and Darius looked at Cashel. He bristled seeing Vijay glance again at Cashel and Cashel dip his head obediently at whatever Darius wanted.

He could imagine; Kashir swung his head to look at him when he couldn't help the low growl from his throat. The wolf disgusted him and the thought of him being anywhere near his gentle omega made Justice want to go and rip his throat out.

Chapter Eleven

Justice knew he would get no respite between matches and even though it disgusted him, he understood immediately why Vijay had gone for the horse. The fight had ended in less than five minutes, and Vijay wasn't supple or fast enough to last a grueling first fight and then almost immediately have to battle in a second.

Justice's name was called and Kashir stepped into the arena amid tumultuous applause. Justice was amused that someone the people didn't know would receive such a welcome, but he assumed the crowd just wanted to be entertained. Sorin was already far towards the north so while the day wasn't quite as bright or glaring, it was still ridiculously hot. Kashir, however was used to it. He was properly rested and hydrated, and Justice had warmed him up. He eyed his opponent, taking in the huge man who sat on an equally big horse. They were both impressive in their own right, but his opponent hadn't made any concessions to his environment, and sported full armor.

Justice wore his halib. A ceremonial white sheath wrapped over thin breeches that were as supple as the soft leather surrounding

Kashir's mouth. The voluminous white covering was secured over his head and fell in soft layers covering his arms and chest, both shielding him from the sun and remaining cool. It was cinched at the waist by a braid twisted in his pack colors. Orange to reflect the heat of Sorin and to ask for her blessing. White in deference to the moon goddess Aylin. Black to protect them against the evil of Surya.

His opponent, Feolin, was a second son from just over the border into Niandes. He was probably five, maybe ten years older than Justice, and he had listened to him explaining to his friends yesterday how his older brother already had three sons which completely removed him from any chance of becoming the Alpha. Justice understood, he really did. He just hoped that the previous bout and quick death hadn't given Feolin any ideas. He didn't want to have to kill anyone. Justice growled low in his throat. He was making no promises with Vijay.

As he rode towards the dais to incline his head in deference to Darius, a prickle of unease ran up his spine. Justice's eyes narrowed at the same time Kashir's head rose and he inhaled. Nothing except the usual scent of sweat and dry heat overlaid with the mild fragrance of the Juno bushes. The blood had completely dried, but Justice's wolf had already dismissed that as inconsequential. Clearly not a threat.

But something was.

The first arrow hit the gamma who stood behind Darius, just as Darius leaned forward to pick up his goblet. Another second and the Alpha would have been struck. Then the sky rained down with them. Screams rose; panicked, the crowd fell over themselves in the rush to get away. Justice clamped down hard on Kashir's flanks in a desperate attempt to reach Cashel, but the panicked onlookers were already obstructing his view. Gaven's furious voice rose higher and he pointed to the three tall buildings overlooking the arena—the only place the assailants could possibly be. He shouted again, only for his words to be abruptly cut off as an arrow found its mark and he fell. Justice didn't see if he shifted successfully. The stands were full of humans crying, wolves screaming, and fully shifted wolves racing away. Justice saw a she-wolf stagger as an arrow nicked her shoulder, but a fully shifted wolf barreled into her and knocked her uncaringly off the dais.

Cashel? Where was he? He felt Kashir tremble slightly but pressed him on and jumped down as they reached the melee.

Heart pounding, he dodged the panicked wolves and took the steps to the dais three at a time, running in the opposite direction as everyone else. He felt the sting of an arrow as it glanced off his shoulder and ignored it.

"Justice?"

Justice zeroed in on the cry and just managed to not be swept off his feet as a crowd of gammas protecting Darius swept past him with the Alpha in their midst. It was chaos, and his heart threatened to stop altogether when he still didn't see Cashel. Then a hand clasped his arm—a hand he knew to be Cashel's the second it touched—and he whirled around, encircling him instinctively.

Even as he did, the sting of what seemed like hundreds of darts peppered his back. He grunted as each one hit, but didn't care so long as Cashel was safe in the circle of his arms. Then they stopped, and as if someone had flicked a switch the screaming died.

"Cashel, *par se vuta*," he whispered and reveled in the smaller arms clinging tightly to his own. Cautiously he eased Cashel back, every sense still on full alert for any threat. Cashel made a strange noise in the back of his throat and alarmed, Justice pushed him back so he could see him. "Are you hurt?"

Cashel shook his head, looking completely stunned. "Are you?"

Happiness flooded Justice, taking in the fear that laced the question. That Cashel cared for him warmed every corner of his heart.

"Alpha?" Justice raised his head at Armand's shout and saw them both catch up with Kashir, Zane taking the stallion's head, and Armand following where Justice had run to get to Cashel. Justice hissed in a breath as he turned, as if flames licked up his back. "Justice," Armand's breath caught. "You are bleeding."

Cashel immediately stepped from Justice's embrace, glanced at his back and sucked in a breath, his eyes becoming round. "Justice, you must shift. You have easily ten wounds on your back."

"No," Justice replied flatly. He could protect Cashel better in human form at the moment. Armand sighed.

"Kashir has three flesh wounds but I think you were both lucky. Zane is taking him to the stables. I am taking you to your room."

"No," Justice wheezed. His breathing not as effortless as he was used to.

"Yes," Cashel said determinedly. "I will take you back." He immediately positioned himself under Justice's arm so he could lean on him. Justice attempted a laugh at the thought that his omega could take his weight but quickly realized he had to save all his breath to inflate his lungs. Armand silently stepped into his other side.

"Tell me," Justice gasped out with a nod to the buildings the arrows had been fired from.

"I would if I knew anything," Armand volleyed. "As soon as you shift I will go and see."

Justice cursed silently. He was Alpha. Territorial Alpha of all Arrides and soon Solonara. If he had to he would take all Askara by force and yet he was struggling to even walk unaided. Justice gritted his teeth as each breath became shallower and his head swam. After a few seconds, he heard Hale's voice and felt a larger arm replace Cashel's. Where was he? He growled long and low and then coughed because he didn't have enough air to express his anger.

"He has run ahead to ready your room, Justice," Armand soothed. But Justice needed Cashel close. His vision was getting darker by the minute and he knew Armand and Hale were all but carrying him now. He just had a second to realize he was in his room before both big men laid him carefully on his bed.

"You need to shift, Alpha," Armand pleaded, but Justice couldn't. He needed to protect Cashel.

"No," he said, but no sound left his lips. Breathing was becoming impossible.

"Cashel," Armand said, and Justice could hear the panic that shook his voice, which was ridiculous. Cashel was safe. Justice had made sure of that. He would always be safe with him. Cool hands cupped his warm face and soft lips whispered into his ear.

"I am safe here, and I am not leaving you. You need to shift before you have to leave *me*. Justice, please."

Justice smiled. As if he could deny Cashel anything. If that was what Cashel wanted, he would have exactly that. The last thing Justice remembered was the heat of the shift rushing through him.

Justice woke to dim light and a feather soft hand stroking his back. He was naked and smiled, inhaling the gorgeous scent of Cashel, knowing in whose arms he lay before he was even fully conscious. "Ow." The stinging slap to his arm brought him fully awake and he blinked as he focused on Cashel's face.

"Don't you ever frighten me like that again," Cashel railed. Justice felt the huge grin splitting his face and the second slap, although not as hard as the first.

"You shouldn't strike your Alpha," he teased.

He heard the amused snort from the corner of the room but didn't bother turning around as Armand appeared in his line of vision. Justice very reluctantly sat up and accepted the pouch of water Armand handed him. It was cool on his dry throat and he swallowed gratefully.

"What do you know?"

"It was the human rebels," Armand said shortly. "We know they have a very active group in Niandes but this has been the first attack here in years."

"But we thought them merely a rag-tag bunch of unorganized troublemakers—"

"Troublemakers?" Cashel interrupted and scrambled off the bed. "Have you *seen* the state of the children from the pits?"

"The quarries?" Justice frowned, not completely understanding.

Armand winced at the horrified look on Cashel's face.

"You're all the same," Cashel said woodenly and slid off the bed to stand. Justice had a second to see more faint white scar lines on his belly he hadn't noticed before until Cashel slipped a shirt over his bare chest and tucked it into his loose pants he always seemed to wear.

"I'm the same as what?" Justice questioned, knowing it was an insult but not entirely sure why. He looked at Armand, who threw his hands in the air and backed away until he reached the door and let himself out.

"All wolves," Cashel replied and took a step away from the bed.

"No." Justice snagged his arm. He frowned. "I have clearly said something you don't like. Explain."

Cashel huffed but stood still. "Solonara's biggest export is silk."

Justice nodded but still didn't understand. The Alpha had his claws in many different pies. Cashel blew out a short breath. "You really don't understand?" His tone was incredulous.

Justice shook his head. "I am aware that Tarik used to contain a large area the silk worms thrived in, but I think it has been moved further to the west. We have spent our greatest time in Salem. We couldn't land at such a place as Lapis because we needed a fishing port to safely hide our boat." He nearly said ships then. But caught himself just in time. He didn't think Cashel would betray him, but while a mere two day acquaintance was enough to risk his own life, it wasn't enough for him to risk the lives of his people as well.

Justice tugged gently and Cashel reluctantly moved closer. "Tell me," he ordered, then tried to smile to soften the order.

"Silk worms are delicate. To extract the strands, they have to be softened in boiling water and then unwound. By hand," Cashel added. "The smallest hands are usually the most delicate and do not damage the cocoons."

It took Justice a minute, but then anger washed first hot and then cold through him. "Are you telling me human…"

"Children," Cashel supplied.

"Are *made* to put their hands in boiling water?" Bile rose in his throat.

Cashel nodded. "You must have seen them—the scars, the missing fingers—unless it is because human children are not worthy—"

"Stop." It was Justice's turn to interrupt. "I am aware of all the horrors your father perpetuates." It was Cashel's turn to look sickened and he lowered his head. Justice winced. That had been cruel and he should have known better. He hooked a thumb under his chin and raised Cashel's face until he was looking into glittering blue eyes.

"But you are right. This is another atrocity amidst many, and not one I was especially aware of, which is my fault."

Cashel brightened. "You need to win and then you can take over from my father. It will probably take some years for all the power to transition…" His voice trailed off as he took in Justice's hard expression. "You do not mean for a gradual transition, do you?"

Justice shook his head. "The children working the boiling pits cannot wait that long."

Cashel swallowed. "Justice, I am not convinced I can give you an heir."

Justice gazed at Cashel. He wasn't about to say he had never given the ridiculous thought of a man becoming heavy with a pup any consideration. He watched in fascination as Cashel's eyes widened and the blue slowly bled to almost black. "What is it?" His voice rasped as he took in Cashel's blown pupils, his body reacting instantly, his heart thudding in his ears.

"What is that smell?" Cashel croaked, but Justice couldn't smell anything. The pure sweet vanilla smell radiating from Cashel drowned out anything else. Justice tried to swallow but his senses swam with the image of Cashel. Happy, smiling, his hands resting protectively over a hugely swollen belly. Justice made a noise in the back of his throat and Cashel's eyes darkened in answer.

"C'mere," he breathed and then he had his arms full of gorgeousness as Cashel buried into him.

"You are stunning," Justice managed the words before he fastened his lips over Cashel's and drowned out everything else. Cashel moaned into his mouth and he swallowed the sound greedily.

Cashel was writhing under him, all trace of hesitation from the previous day gone. Justice suckled the delicate curve of his neck, but he had to know. "I won't hurt you," he vowed. "I will stop anytime you say the word."

"I know."

Justice marveled at the complete acceptance and confidence on Cashel's face, and it humbled him that Cashel would willingly put himself in such a precarious position with someone capable of causing him great pain.

"Justice, please," Cashel begged and Justice tore the pants from Cashel's body, and reached under him only to pause in shock as his fingers came back slick, but then Cashel's pleas spurred him on and he quickly turned Cashel onto his belly and brought his knees up. His hands nearly shook with how desperately the need to be inside of Cashel consumed his body. He took his own rigid cock in his hand and pressed it against Cashel's slick entrance. He told himself to go slow. He must take care not to hurt but as his cock easily slid and breached the first ring of muscle, Justice was helpless not to continue and push all the way. The world stopped. Silence was complete. There were simply him and his lover in a cocoon of heat and sexual energy the like of which he had never ever known.

Cashel heaved a breath. "Move," he begged and rolled his hips in invitation. Not that Justice needed one. He was soon pistoning frantically in and out of Cashel, planting sloppy kisses wherever he could reach skin. He reached out and was helpless to smother the cry that Cashel loosed as cum spurted hot and thick over his hand and then Justice completely lost himself in the maelstrom as his orgasm took over every cell in his body until even his sight dimmed and they both collapsed.

Justice tried to move but he was still hard and thick. He could feel the pulse and the squeeze of Cashel's muscles around him and he sank back down. Cashel whimpered gently and moved restlessly.

"Hush," Justice soothed him because he still couldn't move.

"Oh," Cashel moaned and opened his eyes wide. The groan accompanied more cum dribbling from Cashel's still hard cock, and Justice felt another wave of heat roll over him. How? He almost shook his head in confusion, as desire rolled over him like a wave and he felt his fangs lengthen. A roaring sounded in his ears. The scent of Cashel—that gorgeous smell of sex, heat, and longing—swirled around Justice and coalesced somewhere deep in his gut.

He needed to bite Cashel. He needed to claim the wolf as his own. He knew it and his animal insisted on it even more. The patch of skin on Cashel's neck was just there. Begging to be licked. Begging to be bitten.

Without another thought he bent down and sank his fangs into the delicate surface and sucked. Pleasure exploded in him. He may have orgasmed again, and judging from Cashel's reaction he certainly did, but it wasn't about just that. It was the splitting of two hearts and souls. Each one was broken and then, as if they joined their other half in the other's body, reborn and remade anew.

Cashel went boneless under him as if he passed out. Justice's mind swam as his heart settled its furious clamoring and his cock softened and finally slipped free. He panted in complete exhaustion and just had the strength to wrap his body protectively around his mate's.

His *mate*. Cashel—the prince he had come here to kill. Even as his wolf howled in protest he knew he would never ever hurt so much as a hair on his beautiful head. But what could he do? All the wolves would know they were mated. All his plans that had taken years were for naught, and he had done the very thing he had promised himself he would never, and let his people down. It was the one thing drummed into him from birth. An Alpha protected his wolves. Protected his pack. And he had just put every life he was responsible for in danger, including his mate's.

Sorin's heart. What was he supposed to do now?

Chapter Twelve

Cashel opened his eyes, immediately knowing he was wrapped in Justice's arms. His *mate's* arms. As much as he had doubted yesterday, he felt completely different now. Cashel caught his breath and Justice obviously heard and nuzzled into his hair.

"What is it?"

Cashel had to smile. "Where should I start?" The chest he lay on shook slightly and Cashel felt the rumbling chuckle. "What are we going to do?"

Justice bent his head and brushed a kiss on his temple. "Armand sent one of his hawks yesterday with a message for my people in Salem. We are bringing forward the attack."

Cashel lifted his head. *Goddess.* "My father's army amounts to more than seven hundred trained soldiers, Justice. You cannot take the territory by force." He would die, and whatever happened Cashel couldn't allow that. Not now, not when he had finally found his mate. "Take me back to Arrides with you," he begged.

Justice sighed. "I would love to show you the desert. The wilds of the Patir hills where the horses run free, or the sunset from the beach." Cashel's heart leapt. "And we will someday, but I promised my people a home seven years ago, and I cannot back out now."

"But you have a home." *With me,* Cashel wanted to add. *I could be his home.*

"Arrides can no longer sustain us," Justice carried on. "My people are limited to one child per couple, and the problem is getting worse. One of our largest wells has dried up—"

"I could help with that," Cashel interrupted eagerly. Justice's eyebrow lifted in disbelief.

"My father thinks my omega gift is growing crops in difficult places, but it isn't. It's more than that, but I have never told him. I can tell where there is water. I can—"

"You could find a sustainable water source for hundreds of people?"

Cashel hesitated. He never had. He had pushed his gift deep down, terrified of his father using it in the wrong way and giving him more power than he already had.

"Exactly," Justice said, taking Cashel's silence to mean he was unable. Cashel lowered his gaze. No one ever believed him capable of anything so why should Justice be any different? "I am not doubting you have a gift," Justice said quietly. "But it is too late even if we wanted to try it."

Wanted to try it? Maybe Cashel should prove it. He would believe him then, but the thought that he didn't believe him now hurt.

"Your father knows where we came from. He will not let that slide now that he is aware. I cannot let his forces think they can take Arrides." Justice hesitated.

"But there is nothing there. You said there is just sand and little water."

Cashel watched the indecision battle over Justice's face. There was something important he wasn't telling him. *Because he doesn't trust me.* Cashel tried to slide from Justice's grip but he held on.

"What do you know of the history of Askara?"

The complete change of subject threw Cashel. "What I have read. I am aware the wolves and humans have been battling for centuries. I have read as much as I could about the first Alpha King and his pure omega. Oliver was human, you know."

Justice nodded. "I meant earlier than that."

"Earlier?" Cashel frowned. "I don't know what you mean. The warring has continued for many thousands of years."

Justice took a breath as if making a decision. "Askara was first settled by human travelers from another world many, many thousands of years ago. They had knowledge and skills far exceeding our own, but over time started to breed with the original population of wolves here." Cashel wrinkled his nose, and Justice laughed. "The wolves were already beginning to take on human characteristics. Their population was evolving also. The travelers started experimenting with breeding programs. We aren't sure why they started to want a super race of beings with the physical strength of a wolf and the mind of a human. Maybe they had been forced from their own world and wanted revenge. We don't know as the initial reason has been lost over time but the early experiments failed, and the results were quite hideous. The shifters were born deformed and in great pain. Some of the travelers began to rebel, and the group eventually split. The story was that the group that wanted to continue the experiments left to return to their own world, and the ones that stayed shunned all the technology they had brought with them, and became simple farmers. Fast forward thousands of years and the wolves evolved into the beings you know today."

Cashel was enthralled. "Did they ever return?"

"They never left," Justice replied baldly. "The vessel they had malfunctioned and crashed in the desert. Many were killed outright, and many more died in the heat of the desert. They had not the skills to forage for themselves, and their technology was all but useless without a power source. The ones that survived decided to live in secret and merely concentrate on survival. Wolves, as you know, were banished to Arrides with the expectation of a slow and painful death.

While I am sure that was the case for many, some survived and some bred with the humans."

Justice's face broke out into a wistful smile. "I am told my great, great, great sire was found half dead on the beach by a human girl who nursed him back to health and they fell in love."

Cashel's mouth fell open. "You are a hybrid?"

Justice nodded. "But none of the humans carry any scent. Which is why we don't, I suppose. I smell like a pure wolf as you know. Zane says he can't smell me on you, but I don't know if that has changed now we are fully mated."

"That still doesn't explain why you are afraid of Darius going to Arrides." Cashel studied Justice's expression but the look of indecision remained. "You would make a terrible liar."

Justice's scowl was immediate. "Any deception goes against the very code of my people."

"But you are also sworn to protect them as Alpha and you don't trust me," Cashel said bluntly.

"I—"

But Cashel cut him off. "Oh, I know you would protect me with your dying breath, but so would Hale. I don't need another bodyguard." This time he avoided Justice's grip and stood, pulling on his clothes. He reached for the collar. It was fitting that the collar originally given to Cashel to cover an ugly scar Darius was afraid would mar his looks was now going to cover a different type of mark that up to a little while ago he would have displayed proudly.

Cashel raised his eyes to Justice. For a second he admired the strength and beauty inherent in him, but disappointment still settled heavily in his gut. He knew it was too much to ask, really. He was doing what he had told himself would never happen and romanticizing their mating bond. The bond was simply biology, and biology as Cashel knew only too well could be altered and shaped to make of it what you willed. He wanted more.

"Where are you going?"

"I am expected to dine with my father. The attack was quelled successfully and he will expect me to attend what I know will be a huge celebration."

"No," Justice said, the outrage clear in his voice.

"If I don't attend I will be sent for. If I am found here, you will be imprisoned at best, maybe even killed. You will not be able to lead your people to freedom then."

"Cashel." Justice reached for him and Cashel stepped back. He needed to be alone. He wanted to think.

"I am in no danger and you can get a message to me through Axel. I will come to you when your attack starts."

"But—"

"Don't insult me anymore because you fear letting me out of your sight would mean I will share your secret." Justice reared back at the venom Cashel leached into his voice. If satisfaction would have helped, he would have reveled in it. No one ever thought meek and mild Cashel had a spine of any sorts. Well, his mate was in for a shock. Cashel turned and nearly bolted through the door, pushing past Zane. Axel turned and ran after him.

Cashel could have wept. He knew he was making too much of Justice's reticence. He had told him so much about his people, and he couldn't blame him for not risking their lives on someone he had known barely four days. Even if he was supposed to love and care for that person unconditionally for the rest of his life.

Their mating bond was obvious. It was inherent in them both to care and protect each other, forsaking all others, but that didn't mean love, or any other emotions the humans were so enamored of. Justice would protect him for the rest of their lives, but simply as a possession.

Cashel almost shook his head in exasperation. He was lucky, desperately lucky, to have the protection of such a mate. It was ridiculous to fantasize over any more. He sped over to his rooms only to be intercepted by Hale just as he crossed the threshold.

"Cashel," Hale heaved the word. "My prince, are you well? I have been looking everywhere for you."

Cashel saw how pale the normally tanned gamma looked. "I'm sorry. I was hiding in the stables. Is everyone all right?"

Hale slapped his head. "Of course," he grinned. "I should have known you would wish to see if the animals were unhurt."

This of course made Cashel guilty he had not asked about Kashir, but he knew if Justice was worried he would have been in there himself. "What do you know?"

"There have been nine arrests. There are four still alive and I understand my Alpha will interrogate them himself tonight." Cashel winced. He had seen Darius's interrogation techniques before as a child and it had been horrific. "You are commanded to attend."

Cashel nodded while hurrying inside, and headed straight for the bathing room with Axel. Axel was the only one he could risk seeing his neck.

"My prince?" Helena stepped into his rooms holding his tonic. Cashel sighed and held his hand out for the goblet. His eyes flicked over her as he drank. She seemed to be waiting for something. He nearly gagged as he forced it down too fast and then handed the empty goblet back to her.

"Thank you," he said. He couldn't help the wary tone creeping into his voice. She had seen him with Justice. Helena smiled.

"I understand you may be interested in seeing my hawks."

Cashel blinked at her stupidly. What the hell was she talking about? "Your hawks?" he repeated, hoping she would elaborate.

Hale chuckled. "Helena is more gifted with them than the court messengers. I did not know you were interested or I would have mentioned it earlier."

Except he wasn't especially.

"If it will not be too late for you, I will be exercising them tonight after the banquet. I would be honored for you to see them."

Cashel smiled. "I would, yes." Helena bowed and walked to the entrance of his rooms. It had been some sort of message or an excuse for him to leave his rooms. Maybe Helena knew Justice? She hadn't tried to cause either of them trouble yesterday. It was interesting.

"Helena?" She turned immediately at his soft call, her eyebrow lifting in exactly the same manner as someone he had just left, and he knew. He absolutely knew. He didn't understand, but knew his earlier suspicions were correct. Helena was neither an ordinary human or a pleasure-slave. He opened his hands, palms up in an entreating gesture. "I need some help with my clothes tonight and I am hoping you will have just the experience I need to advise me."

Helena studied him for a second then returned a knowing smile. They understood each other then.

Maybe it was time he started to take charge of his own body. Other people had used him for far too long.

Chapter Thirteen

What had just happened? Justice sat back down on the bed heavily as Zane let himself back into the room.

"I thought Cashel and Axel were staying with us?" Justice glanced up. Zane's face was flushed and his lips swollen. It was obvious what he and Axel had been doing before Axel had to run after Cashel.

"He has to attend a banquet. How's Kashir?"

Zane grinned. "Being mothered. Sanjeli tried to bite me when I dressed his wounds. They are superficial,"

"Did Cashel smell any different to you?"

Zane's eyes widened. "You are mated? Congratulations, but no. I couldn't smell you on him at all." Justice growled. He hated that, even if he was thankful Cashel wasn't in any added danger. Zane gazed at him. "He didn't look happy, and as you are the most honorable person I know I am sure nothing would have happened that he didn't want, which leaves the only other option that you said something to upset him."

Justice sighed. Zane and Armand both knew him far too well.

"He wanted to go live on Arrides. To run away. I explained why we could not."

"Everything?"

Justice shook his head. "He knew I was keeping something back."

"You are a terrible liar," Zane pronounced and helped himself to a banana from the bowl.

"That's what he said."

Zane sprawled onto the nearest chair. "He needs to trust you, Justice. He will need to do exactly what you say in the next day without hesitation to keep himself safe. If he doubts you because he knows you are holding back, it may make him question something."

Justice nodded miserably.

Zane leaned forward. "I have more information from our contact. She was waiting for a chance to speak to him and wants to make herself known."

Justice's head snapped up. His mother? "She trusts him?"

Zane nodded. "There's something else you need to know. Cashel is a grower. It's an omega who can grow crops in hard places, where there is little water or poor drainage for example. Darius knows this but he has been heard to say that the gift is useless because he has enough slaves to work his land."

"He told me," Justice confirmed, trying to remember exactly what Cashel had said. "He didn't use the term 'grower' though, he seemed to think he could source the water and plant the crops accordingly to make the best use of it."

Zane tilted his head in consideration. "I'm not sure I understand the difference but I'm guessing he thought that would be a gift on Arrides."

Justice nodded. But he had thrown it back in his face. Exactly as his father had done for years. Justice groaned. It was no wonder Cashel had left.

"She has also spoken to a healer friend of hers and he told her Cashel's history."

Justice sat up immediately.

"Cashel has had his insides changed."

"Changed?" Justice interrupted. "What do you mean, *changed*?"

"I mean he has had various crackpot healers try and make him internally like a female. Most of his stomach is missing which is why he cannot eat any solid food, and why he drinks that tonic all the time. They have fashioned some sort of pouch for a baby."

Justice lurched to his feet. "That is the most ridiculous thing I have ever heard."

"Except the first ever *pure omega*, as they called him, was human, and so the legend goes pure omegas have the ability to become heavy with pup and even give birth naturally. Every idiot wanting money has been coming to Darius for over two years, and he wants an Alpha-heir so much he is letting them do what they want to Cashel."

"Sorin's heart," whispered Justice. What had they done to his sweet boy?

Zane looked uncomfortable. "One even said that the key was Cashel remaining awake while the healer did it. Apparently, he needed to be 'aware' of his own body. They had to tie him down."

Justice gulped as utter revulsion ran through him. He rushed into the bathroom and promptly lost whatever he had in his belly into the pot. He wiped a towel over his mouth with his shaky hand. Zane followed him in with some water for him to drink. "I had a similar reaction," he said ruefully.

Justice breathed out slowly, aware his hands had become claws. The need to eviscerate Darius was nearly overwhelming. Zane laid a comforting hand on his shoulder. "All competitors have been commanded to attend tonight, even if you never got to finish your fight today."

Justice nodded and straightened up. Tonight, he would wear traditional dress. He would step up and be the Alpha for his people. *All* his people and especially his mate. After tonight, Cashel would never ever doubt he was trusted.

No, he would never ever doubt he was *loved*. Because Cashel had stolen his heart the first time he had ever seen him. Justice smiled.

No, not *stolen*. His people believed that true mates were simply one half of the other's heart, only to join together when they finally met. Justice's heart had always belonged to Cashel. He could not take something that was already his.

"Are you sure?" Zane's eyebrow rose and he whistled as Justice stepped out of the bathing room. Justice nodded; he was done hiding. His ceremonial robes were like nothing he had worn even the day before. The alternating black, orange, and white was stunning. Justice stepped forward and bent to pick up his boots, but Zane beat him to it.

"Allow me, my Alpha." Justice nodded once as he gazed at Zane's determined expression. Zane immediately bent and Justice lifted his feet in turn as the soft leather slid over them. *"Sorin kli-t'am'sardeesh,"* Zane murmured and tied the straps. He picked up the colored woven belt to cinch Justice's robes into his waist. *"Er t'am vuta."* Finally, he tied the matching band around his forehead. *"Er t'am er'di n'ass."*

May Sorin make your journey swift, your heart pure, and your intentions true.

It was the traditional blessing—only ever spoken by a second to his Alpha—and the first time Zane had ever had a chance to say it to Justice.

Justice took a breath and stepped forward to clasp Zane tightly. They had both planned for years. Even before they had brought Armand into their confidence. Yes, they had physically prepared for over seven years, but really it had been at least fifteen. Justice had found Zane crying next to one of the water wells. There had been nothing wrong with the well as Justice had first thought, but Zane had heard his aunt sobbing the night before. Whispering to his uncle as they both had thought he was asleep. She was going to have a pup, but as he listened excitedly dreaming of a younger cousin he understood finally what his aunt was saying, that she would travel to the healer tomorrow and take something to get rid of it. Even as young as seven as he was, all children knew the law. In his excitement, he had just forgotten.

Justice had held Zane as he had cried, and promised him when he became Alpha it would stop. Zane had vowed to be his second right there and then. Neither of them had ever wavered from that promise. The vision of Cashel heavy with his pup had been a dream. A nice one, but there were far more important things to worry over now, and Cashel would never be put through such horror ever again.

Justice stood at the entrance to the great hall ignoring the whispers as the others saw his clothing. He was waiting to be presented in the same manner as the first night. He was close enough to see Gaven standing next to Darius.

"That's a shame," Zane said. Justice agreed. He didn't trust the beta one little bit and was convinced his aspirations were a lot higher. Darius was almost *jovial* if that was the right word, but he supposed capturing the rebels that had organized the attack would have put him in a good mood. The great hall was packed. All visiting attendees were asked to attend but surprisingly both Zane and Armand had been included in his invitation. Armand was still fretting because Orest hadn't returned, but he was here after leaving Kashir and Sanjeli with Valerie's younger brother. Zane and Armand were also dressed in their *halibs*. They stepped forward into the packed room and Justice's eyes immediately scanned the seats for any sign of Cashel. The tables were in a different formation, a large V shape facing the double doors with Darius in the middle. It meant he could turn to either side and see all his guests.

His pulse quickened. Where was Cashel? Justice heard his name read out by the clerk and, as if they had practiced it Justice, Zane and Armand all bowed and gave the traditional greeting to their Alpha...

except it wasn't. A full greeting didn't involve a half-bow from a standing position, even if they still extended their right hand then pressed their first two fingers to head and heart. To truly acknowledge an Alpha, his people knelt down, bending from the waist and extending their arms flush with the floor. To do any less was a mark of disrespect, and all three men's actions were entirely deliberate.

Not that Darius would know that. To the quietened crowd the three huge men made an amazing spectacle, and Darius's eyes gleamed at their pretended show of obeisance. "It is a shame your bout had to be postponed today. I would have enjoyed the fight."

Justice straightened. "I hope to be allowed to further demonstrate my loyalty, my lord."

Darius smiled as if he were pleased but a shiver traced up Justice's spine. He glanced at the beta, Gaven, who stood behind him. "I am glad to see you suffer no ill effects from today."

If Gaven dared growl, he would have—Justice recognized the flash of temper that crossed his face and for a split second wondered what he had done to deserve it. He had no idea why the beta had taken such an instant dislike to him; not that he cared.

Justice, Zane and Armand took their seats. They had been nearly the last to enter but just as they were seated he heard the booming voice of Vijay, and tried very hard not to roll his eyes when the beta was invited to sit close to Darius.

Justice was seriously deliberating whether or not to get up and go see where Cashel was when the door at the back opened and Axel walked through and stood quietly off to the side. Justice felt Zane sit up a little straighter. Four gammas entered in quick succession and stood to attention. Even Darius and Gaven glanced around at the noise. *This is different.* Cashel never made an entrance. He was either already there on display or he scuttled in behind his father. Then Helena stepped through the door and stood next to Axel. Justice took a breath but as Cashel stepped into the room, he didn't take another.

Because Cashel had stolen every breath from his lungs. In an abstract part of his brain, Justice recognized this for the punishment it

The Alpha Prince

surely was. He had on the *am-la-shar*. He heard Zane and Armand take an astonished gasp each, and had no idea how his mom—and it had to have been her—had managed to get a mating robe in less than two hours. But even as the thought occurred to him, he knew the answer. It was hers. The silk was often handed down in families. He had no idea she had taken it with her when she had left though.

Cashel was stunning. The ivory silk had been shortened. On a female, it would be a dress that reached to the floor, but Cashel wore it as a shirt over the tightest pair of black breeches Justice had ever seen. Cashel never wore by choice something designed to show off his luscious package. Yes, everyone had seen him practically naked, but covered here, he was even more attractive. The shirt was embroidered with the images of the desert. Justice knew before Cashel even turned that the sun, the emblem of Arrides would be stitched into the back of the shirt. It was ironic that the emblems of Solonara and Arrides were nearly the same. No, it was lucky. Darius would never have seen such stitching before. He would assume his son was honoring his own pack. It was only Justice who knew better.

Then there were the names of his line, all in Askaran. All the named Alphas and their mates from Sayvan onwards were sewn on, but equally as meaningless to Darius—a thousand years of history in one piece of cloth. It was the quietest but most defiant act of rebellion he had ever seen.

Justice's eyes rose to meet Cashel's. His gorgeous blue eyes were rimmed in kohl, and an elaborate pattern of the Juno flowers had been traced into each cheek. His long hair had been braided with what looked like hundreds of beads.

He felt Zane's hand urging him down and only then realized he had risen to his feet. Cashel glanced at him briefly and then turned and walked towards Darius, bowing low as he stepped in front of him. Darius was speechless for a few seconds and then he waved to his side. The slaves hurried to do as Darius asked as he obviously wanted his son seated next to him. "Justice," Zane hissed and Justice sat quickly, not taking his eyes from Cashel.

He was standing again in barely a second thought as Vijay took the seat on the other side of Cashel. No. Not for one minute would he allow his mate within ten feet of that man. Justice took a step away from the table intending to go and retrieve Cashel when Gaven stepped forward and held a hand up.

"Silence for your Alpha."

Justice hesitated, then reluctantly let Zane drag him back down. Darius glanced around at everyone and stood.

"Bring out the prisoners."

You could hear the chains even before the shuffling footsteps and the clunk of the gammas' boots. Justice looked towards the double doors he and everyone else had entered from as they swung open. There were four human prisoners. Three men and one woman. Justice glanced at Cashel, who was riveted on the appalling sight, his lips parted in horror. The first man was barely able to shuffle forward. Copious amounts of blood covered the torn rags he still wore, and he trailed in some on the marble stone floor. He was beaten so badly his face was nearly indistinguishable. Justice doubted he could see out of either eye by how cut and swollen they were. The second man was older and walked a little better, but his back bore so many lash marks it was impossible to distinguish a clear patch of skin. He fixed his gaze insolently on Darius as he walked slowly forward. The third man walked in carrying the girl. He was in as a sorry state as the others, but the girl's appearance was heartbreaking. Her eyes were open but it was if she was completely unaware of her surroundings. She didn't look at the man who carried her, and took no notice of anyone else. She was naked. Completely so, and everyone could see the blood smeared on the inside of her legs. The only other marks were bruising around her neck and her wrists. She had been held down while she had been raped.

The gammas yanked on the chains tying their ankles together to make them stand when they were a good ten feet away from Darius. "Gaven," Darius said slowly. "Perhaps you can explain to them why they are still alive?"

Gaven stepped up beside his Alpha. "We know it would have been impossible for you to get to the rooftops of the palace without help. I want to know the name or names of the slaves that helped you. You have ten seconds before I kill one of you." Gaven sounded bored.

The second prisoner spoke up. "You have tried individually to get us to talk and we volunteered for this knowing if we were caught it would mean death. Why would you think that anything you can say would change our mind?"

"What's your name?" Darius asked silkily, but the human just remained silent. He nodded to the gamma nearest the last prisoner holding the girl and the gamma simply dragged the girl from his arms. The boy yelled and struggled but the gamma simply backhanded him and he fell to his knees. The girl sank down slowly, seeming unable to stay on her feet. The gamma just held her around her waist and looked back at Darius. He nodded once and before anyone could react the gamma slit her throat. Shocked cries rose, as much from the audience as the other prisoners. Justice shook his head in disgust and glanced at Cashel. As Justice watched, every drop of color seemed to leech from his face.

"Shall we try that again?" Darius asked.

The man shook his head. "We cannot tell you because we don't know."

The gamma dropped the dead girl and marched up to the next prisoner. He was still on his knees but the gamma yanked him upright and held him in the same way as the girl. His knife was still clasped in his other hand.

The other young man—the one holding the girl—shouted, "It's true. We never see anyone. It's all done by messages."

Justice winced a second before the young man realized he'd said too much. "Is that so?" Darius said as if greatly interested. The younger man looked at the older one in consternation.

"So, I wonder how it is you can send messages to each other?" Darius appeared calm, almost curious, but Justice knew it was all a big act. "Perhaps you have those among you skilled with messenger birds?"

Darius said it as if he wasn't really expecting an answer and looked at Gaven. Gaven beckoned to a gamma stationed by the doors and he stepped out, returning with another gamma. Justice had a second to work out what hung from the gammas hand before a pained gasp from Armand confirmed it. It was his hawk. The gamma was holding Orest's leg as it hung lifeless. The bird was huge, and completely different to the black doves the army used.

"As you can see we have two problems." Darius held out his hand and the gamma unfastened the leather pouch attached to Orest's leg. "We have obviously already read the message, but for everyone's benefit I will read it for you all." Darius unfurled the small piece of paper and read it out. "May Sorin see us succeed and the dawn bring us a new Alpha."

He looked at the young man who stared blankly back at him. "We know this message is intended for the rebels and the most amusing thing is that the bird was actually shot by one of the rebel's arrows yesterday. So, the message was never delivered." He hummed thoughtfully to himself. "I want to know where this message came from, and to do that I have no choice but to question the only person who has access to the palace and keeps hawks."

Justice's hand went to his Kataya, waiting for the gammas to turn on them. Armand and Zane stood at the same time but as the gammas moved swiftly he realized they weren't coming for them, they were going for his mother. In seconds, she was surrounded. The gammas dragged her in front of Darius but before Justice could open his mouth, Armand took a step forward. "The hawk is mine."

Darius looked up in surprise and disbelief.

Armand stepped forward. "I was merely informing our pack that we hoped our Alpha would be successful in the games. It has nothing to do with the human rebels. As you know, my Alpha, the humans would never wish for a new Alpha. They wish to eradicate all wolves."

Surely the reasoned argument would be convincing? Justice's fingers itched counting how many gammas stood between him and Helena. Even as every breath he took seemed to court danger, he admired his mother as she stood proud and refused to be intimidated.

Darius's eyes narrowed. "You have never once been seen with the bird. Helena, as we know, flies them regularly. It is an indulgence I have allowed because she runs the pack house."

Darius beckoned to the gamma holding the bird and he drew it close. "Helena? Describe to me the unusual pattern on the hawk's near foot?"

Helena opened her mouth but she couldn't say anything.

"It is a diamond," Armand said instantly. "And he has another just above his left eye."

Darius nodded to the gammas holding Helena. "Let her go." He turned to Justice, smiled, and before Justice had the chance to react, Darius commanded, "Arrest them all."

Justice felt the sword prick his back before he had the chance to attack. They were instantly swarmed by gammas. His Kataya was taken immediately, and his robes pulled from his head and chest to examine for hidden weapons. Darius stepped closer. "All your belongings are forfeit to me," he growled, and Justice went berserk. *Kashir*. Darius had coveted the stallion since he had first seen him. He struggled, howling through his still human throat until pain exploded behind his head as the hilt of a sword struck him and everything went black.

Chapter Fourteen

Cashel was immediately blocked by Gaven. His hand circling his wrist so tight he thought the bone would break. "Sit down," he ordered and pushed Cashel back on his seat. Gammas ran over to Gaven and Cashel jumped up again as soon as his back was turned. He had to get to Justice. They had hurt him. Another hand grabbed his arm and yanked him back.

"You have nothing to fear from the barbarian."

Cashel flinched as Vijay pressed his other hand cruelly into Cashel's thigh. He tried to stand again, but Vijay pressed down further. Cashel whimpered. "Let go, you're hurting me."

Vijay just grunted and leered. "No need to pretend with me." He licked his lips. "I had a very interesting conversation with Gaven. He told me all about you. How you like to play hard to get with us all." He caught Cashel's hand in a vice-like grip and dragged it to his groin. "There, you just feel how that turns me on. This whole contest is a waste of time. I could have you fat with my pup straight away. You'll be begging for it by the time I'm through with you. You need a real man, not these pathetic boys."

"Cashel?"

Cashel had never been so pleased to hear his father's voice and he wrenched his hand from Vijay's grasp. Darius eyed him and Vijay. The beta bowed his head. "Just getting to know your son, my lord," he said jovially.

Darius nodded. "So I see." He pinned Cashel with a thoughtful gaze. "Although omegas have a weak constitution and I can see how this unpleasantness would upset him."

"Perhaps he should retire?" Vijay jumped in. "It would be my pleasure to escort him back to his rooms." Cashel gaped at them both but as the smile widened on his father's face his stomach dropped.

"Perhaps a walk in the gardens first?" He looked pointedly at Vijay. "I would see you aren't disturbed."

Cashel started in horror. "Father!"

Darius leaned down. "Do not make a scene, and don't think for one second I know you wouldn't have whored yourself out for that traitor. I saw how you were with him. Wearing his token earlier. Dressed like the street rats in Salem." Cashel was speechless. He was wearing more clothes tonight than he had done the previous two. Darius looked at Vijay. "Get him out of here."

Cashel was dragged out of the back door by Vijay in a punishing grip. When both Axel and Hale tried to interfere, they were beaten back by his father's gammas. Cashel had a second to see them remove Hale's weapon and yank his hands behind his back before Vijay pushed him through the back doors into the gardens. Vijay grunted as he strode over the grass, dragging Cashel along with him, then threw him on the ground near the trees. Cashel tried to scramble away but Vijay laughed and hauled him back. Pain exploded in his back as he was dragged over the sharp rocks.

"Now, now," Vijay tutted. "What's the point in playing hard to get when I know you're desperate for it?"

Cashel opened his mouth to scream, and tried to summon his wolf, but Vijay clamped his hand so tight on Cashel's mouth it was all he could do to manage to breathe. He felt the first rip on his tunic and could have cried at Helena's precious cloth being ruined. He fought like a madman, doing his best to claw and scratch at Vijay's face as he yanked his breeches down. Vijay laughed. "So, you like a little pain to have a good fuck?" He backhanded Cashel.

Cashel was stunned. The force nearly knocked him out and his vision whitened for a few seconds as he lay limp. He heard the snigger from Vijay and felt his legs being roughly forced apart.

No. Cashel whimpered in fear. Vijay was too strong for him to do anything. He was pinned, and the gamma roughly forced his knees bent, holding him with one hand. Cashel struggled futilely but Vijay was too big and too strong. Vijay grinned and shoved away the torn cloth, then he stopped abruptly.

Cashel stared up at him. The gamma looked odd, as if he were suddenly confused, or doubtful. Cashel held his breath as a tiny red line dribbled from Vijay's mouth. Then he was gone. Pushed off Cashel as if he weighed nothing. Cashel heaved a lungful of air, head still spinning, unable to fully grasp what had happened.

"Well, well, Trik, look what we have here." Cashel frowned in confusion as he stared at the man looming over him. "And there was us thinking we were stopping a slave being raped."

A second man stepped closer to him and stared at Cashel. Cashel reached for his clothes but the man kicked them away. Who were they?

Cashel inhaled. They were both human and as that thought settled he became aware of at least another five or six humans standing behind them.

"If he's a wolf, just kill him." A young girl stepped forward and Cashel's heart sank at the utter hatred on her face.

"Oh, no," the first man said and nodded to Trik and another man. "Do neither of you recognize him? This is Cashel. The Alpha prince as he is called." The woman gasped and Trik laughed. "He comes with us."

Cashel opened his mouth to cry out as he was yanked to his feet, and struggled. "Quick, before he shifts," the first human ordered, and pain burst in the back of his head as everything went black.

Sometime later—Cashel didn't know how much later—he came to with a slight whimper. He really wished sometime his head would stop aching so abominably all the time. Of course, it didn't seem to help that he was lying upside down. *Upside down?* He tried to move but he couldn't. He was also being rocked slightly.

"It's awake." Cashel winced at the bellow, but it woke him up a little and he realized he was slung over a horse and tied down.

Everyone came to an abrupt halt. "Here, give him this to drink." He recognized the voice from earlier and gasped as his hair was roughly grabbed and liquid poured into his mouth. He choked and spat it all out.

"He can't drink upside down, idiot."

"You try then." The man let go of Cashel's hair and his head thunked back against the horse's side. He felt strong arms hold him as he was untied. He also felt a sharp knife press into his back.

"Try anything. I see so much as one claw and I'll cut your heart out." Cashel nodded at the order and suddenly he seemed to be sitting on the ground. He looked up into the man's face who still pointed the knife in his ribs. The man reminded him in a lot of ways of Hale. Large, muscular. Probably similar age. His face was weathered and his short hair was completely gray. He was completely human, though. It was the same man who had recognized who he was. The other man, Trik, passed over a small skin of whatever they had tried to make him drink.

Cashel eyed the skin nervously. "It's water," the older man said brusquely. He was thirsty. Then he shrugged and held out a hand. If they wanted to kill him, he would have been slaughtered in the garden. He didn't know why he had been taken, but getting dehydrated wasn't going to help anyone.

"See, Jon. Our little prince wants to be reasonable." So, the older man was called Jon. Cashel filed away the information and lifted the skin to his lips. It was water, but it was warm and tasted stale. He kept his face impassive though. They were giving him some, which was important. He risked another long drink before anyone could object. Jon smiled.

"You can finish it. We have plenty, and won't be stopping again for a while." Cashel obediently lifted the pouch just as a wave of dizziness hit him, and it slipped from his numb hand.

Jon lowered the knife and grinned. Cashel stared at him but he didn't seem to be able to focus properly. He squinted, trying to wonder why everything seemed blurred. Abruptly he was hauled to his feet, but he was incapable of standing and started to sink down nearly immediately. He heard Jon chuckle again. "Doesn't usually work so fast on wolves."

His head was swimming in lazy circles. "Tie him to me," Jon ordered and Cashel felt himself lifted and strapped to Jon's front. At least he sat astride this time, and he smiled lazily. He felt wonderful. Relaxed. An abstract part of his brain was trying to tell him he should be afraid, but for the life of him he couldn't work out why. He relaxed against the strong body behind him and closed his eyes. Thought was too strenuous and as he felt the horse move underneath him, he let his eyes close.

The next time he woke it was dark. He was lying down on a hard surface and seemed to be alone. He blinked slowly, trying to let his eyes get used to the dark, silently thanking his wolf as his surroundings became clearer. He was in a cave, as far as he could tell, blocked off by solid looking bars. The air wasn't too fresh and it was cold, but Cashel wasn't shivering which seemed odd. He touched his face. His skin seemed pleasantly warm. He looked down, puzzled. All he wore was an oversized shirt and some breeches that were too big for him. Nothing that would normally keep him this warm. His belly rumbled quite insistently which surprised him as well. He had lost his appetite months ago when he stopped being able to eat much food, but right at that moment he could eat a whole chicken. He licked his lips. Make that two.

He sat up gingerly and inhaled. It had been obvious the water

The Alpha Prince

was drugged, but as he felt no ill effects he was glad they had done that rather than knock him out again. Humans, small animals. He sorted out the different scents in his brain, puzzled he seemed to be able to do so easily. His wolf had never—

My wolf. It was there. A strange, almost foreign presence in the back of his mind. He hadn't felt his wolf for so long. Or no, he had, he had just buried it so deep because it petrified him. But he didn't seem to be now. What that the reason his wolf was suddenly making himself known? Justice had made him shift, was that it? He inhaled sharply as the last memory he had of his mate flashed through his mind. One of the gammas had hit him with the hilt of his sword and all three of them had been taken away. What would his father do with them? He had to get back.

Cashel picked up a small sound and stilled. The scent of the human, Jon, became stronger. The torch Jon carried flickered as he grew closer to Cashel.

"What do you want?" Cashel asked calmly before Jon got the chance to speak.

He heard the amused chuckle again. "An exchange, of course. He has two of my men. I don't think that's much to ask for. A son for a son."

Cashel took a sharp breath. He knew which man was Jon's son. The younger one who had defiantly carried the girl. The resemblance was obvious now that he looked. "I'm sorry you lost the other two," Cashel said quietly.

Jon stared at him for a second before he replied. "I didn't lose them, they were butchered at the hand of your father."

Cashel nodded sadly. He was right and he had no idea why people used such a trite expression.

Darius would be incensed at his disappearance. Not because he valued Cashel in any way except for the dream of an heir, but that his palace had been breached by the humans, and they had stolen one of his possessions.

Jon removed a package from his pocket and held it out through the bars. "Bread. We are moving again soon and will have to drug you, but I suggest you eat while you get the chance."

"You don't need to drug me." The words were out before Cashel realized how stupid they were. Like the rebels were going to accept the word of a wolf. Jon scoffed and passed him a flask.

"Your choice. Either you drink it all or I knock you out. You won't be given the opportunity to shift to heal any injury, so I think you'd best be smart."

Cashel took the bread and the flask. Jon pivoted and walked back the way he had come. Cashel inhaled as he unwrapped what he expected to be a dry crust, knowing he wouldn't be able to eat it. He paused in shock as the scent of fresh bread wafted up. He took a breath and then nearly rammed the bread into his mouth in one. He was ravenous, but slowed and broke it up quickly, marveling as he swallowed it with ease. He smelled the water in the flask cautiously. It didn't seem to be too bad, and he understood it made sense for him to drink it instead of getting injured. He needed to think, though. He was going to have to escape, and not because he wanted to cheat the two men of their chance of a rescue, but because he knew absolutely Darius wouldn't stop until he had slaughtered every human that had dared to challenge him. He also had to get to Justice. Cashel took a cautious sip. He needed to drink. They wouldn't trust a wolf.

Another surprising thought entered Cashel's head and he paused before drinking any more. His sight. His sense of smell. The bread he had bolted down with no ill effects, and even the hunger itself. He'd never experienced any of these before, and even if his sharper sense were due to Justice summoning his wolf, that didn't explain why he seemed hungry and why he had eaten more than he usually did.

Cashel took another small sip. He could feel the drug making him feel lethargic almost immediately. Maybe he could pretend? Just take a little to be convincing?

He heard the boots clunking down the passage and immediately lay down and closed his eyes. The gates opened and Jon and Trik stepped in. Before Cashel had the chance to steel himself, Jon reached down and pinched his arm, hard. Cashel couldn't help flinching.

"Nice try, but I have a few more years of experience on you." Jon pinned his arms effortlessly and Trik held his nose. Of course, when he opened his mouth to breathe the water was tipped down his throat. When they stopped, Cashel was barely conscious.

He completely lost track of time. Hours seemed to pass between short periods where he was awake to obediently cram as much food into his mouth as he could before he was carried by a horse again to goddess knew where. The next time he awoke he immediately rolled over and retched. His head swam and he felt the nudge of a skin of water next to his hand. "Please, no more," he begged, and heard a sigh. It was Jon.

"This is just water."

Cashel's lips twisted. "Of course, it is."

The big man grinned. "We have no need to move you now." He stood up. "I'll bring you some food in." He stepped away and Cashel realized for the first time he was lying on a small pallet in some sort of room. He moved restlessly—his bladder was full—but the big chain bit into his ankle. He wasn't going anywhere. The door opened again and a woman walked in with Jon. She put a tray down on the floor and Cashel couldn't help the groan as the gorgeous smell of some sort of broth wafted over his nose. Jon chuckled and pointed to the pot in the corner. "Your chain will reach so you can use that. If you get any stupid ideas about shouting for help, don't bother. We are on a farm, miles from anywhere. No one will hear you, but if you annoy me I'll simply gag you."

Cashel nodded weakly and looked at the other end of the room. He wasn't sure he could even stand. Jon let out an impatient sigh and bent down to haul him to his feet. Cashel was naked and blushed even if the woman had turned away.

"I've been doing this for five days," Jon snapped. "Don't think you have anything I haven't already seen." Cashel's face heated even more but he relaxed as he heard the door close behind the woman and he let Jon help him use the pot. His legs were shaky and he was hungry, but he was alive. At least so far.

He caught another smell but didn't say anything. If he had to guess, the farm—if that was what he was on—was nearer Salem than Jon was going to admit, if the scent of fish was anything to go by.

Cashel sank back down on the bed gratefully and looked at the tray. Jon lifted it and put it on the bed. There were no spoons, but massive chunks of bread he could easily dip into the broth. Cashel dived on the food, marveling at how good it tasted. Jon stood and walked to the door.

"Whoever makes this bread is incredibly talented," Cashel said as he swallowed. "It's the same from the caves, isn't it?" Jon's eyes narrowed. He obviously wondered how Cashel knew. To be honest, Cashel wondered how he was so sure, but he was.

Jon simply nodded and opened the door, shutting it and locking it behind him. Cashel lifted the bowl to drink the rest of the broth. Now he just had to find out where he was and how to get back to Justice.

Chapter Fifteen

Justice groaned and sat up fingering the lump on the back of his head. Without another thought he swiftly pulled off his breeches and rapidly shifted to his wolf. He was back to human and dressing before he heard a sound. He was in some sort of cell and it was dark. He could smell Zane and Armand but knew instantly he was alone in in his own cell.

"Justice?" It was Zane.

"Yes. Cashel?"

"We don't know," Zane nearly growled his answer.

"How long have we been in here? Armand?"

"Here," Armand answered. "We're guessing about four hours."

"Are either of you hurt?"

"No," Zane said. "We saw Gaven once when we were thrown in here, but no one for quite a while."

Justice took a breath and tried to calm his wolf. The animal was ready to eviscerate any who thought to prevent him from getting to his mate and Justice was about ready to unleash him.

"What happened?" But his words were garbled as his canines dropped.

"Alpha," Zane warned.

Justice took another breath. He needed the reminder. Losing control wouldn't help any of them. Justice became aware of another human smell—dirt, but mostly blood. "The human prisoners are in here? They are alive?" He could see nothing but a stone wall beyond the bars.

"And you care, why?" Another voice spoke up. Young. Justice guessed at the man who was holding the girl. He heard a moan and a slight scuffle. "Hush, Max."

"Is someone hurt?" It wasn't a question, more of a confirmation. The boy didn't reply, and Justice couldn't really blame him. They were wolves. The rebels were humans. There was no way they were going to trust him.

Justice looked towards the light as the door opened and heard the boots clunk down the passage. He recognized Gaven's scent before the beta even appeared.

Justice folded his arms casually and leaned on the wall looking completely disinterested. Gaven couldn't know what Cashel was to him, none of Darius's wolves could. Gaven came into view and Justice just managed not to react. There was blood on the man's collar, but more importantly there was a huge claw mark down the side of his face.

"Cashel is missing."

Justice growled and launched himself at the bars as his fingers turned into claws. "Missing? What do you mean missing?"

"I mean kidnapped," the wolf clipped off the word. "Vijay was found stabbed to death in the gardens. We can smell humans, and assume it is the rebels that have taken him."

"Let me out," Justice growled the order. If Cashel was hurt Gaven wouldn't have to worry about just one claw mark. Justice would shred him.

Gaven stepped close and put up his hand. At the same time Justice realized Gaven was alone. It was strange he had come down to the cells with no gammas. "Listen carefully," Gaven rasped. "Darius is enraged. He has just killed two slaves and one gamma." He paused. "He attacked me." Gaven sounded aghast. "I have faithfully served him for years, but he has let this obsession with Cashel take over his life, and it cannot be allowed to continue." He gazed at Justice. "I have seen how you are attracted to the omega. His gift would be useful in a desert. If I release you, do you swear to go and take Cashel back to Arrides and never to return?"

Justice stared back at Gaven. So this was all because he didn't want his comfortable life upset? There was something else. He was sure there was something else. Then he did something he had always sworn never to do a second time. He lied. "Yes."

Gaven nodded, unclipped a bunch of keys from his belt, and carefully withdrew Justice's Kataya. He glanced at the other cells, and Justice knew he was looking at the humans and knew they had heard what he had said.

"I need to question them," Justice said. "They will know where Cashel is."

Gaven frowned. "I cannot risk anyone knowing we have spoken."

"Neither can I," Justice agreed, and held his hand out for the keys and the small sword. "Will the keys be traced to you?"

Gaven shook his head. "I will keep the gammas busy to give you a chance to escape."

"My horse," Justice ground out as Gaven unlocked the door.

"He is still in the stables. Trust me when I say Darius is too upset about Cashel to care about anything else."

Justice pushed the cell door open and stepped out. He nodded to Gaven. "Go."

He took one last look at Justice then pivoted on his thick leather boots and marched away. Justice stepped up to the next cell and let Zane out. Zane immediately took the keys and let Armand free.

Zane nodded to the other cell. "What about the humans?"

Justice gestured for Zane to use the keys. He stepped aside so Justice could walk in.

The young boy immediately stood up from where he was tending the older man and stepped in front to shield him. Justice smiled at the show of bravery. There were only two in the room though. "Where is your other companion?"

"He tried to get free when the gammas hit you, hoping for the distraction. He was killed instantly," Armand said.

The young man's eyes glinted as if he wanted to cry. Justice suddenly wondered how old he was.

"I will be quick," Justice said. "The wolf that was taken is my mate. I am as interested in ending Darius's rule as you are, and I have no quarrel with humans." The boy sneered in contempt but Justice carried on. "Think. You have two choices. We will take you with us and get your companion help, but I need information in return. Decide now, because the gammas will butcher the both of you when they come back."

The boy looked stunned. He glanced at the older man who looked ashen. Blood had stained his shirt but was dry.

"If I agree to help will you leave Max at the village smithy?" Justice nodded, thinking this young man wasn't much of a rebel. Had Justice wanted to kill the humans the boy had just effectively told him where to start. Justice sighed. He was young, but bravery wouldn't keep him alive for very long. He needed to be smart, also.

He held out his hand in the traditional human way and no one seemed more surprised than the boy himself when he clasped it in his own. "My name's Mark."

Justice nodded. Zane was already bent and examining the man's wound. "It isn't fatal," Zane pronounced, "but he cannot travel far. He needs care."

Armand bent and slid his hands under the man's body and Mark jumped.

"I can do that."

Justice shook his head at the retort he was sure was just about to leave Armand's lips. "Let Armand carry him. We need you to direct us, but first we need to go to the stables and collect our things."

They walked out quietly. Gaven had kept his word and there was no sign of any gammas guarding the cells. Justice threw the keys down a nearby drain. Just leaving them would cause problems for someone, and while he was sure Gaven wouldn't get blamed, he knew some other gamma would. They crept cautiously into the stables. Justice stopped as soon as he smelled his mom.

"Justice," Helena gasped and clutched his arms. "We cannot find Cashel."

"The rebels have him." He was ashamed his voice shook. Axel brushed past him and launched himself at Zane as he walked through the door. Zane opened his arms wide as the young man jumped into them. Mark's jaw dropped in complete astonishment. Armand laid Max down on the straw.

"What did you see?"

Helena shook her head. "Darius let Vijay take him to the gardens. The gammas prevented Hale from following, and only let us go when one of the human slaves ran in saying someone was hurt. Vijay had been stabbed to death and Cashel was gone. Hale tried but couldn't track his scent." Helena trembled. "We have to find him, Son."

Zane turned to Justice. "Max needs attention. We need to get him to the smithy."

Justice nodded. "Take the boy as well."

"No," Mark spoke up and everyone turned to him. "You are really going to let us go?" He looked at Justice, incredulity stark on his face.

"I told you I have no quarrel with humans but we are not returning to Arrides. My troops are waiting to take the territory."

"He's telling the truth," Axel interrupted.

Mark nodded. "I hope I'm not making the biggest mistake of my life, but I think I know who has him and where they have gone."

"Let me and Mark take him to the smithy," Axel said. "I know how to get past the gammas and no one would question servants pushing a cart. Any wolf carrying him would be stopped immediately."

Justice looked at Armand. "Valerie?" He had thought Armand would bring her.

His friend winced. "I think she's safer here for the moment."

Justice nodded and turned back to Mark. "Say goodbye to your father. I'll make sure he gets there safely."

"He's not my father," Mark blurted out.

Justice eyed the young man. Did he trust him?

Axel stepped out of Zane's embrace. "We need to go."

Worry slid over Zane's features but Axel shook his head. "I won't be challenged. We had better meet by the south gate. The main ones will be manned."

Justice frowned. "Won't the south ones?"

Axel grinned evilly. "Yeah, but the guards there are slobs. At this time, they'll be drunk."

"I know where the gates are," Helena said.

Zane dragged Axel towards him and landed a bruising kiss on the boy's pink lips and then let him go, quickly. Justice's heart squeezed. He didn't begrudge his friend, but he just missed the taste of another's lips. He stopped in surprise when he saw Armand had saddled Kashir *and* Sanjeli. He had two other horses saddled next door for him and Zane.

"She is fit enough to be ridden?"

Zane nodded. "She will easily carry Helena." That just left Mark and Axel.

"We need two other horses," Justice said.

"I can get them from the smithy," Mark said. "He will help."

Justice hesitated and glanced at Zane. It was a risk.

Mark licked his lips. "If I take you to the rebels, do you promise not to kill anybody?"

Justice sighed. "I cannot promise that. You heard me lie to Gaven when I said I was going back to Arrides, so even if I said the words you really shouldn't believe me."

"And yet, you have kept all your promises to me so far," Mark replied, and Justice smiled. He was so earnest. So trusting.

"I intend to take over the territory," Justice said. "I despise slavery of any kind and would abolish it. There are no slaves on Arrides but the desert is no longer able to support our population. It was always our intention to petition the Alpha to be allowed to settle in Solonara until we found out the atrocities he committed and realized we can't —*I can't*—let that slide.

"I need allies, both human and wolf, as free men to crush a regime that has tortured and enslaved thousands unchecked for years." Justice paused. "But first, I need to find my mate."

Mark's eyebrows rose. "The Alpha-heir is your mate?" Justice nodded and Mark chewed his lip, thoughtfully.

"They likely came to rescue us. If as you say the human alliance has him, then there is only one thing I can suggest and it means travelling to Salem. My father lives close by there and has contacts who would be able to get a message to Christoph Tor." Justice looked blankly at Mark. He said that as if Justice should know the man.

"I don't know who—"

"I do," Helena replied, coming to stand next to her son. "My birds have taken messages to him for years." She turned to Justice. "He is a good man, but the wolves just killed his son. He's out for blood, and I'm not sure how amenable he would be."

"Who is Christoph Tor?" Zane asked.

"He's the leader of the Human Alliance—the rebels—in Niandes," Helena explained, "but he's active in Solonara as well. He was supposed to be joining the locals here to start a proper group, but his son and the whole village he was in was attacked and over a hundred humans were killed."

Mark shuffled his feet, and Justice immediately picked up on the movement. "What is it?"

Mark looked almost embarrassed. "It's just a rumor," he hedged.

"What is?" Helena asked immediately.

"That his son is alive."

"Oh my goodness," Helena put a hand to her throat.

"There is another." Mark was obviously getting braver. "You know the old stories of the Alpha King?"

Helena looked stunned. "Of course."

"What stories?" Justice interrupted.

"That Askara would eventually be ruled as one when the true Alpha King found his pure omega," Helena replied quickly.

"It's supposed to be true. He may be on his way to Niandes now." Mark's eyes were round.

Justice all but rolled his eyes. "This is to do with men having babies, isn't it?"

Helena smiled but shook her head gently. "Do not doubt there is an oasis beneath the sand because you cannot see it," she reproved. Justice swallowed. It was an old saying amongst his people. That sometimes things had to be taken at face value. "Arrides is very sheltered in a lot of ways, Justice."

He nodded, but it was time to go. Cashel had to be found. He could worry about him having a baby when they got him back. Justice wanted to roll his eyes again, but the image he had had before of Cashel deliriously happy and resting his hand on a huge swollen belly just didn't seem to want to go away.

Chapter Sixteen

Cashel was going to die. He was going to die and never see Justice ever again. He rolled over on his back and stared up at the ceiling. Seven days. Seven days he'd been shut in this room. Oh, they'd fed him, and he'd had unlimited fresh water, but every time he saw Jon or his wife he asked if they had heard from his father, and so far, the answer had always been no. He knew Jon was puzzled. Daisy, his wife, was at a complete loss. Cashel wasn't surprised in the least.

The problem was Jon and Daisy were good people, and even though they knew Darius was a monster to all humans, they didn't expect him to be indifferent to his son. They had five children. Mark was away at the moment. Ike, their second son, was fifteen and Semian, the baby, was one. The twins, Aden and Jarelle—or Jelly, as she was affectionately nicknamed—were eleven, and Jelly was the source of all his information.

He was shut in a barn. He'd worked out from what he could hear with his werewolf hearing that the small room seemed to be above the hay barn. There were also chickens that roosted below him every night. The problem was that neither parent had realized that their daughter, Jelly, was either the most curious, or the most reckless child on the planet. Although, it could have been simpler. Jelly had told him that they were forbidden from entering the barn, so of course while Ike worked the land with his father, and their mother ran the house and cared for Semian, there was plenty of time in between chores for Jelly—way more daring than her brother—to decide to go see what was in the barn that they had been forbidden from seeing.

Cashel had heard the soft footsteps which would have been completely undistinguishable to a human ear, and had waited in silence, torn between being afraid someone was going to kill him—completely ridiculous because of course they wouldn't have had to stay quiet—and being filled with hope he was being rescued. When neither happened, he'd became curious himself.

The third day, he had heard the quiet footsteps and then louder ones indicating Jon had arrived. There had been no talking so he had guessed that the owner of the quiet footfalls was hiding. He had assumed it was a child because it had obviously been someone who didn't want Jon to know he or she was there.

The fourth day they had come and after a second, Cashel called out asking who was there. There had been complete silence and then Cashel could hear hurried footsteps as whoever it was ran away. He had been convinced that was the end of it but yesterday he had heard them again, followed by a soft scratching at one of the boards in a far corner of the wall. Cashel had watched in complete fascination as the board had been removed and a small face had peeped in.

He didn't know which one of them had been more surprised. Him to see a cheeky but triumphant grin, or her to see what was being hidden in the room. He crossed his ankle deliberately before saying anything so she could see he was chained. "Are you going to come in and say hello?"

He was answered with a small, but defiant shake of her head. "No. Aden said I didn't dare come and look though, because I'm a girl." Her disgust at that statement was evident.

"But you showed him, huh?" Cashel was completely charmed.

The Alpha Prince

"Why are you chained?"

Cashel thought a minute. "Because my father is very bad."

The cutie wrinkled a freckled nose. "But then he should be locked up, not you. Mama says you need to own up when you did a bad thing."

Cashel thought her mom sounded a wise woman and he nodded in agreement. "I don't think you should be here."

She nodded vigorously. "Papa says he will whip me."

Cashel blanched. "Then for goodness sake, go. Please don't get into trouble." The thought of anyone hurting her made Cashel slightly nauseous, although that could have been the soup he had this morning. It was still churning in his belly.

She giggled. "Papa always says he will whip me, but he never would," she added with complete confidence and crawled through the space into the room. "I'm a con...cond—"

"Conundrum?" Cashel supplied with an answering grin.

"Yes, Ike says that's just another word for a girl."

Cashel thought Ike sounded very sensible as well. "Who's Ike?" Cashel hitched his breath as without any thought or hesitation, she came and sat on his pallet. The thought that he was in actual fact very much in a position to hurt her, made him feel distinctly ill.

"You look funny," she pronounced. "Does your belly ache? Aden looks like that when he eats beans." Cashel was sure he looked as wrung out as he currently felt. "Mama always reads him a story. Do you want me to tell you a story?"

Cashel smiled. "You have no book."

She rolled her eyes. "No one has books anymore. Mama says they're too much money, but I can make them up."

"You can?" Cashel was impressed. He'd always had access to books, but none of them had ever been just story books. Books that were read for pleasure. His had always been instruction books on everything from horse management to strategic troop movement. Those had been his father's suggestions. The ones on history had been his own. "What's your name?"

161

"Jarelle, but you can call me Jelly. What's yours?"

"Cashel."

She had started to tell him this long, involved story about a princess and a wolf. How the wolf had been mean to all the villagers, but he had fallen in love with the princess and become kind, and they all had lived happily ever after.

"Jarelle."

The low pained voice from the door had startled them both. Cashel had been so wrapped up in Jelly's story he had neither heard nor smelled her mother climbing the stairs. When Cashel looked up, Daisy's face was drip-white. Terror for her daughter was etched in the tremble of her hand as she extended it towards her daughter. "Come to me."

Jelly hadn't moved. She just opened her mouth to launch into what Cashel would knew was either an objection at having to move—as she was currently snuggled into his side—or an explanation about the story.

"Jelly"—Cashel dropped a kiss on top of her head—"go to your mama. You can finish the story another time."

Jelly grumbled but did exactly as he asked and when she got within arm's reach of her mom, Daisy cried out and grabbed her close. "Mama," Jelly grumbled as her mom held her tight. Daisy raised a tear stained face, obviously completely at a loss to know what to say. In the end, she just nodded at him and bundled her daughter out of the room. He had been left alone the rest of the day, and had no food or water brought up.

He was rolled up in a miserable ball when he heard Jon's footsteps. The door opened and Jon stepped in with a tray and put it down on the old rickety table in the corner. Cashel hadn't had anything since breakfast which was about seven hours ago, and to be honest wondered if he was just going to be left to starve now Daisy was obviously terrified for her children.

The smell of fish immediately filled the room. Cashel jumped up, not even registering that in alarm, Jon had drawn his knife, only making it to the empty bowl still left from earlier before he retched helplessly over and over. He startled as he felt Jon's steady hand on his back and saw the other holding out a small metal cup of water to him. His hands shook but he managed to take it. "Not a fish lover, then?" Jon questioned before gruffly picking up the bowl and putting it outside the room.

Cashel groaned pathetically and shuffled back to the bed. He turned away from Jon and lay down, just hoping the man would go away and leave him in peace.

"I understand you met my daughter?"

Cashel ignored him. It made no difference. He clearly wouldn't meet her again.

"If you think it's going to earn you any favors, it won't."

Cashel closed his eyes as they burned. Where was Justice? It was like he had been forgotten about. "Have you heard from my father?"

Jon didn't reply, which Cashel took as a negative.

"Do you know a wolf called Hale?" Jon asked.

Cashel rolled over so fast Jon took a step back. "Hale?" his voice croaked. "He's here?"

Jon shook his head. "My team have told me that there is a wolf named Hale who's been trying to contact the rebels around here. Wants to know where you are. Offering a reward."

"Hale was my bodyguard. He's a friend."

"So, he works for Darius?"

Cashel nodded. "But it makes no sense why he would be on his own. Is he offering the prisoner exchange you were hoping for?"

"I understand the prisoners escaped."

Cashel jerked back. "That's impossible."

"Not without help, certainly." He picked up the tray. "I'll see if the missus has something else."

"It doesn't matter," Cashel said. He wouldn't be able to eat anything. Hale? Why was Hale here—and on his own? It made no sense.

Jon left the room and Cashel must have been asleep when he

came back because the next time he woke, it was to see some bread with a little meat spread laid out on the table.

Cashel made himself eat a little and then lay back down as tiredness washed over him again.

The next morning he woke feeling a little better and finished the bread from the previous night. He was just drinking some water when he heard the earth shattering scream from outside, and nearly dropped the small cup. Pounding footsteps came up the steps and the door burst open and two gammas piled into the room.

"My prince," the first one spoke. "I am Captain Rand. Your father sent me to free you as soon as we had confirmation of where you were."

Cashel gaped. *His father?* For a second he was disappointed. He had hoped a pair of boots on the stairs had belonged to Justice.

Rand stepped forward and grabbed one of the chains, heaved, then he simply pulled it in two. Cashel was free.

"My prince, we need to leave. We have surprised the family, but cannot guarantee there aren't more rebels in the area. We are but a small force sent to search the neighboring farms."

Cashel's heart thudded. *Surprised the family?* What did that even mean? As he descended the stairs, his knees shook a little at the thought of Jelly being hurt. Cashel stepped outside and stopped in horror. All the humans were lined up on their knees. Jon raised his face as Cashel stepped outside and Cashel gasped. Blood was running from a nasty cut above his eye, and his cheek was rapidly swelling. Cashel glanced at the young boy who knelt down next to him. His lip was split. The smaller boy, who Cashel knew must be Aden, had distinct claw marks around his neck. Daisy's top was torn and she was obviously trying not to cry. She clutched her baby and Jelly was pressed close to her. Jelly's hurt look when she saw him nearly crippled him. He had been her friend, that look said. She had told him her best story and they had spent the morning cuddled together, and then he had allowed men to come and hurt her family in his name. Of course, she didn't say anything of the sort, but her hurt and confused look was enough.

"Pass me a knife," Cashel ordered the gamma, clamping his lips together before he let slip, "please."

Rand looked surprised, but immediately unsheathed his own and passed it to Cashel hilt first. It was nice and heavy and Cashel held it experimentally. He nodded at Aden. "Make him stand."

Rand hesitated for a fraction of a second, obviously wondering why Cashel would want to take his presumed revenge and anger out on a child. Cashel didn't know Rand, but he immediately went up in his estimation, even if the Captain had allowed his men to hurt the children. Rand stepped forward to drag Aden to his feet and Daisy cried out. He was the only one without a weapon. The other three gammas stood behind the family, pointing their swords at their backs.

"No," Jon shouted, the anguish evident in his voice. "Please," he begged hoarsely. "Kill me. My son has done nothing to you."

Daisy sobbed and pulled Jelly closer to her, trying to shield her gaze from Rand, who leaned down and grabbed the boy. Rand's attention was soon occupied by Aden when he started wailing, and before Jon could even respond to the gamma who pressed the sword to his back, Cashel stepped up behind the Captain and pointed the dagger at his neck.

"Don't move."

Rand let go of Aden immediately.

"My prince?" he queried in astonishment, and tried to turn around.

"I said don't move," Cashel growled and pressed, knowing Rand could feel the blade against his skin. The gamma froze. "I know exactly where this knife needs to go so don't even think about shifting." Rand nodded quickly. "Tell your men to drop their weapons."

Rand swallowed. "They will not, my prince, not to save my life. I am merely a captain. We have instructions from our beta that hostage requests will never succeed."

Cashel knew instantly he spoke the truth, and before anyone

could move, the gamma behind Daisy leaned down and snatched Jelly from her mother's arms. His knife looked bigger than the little girl. Daisy screamed and another gamma turned his sword to her.

The gamma holding Jelly took one step backwards away from Jon, who even though Cashel had a knife, clearly was seen to be the biggest threat. "Drop the knife," he ordered gutturally. Cashel swallowed. The gamma's fangs had dropped. He could easily rip her to shreds. Cashel had played his only hand and it hadn't worked.

A moment before it hit, Cashel caught the faint hiss of a speeding arrow, and Jelly screamed as the gamma toppled backwards with the arrow pointing from between his eyes. She scrambled off him as they were swarmed. Cashel had a second to inhale a scent he knew better than his own, and then he turned around, dropping the knife before he launched himself into Justice's arms.

Justice wrapped his arms around him tightly and the noise and the worry of the rest of the world fell away as Justice's lips fastened over his own. He wasn't kissed.

He was mauled.

Chapter Seventeen

"I didn't think I would ever see you again," Cashel whispered as Justice finally lowered him to the ground. Justice cupped his cheek.

"I always knew I would see you."

Cashel shook his head at Justice's complete confidence and sighed. It was so *Alpha* of him.

Cashel looked around, completely thrilled to see Hale and Armand. The boy was unexpected, especially when he ran at Daisy and she cried out and clutched her to him. The rest of his family crowded around Mark, who had left with his father to join the rebels because of his skill with a bow and arrow.

"Did Hale free you?" Cashel wanted to know.

"No. Gaven."

"Gaven?" Cashel was astonished. "But why?"

Justice shook his head. "Easy life? I don't know. He was very insistent that we disappear. I think he has another reason, but I was too busy being freed to stop and ask."

"And we found Hale trying to find you about thirty minutes before we got here."

Cashel smiled because he had an idea who he was really trying to find, and he wondered if Helena knew. "Why did I not know she was a wolf?"

"Because our omegas carry no scent," a warm voice said behind him. Cashel let go of Justice and threw his arms around Helena.

Helena laughed and held him tight. "Welcome to the family." He had never realized up to that minute how much he had missed having a mom. She inhaled and her breath caught as he stood back and Cashel reddened.

"I haven't been able to bathe properly."

Helena's smile widened and she clasped his hand tight, moisture glinting in her eyes. "My son is so blessed to have you." Cashel hugged her back but still decided to have a wash at the earliest opportunity.

"Zane and Axel have ridden ahead to get a message to my troops," Justice explained.

Troops? Cashel looked carefully at Justice. Just how many wolves did he have? He hoped they'd be fleeing to Arrides but Justice didn't seem to have changed his mind.

An hour later, the family were packed up and ready to go.

Much to Justice's disgust, Cashel hadn't let him kill Rand and they'd left him tied up. Hale had guaranteed the way he was tied would take the werewolf all day to free himself. Rand had said he would give a poor description of the humans and say rebels had attacked them. Cashel had believed him.

When they were ready to go, Jon and his family stood by warily. Jon had imprisoned Cashel, but he had treated him well and saved him from being raped by Vijay. The fact that Mark completely trusted Justice went a long way to easing the man's fear. "If you stay, your family may be slain," Justice had said baldly. "I cannot guarantee Darius's men may not come looking for Rand." The problem was Justice had no intention of taking Daisy and the children, but Jon said they were well known and he didn't trust them not to be found even hidden at a neighbor's, which would then be a death sentence on whoever was hiding them.

"They have to come," Cashel pleaded, as Jelly cuddled in close to him, and gazed at Justice with big eyes.

Justice growled, whereupon Jelly giggled and said he sounded like their old dog they used to have, Benjy. Cashel hadn't been able to stop laughing at Justice's affronted expression.

"We need to move."

"Where to?" Jon asked bluntly. Ike and Aden had just come back from taking their five cows to a neighbor to sell. The chickens had been given away. Daisy had looked sad, but determined. He supposed so long as they were all alive, nothing else mattered.

"Tarik," Justice replied, straightening up from where he had been tying the wagon from Jon's barn. They were taking blankets and food, as the humans couldn't shift to keep themselves warm.

Jon gazed at him for a long minute. "I have fought your kind nearly all my life."

"And now?" Justice asked.

"Now, I think it's time for a change. We can't bring Darius down on our own." He nodded to Cashel. "I like the lad and obviously I've got eyes, but it's his father." His disbelief that Cashel was against his father was apparent.

Sudden tears welled in Cashel's eyes. He spun and darted towards the trees. Justice easily caught him, and turned him around, solemnly wiping Cashel's face. "I don't know what's wrong with me. Darius hates me. I've been a disappointment to him all my life; I have no idea why that should upset me today."

"Because you see how Jon is with his kids."

Cashel nodded. "And your mom."

"She is taken with you," Justice said gently. "I think there's a good chance she likes you better than me." Cashel sniffed in disbelief. It warmed his heart, though.

"And you seem to have adopted a child," Justice added dryly; the trees barely concealed Jelly, who was pretending to hide.

Cashel laughed. "We need to saddle the horses."

"You will ride with me," Justice said implacably. "I have no intention of letting you out of my sight for the conceivable future... if ever," he added after a pause.

The cart trundled slowly with the kids and Daisy. The money they had gotten for the cows bought an extra horse for Ike to ride. The family's horse was pulling the cart and Jon was driving it.

Cashel was thrilled to see Sanjeli carrying Helena with ease. Justice apologized over and over that they weren't able to find him earlier. One thing had gone wrong after another, he explained. Two horses had gone lame and they had to stop to purchase more. He had been out of patience when Mark had eventually led them to his father's.

Cashel didn't care. He sat astride Kashir, behind Justice, and he wrapped his arms around his waist. Cashel snuggled closer and breathed Justice in. The added bonus was the pressure on his cock every time they touched. After a while, Cashel couldn't help the small breathless sounds he kept making. His cock was rock hard.

"I think we need to swap places," Justice said, his voice odd and sounding scratchy. Cashel had no intention of doing anything of the sort but grinned and breathed out a deep happy sigh.

In another two hours, the children were getting fractious and Armand and Hale said they could smell plenty of game in the part of the forest they were riding through. As they weren't meeting up with Zane and Axel for a few hours, it made sense to stop and catch their afternoon meal and let the humans eat. Cashel slid off Kashir so Justice could swing his leg over and jump down. Ike immediately ran over at his father's request and begged to be able to see to the stallion. Cashel nearly laughed knowing Justice would say no, and gaped in astonishment when Justice simply nodded and nearly thrust the reins at Ike. He grasped Cashel's arm and said they would be searching for game to the east so Hale and Armand better cover the north and south. Hale had hesitated as if he still felt he should be with Cashel, but Cashel would hardly be in any danger with his mate. Cashel

The Alpha Prince

flushed bright red when Armand raised both eyebrows, but he didn't have time to say anything as he was nearly dragged away. Justice didn't stop until they got to a secluded nook at the base of an enormous Zari tree.

Justice swung him around and pulled him close, burying his head in his neck. Cashel let out a slow breath, his hand coming to rest gently on the back of Justice's head. He was shaking. "What is it?" Cashel whispered.

"I nearly lost you," he ground out. "I think—" He stumbled and eased Cashel down to the grass with him. "I think it only just hit me when I got you back." He rolled up onto one elbow and looked down at Cashel, entwining their hands. "I have been in control nearly all my life. The only things I could never alter were when my father died and my mother left Arrides." He smiled, shaking his head as if he couldn't quite believe it himself. "And that was only furthering a plan we have had in motion for years. Then you—*erupt*—into my life," his lips tilted in a smile, "and I feel like a thunderbolt has struck me here." He pressed a hand to his chest.

"That sounds like a bad thing," Cashel said doubtfully.

Justice shook his head. "Never." He rolled onto his back and brought Cashel with him until he was tucked into his side, head resting in the crook of his arm.

"I promised you I would let you go," Justice began, "and I don't want you staying with me because you fear for your safety." He paused and Cashel gazed up at him, willing to hear words he was longing for. "I have nine ships moored out of sight near Salem."

Cashel gasped—*not* what he expected to hear—but Justice carried on. "Zane has given the signal for them to land my wolves, then retreat to a safe distance. We aren't worried for them because Darius only has ships for fishing. He has never worried about a threat from the sea."

"How many?" Cashel asked completely in shock.

"Wolves? Three hundred," Justice replied. "We know once we land messengers will be sent immediately to Tarik. They have three days to prepare to fight. They may try and secure the city, but I firmly believe Darius will choose to wait on the red sand. He will want to crush us before we reach Tarik."

Cashel thought quickly. "Darius's army is vast."

Justice nodded. "From what my mother could find out, he has an immediate four hundred and fifty gammas, and could enlist another two hundred from his other pack houses if he can get them mobilized in time."

"That's more than two to one," Cashel whispered, feeling sick.

"One man fighting for his freedom is worth ten forced soldiers," Justice replied. He bent and kissed Cashel's lips, gently but thoroughly, like he had all the time in the world, not like he was about to fight a war. He broke for air. "Darius is hated. The wolves battle out of fear, more than honor and pack."

"But frightened people can do scary things."

"I have no choice. I cannot let Darius discover what is on Arrides." He took a breath. "Do you remember I told you our ancestors travelled from another world?" Cashel nodded, silent, but he kept his eyes wide. "They didn't have a ship. Or they did, but not one that sailed on the ocean."

Cashel looked puzzled. "It travelled overland?"

Justice shook his head. "It sailed the skies. As easily as my mother's hawks."

Cashel's lips parted but he still didn't seem to be able to force any words out. He took a hurried breath. "How?"

Justice shook his head. "The knowledge has been lost over thousands of years. They had to concentrate on survival. My father told me he thought they harnessed Surya's power, but I have no idea."

"And you believed the stories?" As legends went, it was very compelling.

Justice smiled. "I have seen the ship."

"*What?*" Cashel was incredulous.

"Or what is left of it, and some drawings—and other pieces of equipment that do I have no idea what."

"And no one else does?"

"Only Zane. It has always been knowledge shared between the Alpha and his heir only, but coming here I needed to tell someone. Not even my mom knows. They are hidden deep in caves under the Patir hills."

Cashel sucked in another breath as a tiny light flickered with hope deep in his heart. "Why are you telling me?"

Justice's eyes grew warm. "Because I want you to understand how much faith I have in you." Faith? For a minute Cashel was sure he was going to say something else. He trusted him? He trusted him with the most important secret in his life, but he didn't *love* him?

"My mom has sent another message. A plea for help."

"To whom?" Cashel burst out, "because I hope it's someone with an army." His head was reeling with what Justice had said.

"You have no need to be frightened."

But he wasn't, not anymore. He didn't need Justice to keep him safe because of their mating bond. He wanted Justice to not be able to bear to let him go because he needed Cashel. Because his heart would break without him. He gazed at Justice. "Who has she sent the message to?"

"A man, a human called Christoph Tor." Justice slid his fingers under Cashel's shirt.

"Who's he?" Cashel murmured, trying not to get distracted by Justice's fingers.

"The human rebel leader in Niandes."

Cashel stilled and looked up at him. "Wow. You don't do anything by halves, do you?"

Justice smiled and shook his head. His amber eyes burned into Cashel, waiting, almost asking a question... no, that wasn't quite right. He wasn't asking the question, he was waiting for Cashel to supply the answer. Cashel lifted his arms and slid them under his shirt and up Justice's back. The amber darkened, and for the first time in so long Cashel felt powerful. "Kiss—"

But the rest of his words were swallowed by Justice's lips on his.

Fire roared through Cashel, searing need raced through every vein, and heat and want rose up in him until he thought he would catch alight and burn. Lips demanded and tongues cajoled. He yanked his mouth free and arched upwards.

"Bite me, mark me," he demanded, feeling his wolf pace and roar for another. Justice stripped his clothes and yanked his own free. There was no time. This wasn't a soulful easy joining. They weren't making love. There were no shy kisses or low whispered sweet words.

This was anger. Anger, injustice, and desperation. They didn't come together, they didn't issue any invitation, they just clashed. Each demanded and each took. Tongues and claws and teeth. Cashel's fingers were claw-tipped as he raked them across Justice's back, egging him on, thrusting his hips, begging for more, drowning in need and taste and smell. Justice lifted Cashel's legs over his shoulder and took both of Cashel's ass cheeks in his firm hand and separated them. Cashel felt the slick, but he had known anyway. His body had never responded like this, ever.

The first thrust burned and Cashel rejoiced and wanted more. "Deeper," he begged and tried to push up. Faster, harder. *More.* "Alpha," he chanted over and over as his wolf howled in his mind, needing the dominance, craving it.

Justice thrust and dragged back. Sweat poured from them both, their skin slick and hot with it. Cashel moaned. He wanted more, something that seemed just out of reach. Then Justice bent his head to Cashel's throat and the sharp bite sent Cashel over the edge. He was falling even as he lay on solid ground. Pleasure exploded in every fiber of his body, and he shook as something inside him seemed to splinter, only to fall back more joined and at peace than he had ever known.

Cashel became aware of the harsh pants that weren't just from his lungs, and had the strength to smile. Justice had come apart as much as he had. He groaned as he gently lowered Cashel's legs and Cashel held back a pained hiss as he slid from his body. Justice collapsed on the ground and pulled Cashel into him.

The silence between them changed, suddenly not so easy, and Cashel held his breath.

"Forgive me."

Cashel raised his head. "For *what?*" Every part of his disbelief and astonishment colored his voice.

Another beat of silence. "I was too rough."

"I am a *wolf*," Cashel replied.

"*Par se te vuta*," Justice whispered. His voice low and pained.

"You are my life," Cashel murmured in wonder.

Justice clutched him tightly. "We have so much to talk about."

Cashel smiled. *His life. His heart.* Vuta in Askaran meant both. Was Justice saying he loved him?

Justice's amber eyes were dark and he glanced at the sky. "But not now. Now we need to hunt." They did, but Cashel had no idea why he said "we." He had never hunted anything in his life. The best he had ever managed was a fishing line, and his stomach objected strongly at the sudden visual.

He shook his head. "You hunt," he smirked, "I think I'll just lie here and watch you."

Justice growled and in a moment Cashel lay on a huge furry wolf. He had a second to admire the huge black animal before the shift rushed through him and he was as furry as Justice. Cashel froze but let himself be nudged to stand. No pain. The world was brighter. His vision sharper. His sense of hearing and smell both more acute. Cashel inhaled and knew instantly there was an animal close. Justice nudged him gently forward. He wanted him to hunt? *Him?*

Cashel was running before he even thought to set his legs in motion, and he exulted at the sudden speed. Then the wind changed and if Cashel's wolf had a voice it would have been screaming the sudden danger. He didn't have time to react as Justice overtook him and with a deafening snarl leapt and landed on the fully grown Hadrax just as it was charging for Cashel. Cashel immediately shifted back to human, unable to keep his wolf form without Justice's Alpha power. Fur flew, jaws snapped and snarls rose along with the scent of blood. Cashel was helpless to do any other than stare in terror. The Hadrax were almost legendary. The pig-like ferocious creature was one of the few things apart from a hunter's spear that could kill a fully grown wolf. They were few, though, and the wolves had all but successfully extinguished them. Cashel had no idea what this one was doing so close to the human settlements they usually avoided.

Justice rolled with the animal, his jaws trying desperately to avoid the other's and clamp his teeth into the Hadrax's fur. The blood spatter visible even against his black coat. Cashel heard the pained cry and saw Justice and the Hadrax separate. They were both on their feet instantly. Justice bared his teeth as the growl that came from him seemed to shake the very earth they stood on. The Hadrax charged at the same time as the wolf, and they met in a riot of claws and teeth.

Cashel's hands clasped a thick branch next to him and he rose defiantly, and then it was over. The wolf blurred and Justice stood, wonderfully, gloriously naked and very much alive. The body of the Hadrax lay still at his feet. Justice's amber eyes gleamed at Cashel, all predator as he stalked towards him. Cashel smelled the blood, catalogued the streaks of it still running down Justice's chest and covering his arms. In an abstract way, he knew none of it belonged to Justice and he hated the way it marred his beautiful skin. He took a shaking step towards his warrior, the bitter taste of metal on his tongue, the coppery tang of blood in his ears, and suddenly he was back to being a child and his father had just slain the baby girl. The same hard floor hit him as he fell.

Chapter Eighteen

Justice couldn't react fast enough. Even with his Alpha speed he wasn't able to catch Cashel as his knees crumpled. "Cashel," he cried out in alarm and was cradling him gently in seconds.

"Justice." Armand ran into the clearing closely followed by Hale. They skidded to a stop as they took in the dead Hadrax.

"Where is he hurt?" Hale demanded, raking his eyes over Cashel.

"He collapsed," Justice said as he stood, his heart thumping so hard in its bid for freedom. "The Hadrax got nowhere near him." Hale picked up their clothes and tucked Justice's shirt around Cashel.

"It might have been the shock," Armand said. "He's breathing normally, but he's had a bad few days."

Guilt slammed into Justice so hard he nearly stumbled. Cashel had been kidnapped and held as a prisoner after he had been abused and mistreated by the person who should have loved him unconditionally. He had been brave enough to attempt to rescue humans against stronger wolves, and then Justice himself had been far too rough when all Cashel deserved was gentling. Justice's beast had taken over. He might have hurt him, and then he had forced a shift without asking if that was what Cashel wanted. Then he had nearly been attacked by a wild animal and seen Justice kill it. Justice tightened his arms, his heart squeezing in agony and fear. Cashel would hate him when he woke. *Par se te vuta* meant you are my life, but it also meant something else on Arrides. Technically it translated as *you are the life of my heart,* or the reason for it still beating. He had called Cashel his heart, but Justice had stamped all over it. He wasn't fit to hold something so precious.

Helena came running as they walked back to the cart. "What is it?" The others crowded around.

"Leave him," Justice growled as Daisy reached out a hand. She yanked it back quickly and Helena fixed him a disapproving look.

"I will ride back in the cart with him." She smiled at Daisy. "Can Aden ride?"

"Yes. So can Jarelle, but Aden can also drive the cart so Jon can ride guard."

Helena nodded. "Good." She turned to Justice, who was seemingly immobile. "I'm going to climb in." She did quickly, arranging a soft pile of blankets next to her in the cart and Justice gently lowered Cashel down. He moaned softly and opened his eyes. Daisy climbed in the other side with the baby and the others mounted their horses. Armand passed Justice his clothes and he pulled them on quickly. He glanced back at Cashel, who was watching him. He opened his mouth to apologize, beg for forgiveness, explain how he had never loved anything or anyone as much as he did Cashel. He would give up his home for him. He would give up his pack for him. He would renounce his position as Alpha and return to Arrides if that was where Cashel wanted to go.

"I don't know where to start," Justice forced the pained whisper past his lips, but he couldn't bear to wait for the reply. He whirled around and ran for Kashir. He would lead his wolves to victory and then when it was done—if his sweet mate could still bear the sight of him—they would return to the desert for the rest of their lives.

"Did I embarrass him?" Cashel focused on Helena's face.

"He thinks he hurt you, and my son has a huge sense of responsibility just like his father."

"I'm just a responsibility?" Cashel's eyes widened.

Helena tutted. "I need to tell you two things, and both are equally as important. I hope you like history."

"I love history," Cashel said eagerly. Helena un-stoppered a flask of water. "Drink, my son." Cashel's eyes filled at being called that and Helena tutted gently again, but she squeezed his hand, and he drank thirstily.

"I want to tell you about our pack's history and then omega wolves on Askara."

Cashel sighed. "I hate being an omega."

Helena tilted her head. "In the pack, omegas are only second in importance to the Alpha, some say even more so." Cashel tried not to look skeptical but he must have failed because she smiled. "All omegas have gifts, and all are highly valued, female and male."

Cashel looked anywhere but at Helena. "Female—"

Helena shushed him. "There is no distinction. No Alpha can run his pack effectively without an omega, and I know you are aware of your gift. You are just so petrified of your father finding out you have never used it fully. I am an omega."

Cashel's mouth parted in a silent *o*. "You are an omega?" *Of course.* No Alpha ran their pack without mating an omega. He immediately wondered what her gift was, but didn't dare ask. "But..." Cashel gazed at her in confusion. "You are human." He had definitely smelled no wolf.

Helena shook her head. "No, I am a wolf. We are all hybrids on Arrides, but our omegas carry no scent at all." She laughed. "The wolves here don't register a specific human scent. They just know when someone isn't a wolf and make an assumption they are human. It's easy."

Cashel blinked. She was right. He had never thought of it that way before. "Is that why no one has smelled Justice's scent on me and likewise mine on him?"

"No, Cashel. That isn't why. I am sure it is your omega gift, but I am not certain."

Cashel frowned. What had his scent to do with anything?

Helena talked for ages. She told him the history of Askara as had been passed down to her by her mother, about the pack members she knew. About the tragedy that had put all their plans in motion all those years ago. Of Justice and Zane as little boys. Of Justice's father who Cashel would have loved to meet.

"My gift," Helena finally said, "is linked to my position as *enfantata*, or mother-Alpha."

"What is that?" Cashel asked, completely fascinated.

"My duties include helping the wolves give birth, and the safety and nurturing of all cubs." She glanced down briefly and Cashel was struck with how their one cub per family rule must have killed her. It would go against everything she was born to do.

"My gift is knowing immediately when a wolf becomes pregnant, usually even before they know themselves. I can tell if there is any problem with the pup all the time it is developing."

Cashel blinked. "How?"

"Their heartbeat. Only their Alpha and an enfantata can hear it at first, but I can scent it also when an Alpha can't. Me because that is my gift; an Alpha because an Alpha would sense another wolf in his pack."

"That's amazing."

"It is," Helena glanced at Daisy, who had fallen asleep holding her baby, then looked back at him and smiled. "Congratulations."

Cashel stared at Helena. His mind slow to process what she was saying. "Congratulations?" he parroted.

"Yes," Helena laughed. "Of course, Justice will be impossible when you tell him. He will want to wrap you in furs and scurry you away somewhere. But don't let him. Omegas are some of the strongest wolves ever created. A lot of years ago, the Alpha and omega always ran the pack as a team. The Alpha wouldn't ever go into battle without his omega next to him. Unfortunately, a lot of omegas on Askara just behave like spoiled princesses and not the brave warriors they were born to be." She smiled again. "I have every faith you are going to be different. If Justice gives you trouble, you will simply have to be brave enough for both of you."

Cashel wasn't sure he understood a word of what Helena was saying. She sighed. "For an *enfantata* I'm doing a poor job of explaining, aren't I?" Helena gripped both his hands. "You are pregnant, Cashel. In approximately seven or eight weeks by my estimation you are going to give birth to a pup." She curled her nose. "Have some sympathy for humans. You will only have to go through this for a little over sixty days, while human females have to cope with nine months."

Cashel gaped.

"Do you understand?" Helena repeated slowly.

Astonishment, warmth and then awe flowed through Cashel in equal quantities. "You're sure?"

Helena nodded. "When are you going to tell Justice?"

Cashel looked around as the cart drew to a stop. It had neared dusk as he had lain talking to Helena.

He sat up, pulling the covers around him. He heard a shout and the loud thunder of hooves as horses and their riders burst from the trees. His heart threatened to stop until he spotted Zane jumping from one and rushing to greet Justice. Daisy woke up and climbed down with the baby, and Helena followed. Cashel quickly pulled on his breeches, shirt, and a heavy wool tunic. Should he get out and go to Justice? *You will have to be brave enough for both of you.* Helena's words came back to him. He liked the thought of being a warrior. At the very least he could stand by the side of *his* warrior.

Cashel jumped easily from the wagon and met a pair of amber eyes that had zeroed in on him as soon as he had moved. Justice took a step but he was surrounded by his wolves, and Cashel simply walked in between them until Justice drew him close. "How do you feel?" The worry was clear in Justice's voice.

Cashel smiled reassuringly and turned to greet Zane, laughing when Axel squealed and threw his arms around him. Then the poor boy turned every shade of red and apologized to his master. Cashel squeezed his hands. "There are no master and slaves anymore."

He looked up at the sudden silence and was surprised to see every wolf staring at him. Justice cleared his throat and pulled Cashel back to him. "Warriors, greet your omega."

Cashel stood still as every huge wolf immediately went down on one knee and bowed their heads. He looked at Justice in complete panic. What did he say? He glanced at the bent heads. "I am thrilled to meet you all, but I am hungry as I am sure we all are. How about we concentrate on getting everyone fed?"

The wolves all grinned their approval, and Justice chuckled. In no time, there were two huge fires blazing. Justice brought his beta-commanders up to date. The rest of the wolves then left to join their men and would all meet at the red sands in two days. They had decided to split in case any one group ran into problems. Justice told them all what to expect, warned them of the Hadrax they had come across, and introduced the humans.

Jelly was utterly and completely fascinated by everything. She had gazed in astonishment when Justice had introduced Cashel to Xyanna. Beautiful, fierce, and clearly female, Xyanna had charmed Cashel immediately around the same time as he had lost his shadow. Jelly now had a new hero. The knowledge that Xyanna was not only a warrior, but commanded a ship completely stunned the little girl. She was only used to females cooking, cleaning, and having children. Not that Xyanna pressed upon her that there was anything wrong with that. She also told her that the thought of looking after babies was truly terrifying, and learning to wield a sword was much easier and less painful than childbirth.

Jelly didn't look convinced and followed Xyanna around all evening much to the teasing of the other betas.

Justice accepted the huge plate of food from Daisy with thanks, and turned to share some with Cashel, only to stop and stare in astonishment as Cashel not only got his own, but tore into it with gusto. He was starving.

He was starving? When had Cashel ever been hungry? Glancing at Justice, who was still looking at him in shock, reminded him they needed to have a conversation, and soon. It was likely Justice would already be able to hear the heartbeat, or even sense the presence of another wolf. Arridian wolves, Alphas especially, were so tuned into the needs of their pack. Justice would realize something was different quite quickly, and the second before he walked into battle may not be a good time to share. In fact, Helena had insisted it was only because they had been apart and then so busy that Justice had not stopped to listen. Cashel had hoped to wait until after the fighting, but that was simply not going to be possible.

He had asked Helena to be on hand for him and Justice. He wasn't completely sure Justice would believe him. If it hadn't been for Helena's complete confidence he wasn't sure he would believe it himself.

Cashel sought out Justice and waited until he had finished talking to his commanders. "Can I talk to you?"

Justice smiled immediately, and Cashel glanced at Helena, who nodded. She had said she wouldn't intrude on what should be a private moment, but she would stay close in case he needed her.

Xyanna asked Justice about the timing of their attack. Cashel smiled and said he would see him by the horses. He walked up to where the horses were tethered and saw immediately they had drained their water buckets. He looked over his shoulder quickly to make sure no one was watching and quickly stared at the patch of ground in front of the horses. Slowly the ground darkened, the sudden moisture evident. Cashel stretched his palm out over the ground and water bubbled up over the grass. One of the bought mares snorted but Sanjeli immediately put her head down and drank.

The other horses quickly followed suit. He chuckled. "That should satisfy you until I can get your buckets filled."

A twig cracked and he whirled around to see Helena staring at him with her mouth open. He licked his lips nervously. She had seen what he did. "I—" but Helena's wide smile stopped him, and before he had the chance to say anything else Justice ran over.

"Just seeing that you are safe," Helena beamed and stepped away.

He forgot Helena, as he gazed at Justice, staring into his eyes, his courage completely leaving him. He simply had no idea what to say. "Can you hear anything?" he blurted out, and Justice immediately whirled around, his hand going for his Kataya.

"Not out there," Cashel said, and he brought Justice's hand to press it to his gently rounded belly.

"What's the matter?" Justice's eyes widened and he clutched at Cashel's shoulder with his free hand. "Did I hurt you? I did, didn't I?" His face was twisted in anguish and guilt.

"No," Cashel shook his head and gently cupped his face. "Listen."

Justice's face changed, grew puzzled. He lifted his chin and scented the air, and then he looked back at Cashel, tilting his head to the side. He was listening.

"What is it? I can't hear anything." Justice's voice cracked.

"Our pup," Cashel whispered. "But it may be too early for you to hear."

Justice sighed. "Cashel, sweetheart. You are my mate. A pup doesn't matter."

"Doesn't matter?" Cashel parroted. "No, you don't understand. I know it's hard to believe, yes. But—"

Justice raked both hands through his hair. "It's impossible, sweetheart. Your father was obsessed. I can understand how that would upset you."

"No, it's because I'm an omega. It's linked—"

"To you growing crops?" The disbelief was almost derision. Cashel took a breath. Tried not to be hurt.

"It's more than that."

"How is finding water anything to do with getting pregnant?" Justice snapped. Cashel could see the pulse point beating frantically at the base of his neck. He was scared. Cashel took another breath. His big strong Alpha was completely panicking over something he didn't understand. If it hadn't been so important, it would have made him smile.

"Omegas used to be different to how they are today. They rode into battle with their Alpha—"

"Absolutely not."

Cashel forced his annoyance down. This wasn't going how he expected. "I didn't mean I would. I just meant—"

"Well that's a relief, because you really showed that Hadrax what you were made of, didn't you?"

Cashel hissed in the hurt. Swallowed it down.

"Cashel," Justice stepped forward. Regret and confusion etched in his face. "I'm sorry—"

"No." Cashel put up a hand to ward him off.

"That was unforgiveable of me." Justice took another breath. "I know you went through hell because of your father, but an heir isn't important to me. I hate that territories are granted by birthright and not ability." He took a step closer. "I hate even more what you had to endure because of his obsession to get you pregnant, but that's over now. You don't ever have to put yourself through that ever again."

"Cashel?" It was Axel. They hadn't had the chance to speak earlier.

"Coming," Cashel shouted back. Justice grabbed his arm, but Cashel shook it off. He wasn't hurt, he was furious. "Let go of me."

"Cashel, I'm sorry. I know you want a baby badly. Let's go talk to my mom. She may have an idea."

Cashel shook his head. "You think I'm making this up?" he wrapped both hands around his middle protectively.

Justice swallowed, obviously trying to think of a tactful way to say that yes, he did think Cashel was delusional. "Let's get some sleep. You've been through an awful lot in the past few days."

Cashel nodded, backed away when Justice took another step forward, and turned and hurried back to the camp. He immediately hurried back to Axel and, completely oblivious to the storm that was roaring through Cashel, Axel eagerly shared his news. Zane loved him, and wanted them to mate.

"I am so thrilled for you," Cashel hugged his friend, but as Axel carried on excitedly he was ashamed to admit he tuned most of it out.

Chapter Nineteen

The next day started with difficulty. Daisy and Jon's baby sickened. Helena helped as much as she could, but it was heartbreaking to hear his cries of pain. They seemed to be through the worst of it by late afternoon, and Justice heaved a sigh of relief. He'd sent Xyanna and her wolves on up ahead to make sure everything was safe, and when they finally stopped for the night, everyone was exhausted. Justice hadn't had a moment to speak to Cashel all day as he had kept Jelly and Aden close to him, upset as they were over their brother.

He stood on the edge of the campfire, heaving a sigh of relief that finally the crying had stopped, wondering how new parents ever coped.

"I'm impressed."

He turned to his mom and smiled. "You look tired. How's the baby?"

"He will be fine."

"And why are you impressed?"

Helena looked at him oddly. "Because you haven't had Cashel glued to your side. I thought he would be lucky to be more than an arm's length away from you, but I suppose he has been looking after the little ones."

Justice nodded. "It's hard, but I'm trying to give him some freedom. After all his father put him through…" He trailed off, deciding to ask his mom for advice. "I also don't think I'm his favorite person at the moment."

Helena snorted. "That man loves you with everything he is. He will make a terrific dad, but then so will you." She leant and brushed his cheek softly.

Justice caught her hand. This was going to be hard, and he hoped his mom would be supportive. "I wanted to ask you a favor."

Helena laughed. "That's a first. You're my Alpha, you can command what you will."

"It didn't stop you leaving Arrides."

She leaned forward. "Because it was the right thing to do. I have learned so much about the humans, the other territories. You will need all that, Son."

Justice nodded. "I told Cashel if he wants, then once I have taken the territory we will return to Arrides." He squirmed a little. "He has this small gift."

His mom regarded him in confusion. "I would hardly call it small. He has the capability of preventing starvation."

"He does?" Justice was confused. "Well, I guess finding a little water—"

"Stop." Helena put her finger over Justice's lips. "You have talked about this, haven't you?"

"He told me he was a grower." Justice shrugged but Helena shook her head,

"He's not just a grower, he's a diviner as well. But even more than that. I think—"

"A diviner?" Justice interrupted, completely confused.

"Son, do you not remember anything you were taught? By the goddess." Helena closed her eyes. "I bet that bastard Darius never even told him."

The Alpha Prince

"Told him what? What's a diviner?"

"Of course, there is the slight chance Darius may not know, although unlikely."

"Mom," Justice growled.

"I know because I found a report from the healers to Darius. They always reported directly to him. And of course you always hated history, and there hasn't been a powerful diviner born in hundreds of years."

"Mom," Justice snapped. "What is a diviner?"

Helena took both his hands in hers. "Son, a diviner is one of the most powerful omegas to exist. It means Cashel only has to touch the ground to know what's underneath it. Water, Tanzanite, you name it. There was an omega recently in Caedra who claimed to have the same ability, but she's been tested and it only works in small areas and for certain things. There hasn't been a true diviner for over a thousand years."

Justice let his arm drop. The possibilities were endless. No more poverty or starvation.

"And not just that."

"There's more?"

Helena nodded. "It's true that a diviner often is confused as a grower. They have similar talents. They can both tell you to plant crops in that field because it is fed by an underground stream you cannot see, or there is a vein of precious metal running through that cliffside—"

"But—" Justice interrupted. There was more, he knew there was.

"A diviner doesn't have to tell you which field to plant crops in because the water is already there, a powerful diviner can *bring the water* to the field."

Justice. "Bring—"

"And I don't mean carry it," Helena said with a smile. "I mean divert it from its source. And not just water either, although it's been so long since one was born, I would imagine no one will truly know all Cashel can do until he tries it."

"How do you know all this?" It was unbelievable.

"My birds. I have been communicating with two historians from Caedra. We don't use names as it's too risky, but the amount of history I have discovered is phenomenal."

"And Darius doesn't know?"

She shook her head. "He won't have cared. His real obsession was getting an heir. I would think jewels and money may have ranked lower in significance as he has so much already, and as soon as Cashel was labelled as a grower, Darius was uninterested."

Justice nodded then shifted uncomfortably. "About the heir part, Mom." He sighed. "I need you to stop encouraging him. It's not healthy and he's becoming obsessed."

Helena frowned. "What do you mean?"

"I know you mean well, but he has to get this idea of having a baby out of his head. It's not good for him."

Helena paled and Justice was immediately worried he had hurt her. "What did you say to him?"

"Just that we would talk to you if he wants a baby so much. That I really didn't care about heirs. That ability, not birthright, should decide who rules a territory."

Helena closed her eyes as if in pain. "You told him you didn't care about your baby?"

"No," Justice shouted, but immediately lowered his voice. "I told him I wanted him to stop worrying about having one in the first place. It's ridiculous and he's been through enough."

Helena opened dark, angry eyes. Her eyes were brown, but right then anger made them glow a dark gold. Justice swallowed. She was furious. "This is partly my fault, my Alpha." Justice's eyes widened at the formality. "As enfantata I should have offered suitable congratulations and a *raykia*." Cold washed through Justice. A raykia was a gift—something small—always given to a she-wolf when she found herself expecting a cub. It was traditionally a gift from the enfantata and her Alpha.

"What?" His voice cracked wanting it spelled out, but he knew. Of course, he knew.

"Your mate is expecting his first pup in seven, maybe eight weeks. I have heard the heartbeat myself, and if you weren't a sorry excuse for a mate, and a worse Alpha-father, you would have known yourself. Didn't you listen?" She nearly screeched the last words, completely incredulous.

Justice froze. Cashel's soft hand pressing to his belly. The slight round of it that had changed from last time. His scent. "But," Justice started desperately. "They formed a pouch, for goodness sake. He has had idiot after idiot doing mad experiments. He wouldn't be able to carry a child."

Helena sighed and stepped close, cupping his cheek. "Son, have you or have you not made him shift?"

"Well, of course. When that fool made him sit in the sun and he became sick. He told me he was forbidden..." Justice trailed off and wanted to smack himself, hard.

"Because the shift will have undone everything the healers attempted. He was healed, and because yours is a true mating you were able to get him pregnant. I won't embarrass you, Son, but I would guess your knot formed?" Heat flushed through Justice and he could feel his face burn. He just thought it was because Cashel affected him so. He had no idea it was because his wolf recognized its true mate and wanted to impregnate him. Helena smiled. "There are some male omegas in the northern territories, but from what I have found out their ability to have a pup has been prevented because they aren't true mates—to the point most wolves don't even know it can happen. Mating had degenerated into something artificial for wealth and power. You and Zane are the first wolves on Arrides for a long time to want to mate with a man. I think that's because everyone is too desperate for their one pup not to risk not mating a female."

Justice's legs gave out and he collapsed onto the ground. What had he done? How would Cashel ever forgive him now?

His mom bent down. "I'm thinking you just need to do some groveling." As if she'd heard his thoughts.

"I can't believe I said what I did. How could I doubt him?" Cashel had tried to get him to believe him twice. Firstly, about his omega abilities, and secondly about their pup. He hadn't believed him either time. He deserved to be whipped, but mostly he didn't deserve to have Cashel's love.

Pain ripped through him as if someone had taken his Kataya and plunged it in his chest. Cashel's love? Cashel had never heard that from him. He had told him he had *faith* in him. Justice lost his temper and drove his fist hard into the trunk of the tree. The wood splintering was very satisfying. "Go find him, Justice." He nodded and grabbed her, burying his head in her neck. "He loves you. He will forgive you." Justice stepped away and turned around. *Please let her be right.*

Cashel hugged himself. He was alone at last. Justice was taking first watch and he hoped to be asleep by the time he returned. Cashel had walked past the cart, as he needed some time to think. What should he do? Justice hadn't given him a chance. In fact, Justice had behaved much like his father. Neither of them believed Cashel was capable of anything. He expected Justice to defeat his father and become the great Alpha he knew he could be. But where did that leave him?

He didn't know. They were mates, that much was obvious. A small smile pushed through his worry as he thought about the tiny life that was growing inside him. It was a miracle, and he knew deep down that Justice wouldn't ever take the baby away from him. In fact, Helena had described how the baby was swaddled to the she-wolf for the first few days, and he liked that idea very much.

"Cashel?"

He glanced around at Hale and smiled. He should have known Hale would have been watching him. Hale was a family man, and had said how important his children were to him. Cashel didn't think he could do better than have someone like that to look out for him.

"I heard you'd been sick?"

Cashel blushed and rubbed his belly. Hale's eyes immediately followed the action of his hand. "It was a bad memory." He shrugged.

"Can I get you any food? I can't believe I didn't think to bring you any of your tonic. Some bodyguard I am," he grumbled. Cashel felt guilty. Hale was castigating himself over something unnecessary.

"I don't need it anymore."

Hale looked confused. "But your father said—"

"Hale, I'm fine." And because he was so happy, excited, and wanted someone to be thrilled for him after the reaction he had gotten from Justice, he made the biggest mistake of his life. "We *both* are."

Hale's eyes widened as he stared at Cashel's hand. "You mean?"

Cashel nodded, feeling lighter. At least someone was pleased for him. "Yes, in about six weeks."

Hale gaped. "But how do you know?"

"Helena told me."

Hale looked skeptical. "Is that why she came after you? She would have been much safer back in the compound instead of running around with all these rebels," he grumbled.

Cashel grinned. Typical wolf and his mate. "Don't let her hear you say that. She has definite ideas on how omegas should be treated."

Hale smiled. "I am surprised a human female would make that definition, but she is a caring woman. I am hoping she will meet my children soon."

What? "Helena isn't human, she's an omega." Cashel hadn't realized Hale didn't know, but of course in all the excitement yesterday and with the baby sick today, Justice and Helena had barely been together. "Hale, Helena is a wolf. She is Justice's mom."

"W-what?" the poor man stammered.

Cashel smiled gently, because he was worried Hale might be in shock. "It's been planned for years. I'm sorry, I'm sure she wanted to tell you herself. I know she counts you as a friend."

Hale shook his head as if he couldn't believe what he was hearing, then ran a hand over his shorn hair. "I don't know what to say." It wasn't the reaction he'd hoped for. He thought he would have been pleased.

Hale shook himself, smiled, and opened his arms. "Congratulations."

Cashel grinned and stepped into them. He had a second to process the sharp point pressing into his side and fear washed over him in a sickening wave.

"Keep your mouth closed or my knife goes right through your pup's heart." The growl that accompanied it was full of anger, frustration, and something else.

"Hale, what are you doing?" Cashel instinctively tried to step back.

The knife jabbed a little harder and Cashel immediately froze. "Do as you are told," Hale ground out.

"But—"

"Be quiet. If you value your pup's life you are going to walk with me to the trees and get on one of the horses. One sound and the pup's dead."

Chapter Twenty

Justice had to keep watch by the trees until Jon came to relieve him, and every second he was away from Cashel was one too many, but with sending the others on ahead, he needed every able person to watch, including himself. His first choice wouldn't have been a human, to be honest, because a wolf had such an advantage with sight and scent, but that wasn't the point. The wolves and the humans had to work together, and Jon was determined to do his share.

Justice walked back to the awning where the humans were huddled in bed rolls intending to see if he could get to Cashel. He didn't want to wake him, just to be with him. He'd gone from refusing to hear anything earlier, to wanting nothing more than to listen to that tiny heartbeat. He was to be a *father*. Panic had him catching his breath. What sort of dad would he be? Better, he hoped, than he was currently turning out to be a mate.

"Justice?" He turned at Zane's quiet voice. "Have you given Hale any extra duties?"

He shook his head. "No, what do you mean?"

"He was supposed to take over from Daskid and he hasn't

shown." Justice swore and turned away from the awning. It was probably good he didn't disturb Cashel anyway. His mate needed the rest.

"He may have gotten the times wrong, or been distracted."

Zane quirked an eyebrow in disbelief. "Hale has been a gamma for over forty years. There are not many with his experience."

"Zane!" Axel and Mark came running towards them. "There's a horse missing."

A chill ran through Justice and he pivoted, running back to the awning. His heart pounding faster than his feet. The noise had Helena sitting up in concern.

Justice's eyes raked over the occupied bedrolls. "Where's Cashel?"

"I thought he was with you." She jumped up, which woke everyone except the children. Zane stepped up and started issuing orders to search for Cashel and Hale. Justice seemed to be incapable of either.

"Justice." It was his mom. He tried to force his fear down.

"I don't understand why Cashel would want to go. I mean I understand why he would feel Hale was the only one he could trust, but—"

"Are you sure?" Helena asked bluntly.

"What do you mean?"

"I mean, are you sure Cashel asked to go?"

"But he's his bodyguard." Justice was having difficulty wrapping his head around what his mom was asking.

"Who has known Cashel as long as you have. Hale didn't accompany Cashel from Lapis, he was assigned when Cashel arrived, and there was more than one wolf that thought it odd...including Gaven."

"But surely Gaven assigned him?" Zane asked.

Helena shook her head. "As I understand it, the order came directly from Darius. Hale was a low-level gamma who just seemed to do the minimum to draw his wage. He was simply kind to Cashel on his first day, which is the reason everyone assumed he got assigned." She frowned. "But that would make no sense. Darius wouldn't assign someone a task because they were *kind*."

"When was the last time anyone actually saw Cashel?" To Justice's horror, he realized it had been him, and that had been over four hours ago. No one recalled seeing Hale any time after they had eaten.

Justice clasped his mom's arm and took her a few feet away from the others. "We haven't talked about this, but Hale obviously likes you."

Helena smiled and cupped Justice's face. "Your father will only ever be the wolf I love." She frowned. "I thought we were friends, but he would know as a supposed human we could never mate."

Justice growled. "But surely he knows you are a wolf now."

"He may, but that didn't bring him here. He only found out when we met up."

"Alpha?" Armand stepped closer. "What do you want us to do?"

Justice stared helplessly at his friends. What he wanted to do and what he must do were two completely different things.

"Can you track his scent?" Zane asked. "No one else can ever scent Cashel."

Helena glanced thoughtfully at her son. "Do you remember your father's words? That a source would save your people?"

"But he never found anything, Mom, and I have no idea what I am supposed to look for." Justice looked blankly at his mom.

"Because I don't think it's an object, Son. I think it's a person. I've heard of diviners, but Justice, Cashel didn't just find the water, he made it run over dry ground. I have never seen anything like it. It was as if he pulled it from the earth itself."

Justice tried to grasp what his mom was saying.

"I have lived here for five years. We never have rain in the dry season, ever. I'm not sure about the other times, but at least twice it rained when Cashel became upset."

"The horse challenge," Armand murmured.

Zane nodded carefully and looked at Justice. "It was raining the first time we saw him, the day he arrived. And the night after the first banquet there was a terrific storm."

And Cashel had appeared covered in bruises. He glanced at Armand. "Please ready Kashir for me." He stopped Zane before he could object. "I know we can all scent Hale, but only I can scent Cashel. On the off chance they are not together, only I can do this. Carry on with the journey tomorrow. I will meet you at dawn on the third day at the entrance to the south gates along with the rest of our wolves. I cannot stop the battle, nor do I want to, but I want to ride on ahead. If there is the chance of catching up with them, I have to take it."

He turned to Zane. "I will see you at dawn."

Zane clasped his arm. "Re kitech." *Be swift*. But in Askaran it also meant be safe, and be successful. Justice prayed he was right.

"Son." Helena stepped close. "If I am right, he is incredibly powerful, but has no idea how to use his gifts. So far they have only happened when he has been distressed."

Justice drew in a long breath and quickly hugged his mother. It was something he had to think about.

Kashir took Justice safely through the woods and onto the fields. He couldn't risk the main road between Salem and Tarik, and he doubted Hale had done so. His biggest advantage was that Hale's horse carried two and wasn't as fit as Kashir, but a four-hour start was a huge gap he wasn't sure even Kashir could narrow.

Cashel had been so happy, so excited. His blue eyes had sparkled as he had pressed a hand to his belly where the baby slept, warm and safe. He had asked him to listen, and Justice had refused. He didn't blame Cashel for running if that was what he had done. For a brief moment, he was selfish enough to hope that Cashel hadn't gone voluntarily because that would have meant he didn't want to leave Justice, but then cold, sick, fear rushed through him as he pictured Cashel forced to go back to his father, helpless and terrified.

When dawn broke, he walked around the outskirts of a village. He wanted to shift and eat, but he daren't leave Kashir unattended,

The Alpha Prince

but the horse needed a rest. He had a huge heart and would carry Justice forever but they had also a coming battle. No, the horse needed rest. He stopped on the edge of the village some distance from a human farm and let Kashir graze. He was thinking about Cashel when he heard the cry before he smelled anything. A high-pitched child's wail, full of fear. Justice didn't think, he ran. He smelled what the problem was nearly immediately.

Tamir cats, and a human. Presumably the one that had cried. Justice shifted without pausing, his shirt and breeches both ripping and falling off. His heart pounded as he leapt over a small brook and bounded into the trees. It was a little boy—four, maybe five, and he was backed up against a tree holding a Tamir kitten. As kittens, they were easily mistaken for domestic cats, but the fully grown female—the size of a large dog—teeth bared, hackles raised, and vicious claws, was advancing on the child and looked suitably petrifying. Justice shifted, making a lot of noise deliberately, and the female swung around wildly. "Put the kitten down," he instructed the boy, not taking his eyes from the cat for one second.

"But they were crying," came back the small voice.

"Because they were hungry. Their mother is back to see to them, but she thinks you are going to hurt them." The boy thankfully put the kitten down, and it wobbled back to its brothers and sisters. The female snarled again, and Justice immediately shifted back once more. He couldn't risk still being in his human form if the cat decided to attack the boy. He was faster as a wolf. Justice immediately ran over to the tree and put himself between the boy and the cat. The cat breathed out. She could get to her kittens. Justice turned and nudged the boy, and they both backed away.

"I thought it was gonna eat me."

Seth, Jay's father, shook his head in consternation. "I canna believe it didn't."

Justice had changed back as soon as they crossed the stream, and

Jay had burst into tears and flung himself into Justice's arms. Justice managed to use his ripped breeches to cover himself enough to go to the small farmhouse near where he had left Kashir.

Of course, Seth, and Amy—his wife—had known instantly what Justice was as soon as he had taken Jay back and Jay had told them both how a huge wolf had saved him. Justice was surprised to find out that to Jay him being a wolf didn't seem to be as scary as encountering a Tamir cat—but then, Justice hadn't growled at him. His mother, on the other hand, was obviously scared to death.

Justice sighed. "You have nothing to fear from me." Amy didn't look like she believed him, but she stopped shaking.

"Now," Seth had said when they calmed down a bit. "My eldest son's tall. I reckon we will have some clothes that should fit."

At the words, Amy snapped into action, immediately offering Justice some food and ale. Justice said if they could spare some bread he would be very grateful, but he was in a hurry.

"You don't want meat?" Seth asked in astonishment.

Justice wasn't sure how to reply. He would never insult their hospitality. "I wasn't sure you would have any to spare." Justice glanced over at the young man who had been standing in the corner for a couple of minutes. By his size he guessed this was the owner of his borrowed clothes.

"I will make sure the clothes are returned."

The young man scoffed, but Seth turned angrily. "You will not insult a guest in my house." The young man stared at his father in complete astonishment.

"But he's a *wolf*."

"And you were brought up to be better," Seth snapped and then realized what he'd said. Seth had insulted Justice more than his son had.

"I—" Seth looked horrified turning around to look at Justice, but Justice smiled and put his hand up.

"I take no offense."

Amy put a plate on the table and smiled shyly at Justice. She pushed it towards him. "Please."

Justice looked down. Three small loaves and some spread. There was a little meat that was probably a wild bird. He could see Kashir from the window so he sat down. "You're very kind."

Seth poured him some beer from a jug. Justice tore into the food, but looked up at the young man. "What's your name?"

"Kris." Justice nodded and held out his hand in the human greeting.

"I am pleased to know you. My name is Justice."

Kris hesitated for a fraction of a second before clasping Justice's hand. "Is that your name or your job?" Justice paused, immediately reminded of when Cashel had asked him nearly the same question.

"Both," Justice replied. "I am an Alpha." The disbelief was apparent on Kris's face. His father didn't look too convinced but at least he wasn't insulting. "Tell me what dealings you have had with the wolves."

Seth shot Kris a warning glance. "We don't get to see them much out here, except market day o'course." Then he winced as his son huffed his disgust. He'd obviously mentioned something that was a sore subject.

"Market day?"

Amy made a small scared sound. Justice rubbed his head.

"What happens on market day?"

"The wolves take what they want without paying, that's what happens," Kris said bitterly.

"Kris," his father bit off in warning.

"It's true," Kris yelled back. He looked at Justice. "Mom makes the best pies in the world. She used to sell them so in the winter we had some extra cash, but the wolves got a taste of them, and they took everything. She doesn't bother no more."

Sometimes the thought of what he needed to accomplish was overwhelming. "I am leading three hundred wolves to march on Tarik. We face Darius and over four hundred gammas tomorrow at dawn on the red sands to fight for the territory. We have a human rebel leader riding with us, and we are gathering as many human supporters as we can. Birds have been sent out to issue as many warnings and to ask for as much help as we can get." Justice drained his beer. It was good.

"I cannot convince you in such a short time my words are true, or that you can trust me to keep them." He stood up and took a gamble. "Do you know Jon Wilde?"

The silence stretched out. Justice smiled but Seth recovered from his shock first. "There's some Wildes about a day's ride away from here, farmers. No idea if that's the one you mean." Seth wasn't fooling anyone.

Justice grinned. "His entire family are travelling with my wolves. When I left last night, Jon was taking his place on watch. His daughter Jelly is very fond of my mate." He paused, letting that information sink in. "I have a more immediate problem, however. We think my mate has been taken by a gamma loyal to Darius. He is around three hours ahead of me. Both riding the same horse. I would be grateful—"

"I've seen him," Kris blurted out. He looked at his dad. "Out by the old barn. They were moving, but I knew one was a wolf with the uniform..." He trailed off.

Justice's pulse beat a tattoo so loud he thought they would hear it back in the desert. "He's young, about your age."

"He wasn't happy. Neither of them were. I never thought it odd until they passed and saw the young one had his wrists tied."

Justice felt the blood drain from his face.

Seth stepped forward. "You saved my son. In all my forty-three years, I've never seen a wolf go out of their way for a human, never mind save a life." He nodded to Kris. "Take him to the old barn in case they stopped to rest. I'll have messages sent. Where are we meeting?"

"Just before dawn at the derelict entrance to the red sands."

"Dad?" Kris looked at his dad. Justice could tell he was troubled.

"Go, son. I don't want to lose you in a war that if nothing changes will still be being fought when I'm an old man." He glanced at Justice. "Have you heard the rumors of the King?"

"The new one?" His mom had mentioned him.

"He's meeting with the rebel leaders so I understand. It could be a very good thing or we could all be fucked."

Justice stood and held out his hand. Seth grasped it. "Let's hope it's not the latter."

Justice could have cried when he got to the barn. It was empty. There were only two walls standing and some of the roof, but he smelled Cashel as soon as they got close. Smelled him and instantly knew he was no longer there.

"What do you want to do?" Kris jumped down from the big cart horse and looked around in frustration.

"You need to go back and help your dad. He may need messages sent to people."

Kris looked over at Justice. "What are you going to do?"

"I'm going to meet up with my wolves at dawn and defeat an Alpha, but first I'm going to get back my mate." Justice watched Kris scrunch his eyes as the young man regarded him in disbelief.

"You're very sure."

He was. His people needed him and he had no intention of letting them down. His people believed in him, and he believed in Cashel. And he had given Zane some last minute instructions. If things went wrong, Zane's responsibility was to Cashel. To keep him safe.

He also needed Darius to want to show his complete domination. To want to prove to his enemies he was invincible. Except he still had a good four hours of riding and no way to get into the pack house when he got there.

Well, there was one way. The only way of guaranteeing he would get in.

He would have to let himself be caught.

Chapter Twenty-One

"You really thought your place wasn't anywhere I chose it to be?"

Cashel was kneeling in the great hall. His hands and wrists were tied behind his back. Everyone was silent, with the exception of his father. He refused to bow his head, though; he was finished with all that.

Gaven stood next to his father. Hale was next to him, a pained look on his face. That was one of the things that saddened Cashel the most. He had thought Hale was being kind, that he would be a friend; and all the time he was his father's spy. "What do we know?" Darius turned to Hale.

"That they will be at the red sands at dawn tomorrow, my lord. From what I could learn he has three hundred gammas landed from nine ships."

Darius's growl echoed throughout the great hall. He banged his hand down on the arm of the chair and it splintered. "Why did we not know this?"

"It would have been impossible, my Alpha, without actually

taking an invasion fleet of our own to Arrides," Gaven put in smoothly.

"I want ships built," Darius demanded, "or bring the fishing fleet down from Re-Pal. I don't care what it costs. I want every wolf slaughtered immediately. There is to be nothing left, do you hear me?"

Cashel winced at Darius's words but he hadn't given up hope. Justice had to win tomorrow, he had to.

"And your son?" Gaven asked.

"Take him to the cells, but I want reports from the healers. I want to know exactly when the pup can be extracted."

"What?" Cashel gasped. *Extracted?*

Darius smiled. But it wasn't happiness, or even something as simple as amusement that caused the curve of his father's lips. It was glee. Something cold snaked its way down Cashel's back. "Once I have the heir your services will no longer be required."

Cashel didn't make a sound. He'd always known really. He'd thought he was a disappointment to his father for years, but in a small sadistic way this was even worse. His father didn't care one way or the other about him. He was an inconvenience to get rid of. What he wouldn't give right this minute to have Justice's arms wrapped around him, his hot breath on his neck, his lips firmly molded to his own. But their last words had been spoken in anger, and he might not get the chance to ever speak to him again.

Cashel stayed silent while his father railed again. Some competitor hadn't gone home from the games and was insisting they be completed. Gaven should send a gamma to his room with a knife.

He's mad, Cashel thought, and shot a look at Gaven. Justice had told him Gaven had released him but his face was a smooth mask. Gaven had risked a lot to free Justice and he still didn't know why, not really. But it wouldn't happen again, he knew that. His father still spat out nonsense. Who he was going to kill. How he was going to do it. Cashel could almost tune him out.

"It would be impossible for the traitor to plan all this unaided. Who is it? Who here helped you?"

Cashel jerked. The question was suddenly directed at him. Darius gestured to Gaven and Gaven stepped forward and hauled Cashel to his feet. Feet that were numb, and he stood awkwardly. Gaven firmly clasped his arm.

"Who is helping you?" His father nearly spat the question at Cashel, and Cashel didn't dare look at Gaven. He could say Gaven had released Justice. The beta had always shown how he despised him. How he thought Cashel a pathetic waste of space who was not good enough, would never be good enough to be an Alpha. But even as Cashel thought it he knew he never would tell. Gaven hadn't freed Justice because it was the right thing to do, he had just done it to make his own life easier, and even if Cashel lost his life, Justice was safe.

"You can still deliver a pup with two broken arms." Darius nodded to Gaven.

Cashel cried out as fiery pain shot up his arm as Gaven twisted it.

"It was the humans," Cashel lied. "The small one was an accomplished thief and picked the lock, but the top door was too strong. They had to let Justice and the wolves go because they needed an Alpha's strength to break it."

Cashel was on the floor before his mind had time to process what had happened. His head pounded and his cheek throbbed.

"My lord," Gaven cautioned. "The pup."

"Never refer to that abomination as an Alpha." Darius growled and Gaven took an instinctive step back, but before anyone could say more, a gamma suddenly ran into the room and straight up to Gaven. His eyebrows rose as he listened to what the wolf said.

He turned to Darius. "We have him."

Cashel dragged himself upright and Gaven nodded to the gamma that had delivered the message to guard him. He gripped Cashel's arm but he wasn't rough.

Cashel's head was spinning with the force of his father's hand, so much so he imagined the floor starting to shake. The doors opened once more and a deep growl echoed loudly in the hall, so loud he wanted to cover his ears.

Cashel froze. No, no, *impossible.* He hardly dared raise his eyes to look but then a snarling, angry, totally beautiful, black Alpha wolf was led in, chains pulled taught by six gammas that looked like they were struggling to hold him.

Justice? What had gone so badly wrong that he was caught? He should have been miles away, and then he knew when the deep amber eyes fixed on his and shone in triumph. His Alpha had come for him. He would only have allowed himself to be caught for one reason...

Me.

Moments seemed to pass. Words were spoken, but Cashel didn't hear them. None of it mattered. For all time Cashel belonged to Justice, and he should have known that.

Justice blurred and stood up completely human. He sneered at Darius.

"You will lose tomorrow. Just so you know."

The first gamma's fist that connected with Justice's face made Cashel cry out, but Justice barely moved. He stared defiantly at Darius. It was almost as if he was baiting him. Darius roared in anger, claws breaking through the hand as he pulled it back.

"Alpha," Gaven urged. "You want him defeated tomorrow, not killed tonight. He needs to be slain in view of his pack and the humans. Humiliate him. *Destroy* him. Teach everyone what happens when they dare to question your authority."

Darius heaved in a breath. His nostrils flaring with the effort to contain himself. His hand fell and his claws retracted. Cashel took a shaky breath. "Lock them up but triple the guards." He looked at Gaven. "I want him chained and brought to the sands just before dawn. Then they can all see what it means to think to defy me."

"My lord?" Hale took a step. "And what I was promised?"

Darius turned incredulous eyes to Hale. "You are lucky you are not being put to death alongside him."

"B-But, you agreed," Hale's face was ashen.

"Of course I agreed," Darius scoffed. "You come to me and tell me you are trusted by them? That you can get close to the traitor and return what belongs to me—and then you tell me that the slave you lust after *is a wolf?*" The last words he nearly screamed.

Helena? Was all this about Helena?

Hale didn't move. He looked completely defeated.

Cashel watched as Hale nearly crumpled before his eyes. He had thought he would get Helena. It had to be some agreement between him and Darius, but when Cashel had revealed who she was, he had decided to take Cashel anyway, hoping that Darius would relent. The foolish thing was that Justice's victory would have given him the right to pursue Helena.

Unless... and Cashel suddenly understood. Hale was a gamma. A human slave was nothing, and easily accessible. A mother-Alpha, however, was a completely different thing. Was that it? Did Hale think once he had found out who Helena was she would be inaccessible, or even worse—he had never thought about Helena's choice at all? It was more likely Hale was sure that a human female didn't have any. Helena had never shown any interest in Hale in Cashel's presence, and according to what Helena had told him yesterday, omegas mated once, and for life.

Gaven bent down and Cashel was dragged to his feet. He stumbled after Justice as Gaven led the procession back to the cells. The gammas threw them both into the same one at Gaven's instruction and locked the doors. Gaven gestured to them to leave and he waited until they had left. Cashel's pulse quickened. Was he going to release them a second time?

"You fool," he spat at Justice. Justice leapt to his feet from where the gammas had thrown him in. He looked at Gaven very intently.

"There is nothing I can do this time." He glared at Cashel. "I hope he was worth it, because not only will you lose your life tomorrow, you will lose the battle."

Justice ignored Gaven. He turned and looked at Cashel. "Really?" he said quietly. The amber eyes burning in their intensity. "Would we all not risk everything for those we love?"

"There is nothing more I can do," Gaven said in disgust, and he whirled around, shouting for the gammas to open the massive door at the end. Cashel heard it clank shut. He opened his mouth to say something, but Justice moved so fast to cradle his face gently in his big hands he was silenced.

"My love," he breathed.

"What have you done?" Cashel cried. "You came deliberately." He shook. "They will kill you," he whispered and his knees gave way and his voice broke with the horror of it all. Justice held him close as the tears ran unchecked down his face. He clasped Justice tight, overtaken by harsh sobs, crying out at the futility, the helplessness. He wanted Justice to live so desperately. Justice just held onto him and whispered how he was loved, and that he would never, ever, let Cashel go ever again.

"My darling, can I?" Justice whispered as Cashel's sobs quietened. Cashel raised his head and stood up.

"Can you?" Cashel queried, but Justice was already on his knees, his hands clasping Cashel's hips, his face hovering just in front of Cashel's belly, and he gently tugged his shirt up. Reverently he leaned his face forward, lips hovering and he pressed the lightest, sweetest kiss on the slightly rounded skin. Tears welled up in Cashel's eyes again as Justice closed his own and grew quiet, and so still.

After what seemed like forever he opened them, looked up and Cashel was lost in burnished gold that filled him, bathed him, and settled his heart. "She's strong. She has a pure heart."

"She?" Cashel repeated weakly.

Justice nodded. "The Enfantata told me." He smiled. "My mom," he added. "I am so sorry I doubted you."

Cashel drew in a quick breath. "But you didn't doubt your mom." He believed her, not him. He tried to step away but Justice wouldn't let him.

"I was so wrong, and so foolish. I will never make that mistake again."

Cashel eyed him in complete frustration. "But you did. You got yourself caught. You need to lead your people to victory tomorrow, and you can't do that in here."

"I have every intention of leading my people tomorrow, and we will be victorious, but I could not risk you left in here." Justice rose smoothly to his feet and cupped Cashel's face. Cashel pressed his lips together. He badly wanted Justice to wrap him in his arms and tell him everything was going to be all right, but he was very much afraid it wasn't.

"I have ached for your touch," Justice murmured, his voice full of gravel, full of need, and Cashel swayed closer, an invisible thread pulling him close. "I have dreamed of your kiss." Justice bent and pressed his lips to Cashel's neck. "I need your touch—every part of you—for the rest of my life."

Cashel twisted his face away. "Which could quite easily be over at dawn," he said desperately.

But Justice was unstoppable and whispered that he wanted to kiss him forever so he might as well start right now. Justice slid his warm hands over Cashel's back and tugged at his shirt, pulling it over his head. His amber eyes shone just before he dipped his head and drew one of Cashel's nipples fully between his lips. The scrape of his teeth making Cashel arch in pleasure. "Come lie with me," he said huskily and drew him to the pallet.

"Shouldn't we—" But his words were lost, drowned in emotion, heat and want. Justice laid him down and leaned in. There was barely room for them both, but Justice didn't seem to care. He dipped his head to mouth Cashel's skin. His neck, shoulders, chest.

Cashel's arms slid up and around Justice as he worked magic with his lips.

Soon Cashel was writhing underneath him, planting kisses wherever his lips met skin. His body ached and his skin felt on fire. He couldn't move and Cashel unleashed a frustrated growl that sounded loud in the quiet of the cells.

Justice lifted his head, lips swollen, the faint flush of need on his throat. "You growled," he said in complete astonishment. "I have never heard your wolf before."

Cashel nipped along the line of his jaw. "You're gonna feel him in a minute if you don't move." Justice smirked and Cashel laughed. It was madness, but he suddenly felt so much lighter. That they could laugh, if only for a second.

"I'm frightened of squashing you." Justice huffed a sigh.

"Lie down," Cashel instructed. Justice quirked an eyebrow at the order, but obediently lay on his back as Cashel sat up. "You know I don't need slick with you?"

Justice's pupils widened and he growled deep and low. Cashel was very satisfied at the reaction to his innocent sounding question. "Why is that?"

"I don't know any other male omegas. Your mom says there are some up north, but I'm guessing it's something to do with that."

Justice was silent and Cashel could nearly see the consternation as it flashed across his face. "And no, before you ask—it's only with you." His breath hitched. "Because it's a true mating, not an arranged one."

Cashel marveled at the huge smile that spread across Justice's face, but didn't say anything more. He stretched his leg over Justice's thighs and straddled him. Justice gripped his hips to keep him in place, but Cashel wasn't going anywhere.

He kneeled forward. "You just need to feel me," he whispered, and brought Justice's hand behind him to press a finger near his hole. He didn't try to hide the whimper as Justice's finger grazed his entrance.

Justice swallowed. "That's incredible." Cashel flung his head back as he thrust his hips forward, wanting friction. Justice immediately obliged and took hold of his cock with his other hand. "Sweetheart," Justice said in wonder, but the word trailed off into a long moan when Cashel bucked against Justice's length.

"You're stunning," Justice whispered, as he swirled his finger around Cashel's slick entrance and dipped the tip inside. Cashel groaned and rolled his hips, his cock swelling and throbbing under Justice's tight fingers. "I want to be in you so bad."

Cashel nodded. "Lift me," he begged.

"Too soon," Justice answered and slipped his finger all the way.

Cashel cried out and pushed against Justice. "Please," he cried out. "I can't—" He was on the edge already. Justice had taken him from interested to desperate in barely moments.

"We have all night," Justice soothed, but the words gripped his heart and reminded him they may only ever have that.

"Make me forget." Cashel's tears ran unchecked again. He wanted to forget. To be lost. To drown in urgent, throbbing need that stole his breath and drowned his fear.

Justice growled, the sound urgent and full of understanding. His massive hands cupped the side of Cashel's hips as he lifted him. For a second, Cashel was suspended and he stared at Justice. He was safe, needed, loved. Everything swirled in those deep amber eyes. Every promise Justice could make was written there, indelibly, because it came from his soul. Justice lowered Cashel, inch by breathtaking inch, as he slowly impaled him on his ravenous cock.

Cashel gasped as Justice eased him down. Full as he had never been. Cashel moaned and closed his eyes against the sparks that seemed to burst in his belly. Justice lifted him once more and Cashel cried out as Justice's cock touched places inside him that lit him up, and bled ecstasy into every corner of his soul.

"Touch yourself," Justice commanded and Cashel curled his fingers around his hot, rigid length.

"Justice," Cashel stammered, quickly surrendering to ever urgent pressure in his body. He couldn't wait any longer. He had to come.

For a final time Justice thrust up as Cashel dropped down. Brilliance exploded around him as pleasure tore through his body.

"*Ma vuta,*" Justice cried out as he froze for a heartbeat, before Cashel felt a frantic pulse deep inside him and then incredible heat as Justice thrust again and again. *My heart.*

And Cashel knew finally, he was.

Chapter Twenty-Two

Justice lay awake long after Cashel had finally closed his eyes. If his mom was correct then because Cashel had suppressed his ability for so long, only a huge emotional trigger would enable him to find his gift and use it.

And the only thing Justice could think of was the likelihood of his death. It was a gamble. A huge gamble. But Justice wasn't concerned with himself. He was deeply worried about the stress to his pregnant mate and the effect of such a situation on the baby. But he was all out of other ideas. He knew Darius would kill not only the pup but also Cashel if he thought he would lose tomorrow, to stop there ever being any chance of Justice having them, and Justice simply couldn't take that risk.

Cashel had thought him mad when he had tried to explain to him he could summon energy from the earth itself. He had only ever pulled water from the earth to help the animals in the drought of Solonara's summer. He was so relieved Darius had never been interested enough to further pursue Cashel's gift, and just assumed he was a grower like everyone else had.

Justice cupped the mound on Cashel's belly. It seemed more

The Alpha Prince

pronounced than even two days ago when Cashel had tried to show him. He knew pups grew at an amazingly quick rate, but their pup couldn't be born before sixty days and survive. Whatever Darius's plans were, he simply couldn't let that happen.

He would die himself first, and if everything went wrong tomorrow, he prayed his last desperate message he had gotten Jon to send reached the so called Alpha King. He didn't have the faith that this King was the answer to everyone's prayers, but whatever else he was, it just wasn't possible for him to be worse than Darius.

He heard the outside door's bolt slide back and kissed the top of Cashel's head to wake him. Gaven, Hale and five gammas all appeared at the cell door.

Justice stared at Gaven. The beta stared back. Justice could see some measure of regret, but it wasn't enough.

Cashel got up and Justice rose to his feet, tucking Cashel near him as the gammas unlocked the cell door. Gaven dragged Cashel from him as gammas swarmed Justice, clamping thick chains around each ankle and each wrist. Lastly, they fastened a heavy metal collar around his throat and looped all the chains through a ring. Much to his frustration he couldn't stand tall or take long strides because the chains were simply too short to allow him to raise his head. He knew bent over and hunched was the image Darius wanted to present of him to his people. His growl echoed warningly.

He panicked when he couldn't see Cashel as he was roughly pushed forward towards the small cobbled area with an enclosed high fence. He smelled Darius immediately along with the four massive gammas that stood next to him, and knew immediately that the iron bars they all held were weapons.

"You are here to teach your people a lesson."

Justice opened his mouth to point out sarcastically that his people weren't here, but the first gamma stepped forward and took his legs out from under him with such force he was sure the bones had snapped.

"Not his head," was the only instruction Darius gave as blow after blow rained down on him. He heard Cashel sob, but there was nothing he could do, as sheer, blinding white-hot agony ripped through his body with such violence it was all he could do to breathe, and then because his chest was like a vice he stopped doing even that. Time held nothing. No meaning, no progression. He was no longer anything but the torment itself. Pain wasn't something happening to him, an experience. It was him. His whole body was a raw, bleeding nerve ending and his suffering would never end.

He must have passed out because he was being held between two gammas. *In. Out.* The force of trying to get oxygen into his lungs. The air even stung as it passed his lips. He knew his face was wet. Was he crying? No, he didn't think he had the energy, but he felt the water sting as it landed on the cuts on his face.

It's raining.

"Much better," came the satisfied words. He took another breath and wished it were his last, but his body betrayed him once more and he had to take another.

He opened his eyes to near blackness. He'd thought the dawn was nearly upon them, but the sky looked inky dark.

"Good," Darius said flatly. "Throw him in the cage and we will get moving. Then when we see his wolves I'm going to make them surrender...and then I will kill him anyway."

The two gammas roughly pushed him forward. He immediately stopped at the sight of the metal crate loaded onto a cart and started struggling, but he could barely stand so his struggles were ineffectual. He heard the sobs and managed to focus on Cashel. He wanted to tell him everything was going to be all right, and with an angry snarl summoned the miniscule bit of fight left in him. He would not be locked into a cage, but Gaven simply drew his knife and pointed it at Cashel until Justice stopped and allowed the gammas to lock him in. Cashel was dragged onto another cart with two gammas, but at least he wasn't caged, and the rest of the gammas mounted their horses to begin the ride to the red sands. It was a good two miles from the city and the oppressive silence crept over him as he tried to summon his strength as his head began to clear.

It was eerie here. He knew the sands had been the sites of the silk cocoons years ago when Darius's predecessor had started harvesting them, but the Nay'eth flies had killed them all and they could do nothing with the dry cracked earth that was left. His mom had told him that the humans refused to work in the area, convinced the very ground was still infested. Nothing ever grew, and the horses spooked when they were made to cross. If it had just been the humans who were reluctant, Darius would have forced the area to be used, but even the wolves hated it, and Darius had enough other land not to care about a dry barren area far from the south of the city.

The wind whipped around them, and the silence was ominous. Even barely conscious he caught the nervous looks of the gammas positioned on each side of the cage. Something was spooking them.

Justice tried to look at Cashel but the big gamma walking at the side of the cart with him completely blocked his view, so he turned to the expanse in front of him as the twin suns rose from the south. The horses snorted as the ground changed color from the dark packed earth in the city to the red of the sands and he could see the rolling black clouds as they passed overhead. He could see the far gate and wondered if any wolves bothered to guard what was left—an enormous, crumbling wall, once the entrance to the garrison when Tarik just housed the army. It stood forgotten now. The gates had long since rotted and the entrance moved to the east years before.

Justice smelled the wolves before he saw them and looked up. Darius had brought his entire army. Hundreds of wolves in long lines all sat astride horse after horse and moved nearer as one.

He nearly laughed in despair. They had been wrong. There were more than four hundred wolves in Darius's army. It was more like a thousand.

The black clouds parted for an instant and the horses nearest to him shied. Another scent hit his nostrils but this was familiar. Justice turned to the derelict gates. His wolves—every one of them—stood silently, their horses shoulder to shoulder. They had made no noise. It was as if they had simply just appeared.

Justice smiled. He knew it was a trick of the light, as if they hadn't been there moments ago, but he had wished he had been close enough to witness Darius's reaction when he had first seen them. He smiled again as the horses all took two steps forward in perfect synchronization and then he saw the second line behind them.

Humans. As far as the eye could see men stood or rode the odd cart horse. Hundreds of them. They carried no fancy swords. No jewels encrusted the makeshift spears or forks that would normally be tossing straw and hay. But one by one they stood as determined as the wolves next to them.

Together. Man and wolf. Just as it should be.

"My lord," Gaven stammered, the fear apparent in his voice. Justice could see Darius's betas all glancing at each other. They had been expecting a swift victory. They hadn't been expecting a fair fight.

Zane sat at their head on a large black horse, but significantly, Kashir—untethered and unmounted—was next to him. Justice had left Kashir by the gate before he had walked into the city. He knew the horse would wait until Zane and his people arrived. To his people the horse was significant and showed their absolute confidence that Justice would be riding him to victory. Darius was simply being shown what he would never have.

Darius's stallion shied and he yanked it still with a snarl, but glanced over at Justice's wolves. "I am Darius, Territorial Alpha of all Solonara," he bellowed. "You will all kneel before me and offer your submission. In return for your pledge, I will spare the life of your Alpha."

Justice watched as Zane walked his horse forward.

"You speak for everyone?" Darius asked.

Zane shook his head. "My Alpha speaks for all his people but I will confirm his words. Today isn't just about one person. Today is the righting of a great wrong that has been perpetrated against all the people of Solonara. Wolves and humans equally. My Alpha has commanded we rise against you, and nothing you can do or say will alter that course."

Justice heard Cashel's gasp of horror, but he kept his gaze fixed on Zane. His fingers became claws as he struggled to contain his wolf. The collar would cut off his air if he couldn't break it, but it wasn't just that. Everything in him screamed to look at Cashel. Everything in him screamed to offer comfort, reassurance, protection.

But he couldn't. Because whether Justice was going to die or not, Cashel had to believe he would.

Cashel's face was wet and in an abstract way, he wondered how it was possible he had any tears left at all. Justice must be thinking the worst. He wouldn't look at him. He must have been convinced he was going to die and trying to keep that from him. Cashel looked beseechingly at Zane but all the beta's attention was on his Alpha. Cashel didn't blame him.

"You either kneel before me or your so-called Alpha dies," Darius repeated.

Cashel watched the sadness leech into Zane's eyes. He heard the rasp of metal as one of the gammas drew his sword and the four gammas each pulled Justice's chains taught. Zane moved restlessly and Kashir danced. Both sensed Justice's life was on a knife edge of his own choosing.

"No," Justice's voice carried clear and compelling to his wolves. Every one of them heard the order and every one of them understood. The low growl from his throat held every bit of anger, humiliation and desperation for his people, but he would not surrender them. He would die fighting for every wolf. Cashel understood that, as much as every one of Justice's people.

"You will submit to me," Darius screamed and jumped from his horse, striding towards where Justice was being made to forcibly kneel, his arms outstretched. One of the gammas yanked his head back with a fist to his hair. Darius pulled his Kataya from his belt and laughed wildly, looking to the sky as water rained down on them all.

Murmurs rose from Darius's army as they looked upwards. Thunder echoed in the still of the morning. More horses shied, their riders desperately trying to quiet the animals that were becoming as panicked as their riders.

Cashel glanced at Justice's wolves. Not one of them was moving. Every horse was as still and calm as its rider.

Cashel wasn't. He struggled as the gammas held him tight. Justice's wolves were all going to let Justice die under his father's sword. No one was doing anything.

Another crack of thunder seemed to come from nowhere. Gaven's horse reared but Darius didn't even seem to notice.

"Justice," Cashel cried in desperation and looked at Zane. Why were they not moving? Why weren't they attacking? Why was no one lifting a weapon and charging?

Then another horse moved closer to Zane. It was Sanjeli and Helena. Cashel's heart jolted in his chest, and he heard the gasp to his side. It was Hale, and he was gazing bereft at what his greed and selfishness would forever prevent him from ever having. For a second Cashel wondered why she was here. She wasn't a warrior. She was...

An omega.

Suddenly, as she stared right into Cashel's eyes, he understood. Everything Helena had said rushed through him. Omegas rode into battle with their Alphas. They weren't pampered princesses, they were warriors. He was a warrior. A warrior of the desert. A warrior of Solonara.

A warrior of Askara.

Cashel stopped struggling to free himself and looked at the black sky. The wind whistled around him. Sand rose and whipped itself around and between Darius's army. Thunder roared and the rain hammered down on them. Cries went up as horses skidded and broke formation. Riders fell. Huge rents appeared in the packed, red earth and many gammas abandoned their lines as they tried to stop their panicked horses from bolting.

And yet in all the chaos, the noise, the panic, the white stallion stood as immovable as the rest of Justice's wolves and simply waited for its rider.

"Darius?" Gaven jumped down from his horse, intent on his Alpha. "This is madness, we must flee."

Darius snarled. "Flee?" he said the disgust dripping from his voice. "Flee where?"

Gaven rushed nearer, his eyes beseeching. "I have it all planned. A ship waiting to take us from Salem-dar. It is already provisioned, loaded with gold. We can finally find somewhere to be together—" He stopped, seeming to realize his mistake as soon as the words were uttered.

"Loaded with whose gold?" Darius asked, snarling. Without warning, he brought his arm down, his Kataya cutting a red line across Gaven's chest. The beta glanced down in horror as he staggered, seeming stunned at the huge wound that opened across his chest.

"Darius," he choked, bloody froth forming at his lips, "my mate..."

"Mate?" Darius sneered.

Cashel watched in horror and realization. It explained why Gaven had remained loyal to his father for so long. Why he had wanted Cashel and Justice to leave. Why he had never had any other ambition than staying with his Alpha. Cashel had always known a breeder had birthed him, and realized why Darius had never taken a mate: Gaven was his mate, and in all his greed and insanity striving for more wealth and more power he hadn't taken the one person who could make him whole.

Gaven reached out blindly to Darius, but Darius had already forgotten him as the beta sank to his knees. Claws erupted from Gaven's hands and his cry became a howl as he tried to shift.

But he hit the sands as a human. A dead human.

More horses panicked and broke formation; the gammas holding

Cashel had long since run. The gammas holding Justice looking ready to bolt as fast as the horses.

"Hold him," Darius screamed as he whipped around toward Justice. The gammas tightened their grip, claws erupting and digging in to Justice's shoulders making the blood run, and Cashel had a second to take a breath as his father lifted his sword to cleave Justice's head from his body. Cashel raised his face to the sky and reached out his hands in silent demand as if he could bend the sky itself to his will.

Something, in his head, in his heart—*in his very soul* —stirred, and he just knew. Justice, his mate, his whole life balanced on the whim of a madman too unstable to be allowed to live, and Cashel was the only one with the power to end it.

The sky seemed to explode.

A huge bolt of lightning ripped the clouds in half and shot down, spearing Darius even as he brought his sword down. Darius lit up, his mouth widened on a silent scream, his body frozen as millions of jolts tore through him. His arms flung back and his body arched as the power of the very earth he was standing on finally rebelled at his cruelty.

The wolves holding Justice sprang away and he leapt to his feet, snapping his chains.

Darius was dead before he toppled to the ground.

Cashel's knees gave way but Justice was faster and his strong arms scooped him up safely. Cashel smiled. There was no water on his face now, but what seemed like a million kisses raining down on him instead.

"Justice," Cashel breathed out his name, exulting in being held, in being safe, in being loved... Cashel lifted his face as the clouds parted and the sun's rays shined down. Horses stilled and one by one what was left of Darius's army came to stand together. Everyone stared at Justice as if waiting for something.

Justice smiled down at Cashel and carefully helped him upright. "Come, my omega warrior, and meet your troops."

The Alpha Prince

Cashel accepted Justice's hand and they both turned to where Zane sat astride his horse. Justice straightened and watched as all his people stood still. Wolves watched. The humans kept silent. Then the nearest of Darius's gammas abruptly went down on one knee. He bent his head, and brought his fist to his chest. "My Alpha."

It started a wave. A huge crescendo of words and movement as every wolf and human did exactly the same, and in the resulting silence the white stallion calmly walked forward to be reunited with his rider. Justice placed a gentle hand on Kashir's muzzle and then bent and swung Cashel up and astride the horse. In a second Justice was behind him.

Together they walked to greet their people.

Epilogue

Seven weeks later

T he doors to the grand hall banged open and Justice looked up in consternation. He was having what was probably one of the most important meetings of his life and now wasn't the time for any of his new staff to simply barge in.

Luca chuckled and his eyes lit up at the young man who strode into the room. Justice relaxed and leaned back in his chair, smiling also. In the week his King and pure omega had been visiting, he was getting used to Kit's sudden bursts of energy and seeming ability to interrupt Luca and his advisors every moment he could. Sam, Luca's beta-commander, groaned quietly and rolled his eyes.

"Don't you roll those eyes at me, Sam," Kit warned and strode right up to Luca, who pushed away from the table, giving enough room for Kit to sit on his lap.

"What can I do for you?" Luca nuzzled Kit's neck.

Justice grinned. The words were as optimistic as they were suggestive. He stifled a groan as the gorgeous vision of Cashel popped into his head. Justice had managed to creep out of bed this morning without waking his mate. Between his inability to get comfortable, and their daughter's acrobatics all night, his poor mate hadn't gotten any rest. Justice just managed to stop adjusting his breeches—they seemed to be a lot tighter than they were a second ago.

He rose. The meeting was nearly at an end anyway and he wanted to see Cashel. His territory was secure and as soon as the baby was born and Cashel was fit to travel, they would be heading for Naera. Luca and Kit had decided to delay the coronation until all the territory Alphas could be there, which basically meant when Cashel had birthed their daughter—due now any day.

"You," Kit leaned forward and brushed a kiss on Luca's lips, "can't do anything for me at the moment." Luca pouted, if that was possible for a king. Kit glanced over at Justice. "Justice, however, can get his Alpha-butt upstairs to where his mate is about to give birth."

For a second Justice seemed to have forgotten how to breathe, but then his legs sprang into action without any conscious command to tell them so, and he was running from the room.

He heard the chuckles from everyone as he raced up the stairs. He nodded to the gammas on duty outside their rooms and quickly strode through. Helena stood up from where she had been sitting on the bed and Cashel turned his head to look at him. He lifted a hand and Justice strode over quickly and caught it, bringing it to his lips.

"It's time, Son," Helena said. It was the echo of the very same words his mom had spoken to him six long years ago, but this time they were accompanied by a smile.

Justice gazed at Cashel's flushed face. "Are you in pain? Can I—?"

Cashel had started to shake his head but then he grimaced and squeezed Justice's hand so tight, Justice winced.

Helena sprang into action and started ordering Justice to strip the covers off Cashel. Make sure the fire was lit so the room isn't cold. Make sure Cashel has cold water to sip. Rub his back. Rub his feet. Sit behind him when he wants to lean back against Justice. Hold him when he wants to get on his knees.

Hours passed. Kit kept popping in to sympathize and help, but Helena had everything organized and didn't seem to worry in the least. Apparently, she had communicated with Luca's younger sister, who had experience and knew what to expect when a man gave birth.

Justice didn't want to know. When Kit had regaled them with the story of his twins' birth, Cashel and Helena had listened with rapt attention. Justice had just felt nauseous. He was staying firmly at Cashel's head and avoiding the business end of the proceedings. Cashel had even managed to doze as Justice gently cradled his head at one point during the long, long day.

"Arghh," Cashel screamed again and pushed against Justice. Justice sat behind him, holding him carefully. He glanced at his mom's flushed face. Surely this was going on too long?

Another ripple raced over Cashel's belly and Helena cried in delight. She glanced up at Cashel. "Push, sweetie. I can see a head."

Justice had no idea where Cashel got the strength from so suddenly. He had thought his mate exhausted, but four pushes later and the room was filled with indignant wails as his mom laughed and wrapped a wriggling, squalling bundle of humanity up in a soft drying cloth and laid her tenderly in Cashel's arms.

Tears were running down Cashel's face as he gazed at their daughter in awe. Justice bent down and brushed his lips on her damp forehead and then kissed Cashel too.

The Alpha Prince

"She's beautiful," Cashel sighed.

"You both are," Justice vowed as he gazed at his exhausted but contented mate. He cupped Cashel's face gently and stared into the blue eyes he loved so much. "Did I tell you how much I love you this morning? How much I adore you? And how lucky I am?"

Cashel smiled and relaxed back into Justice's arms. "You just did."

"And I will keep on doing it. Every morning for the rest of our lives," Justice promised.

"What's her name?" Helena asked, reaching over. The fingers on her granddaughter's tiny hand wrapped around hers.

Justice looked at Cashel and Cashel smiled and nodded.

"Tar-el-sami," Justice answered. "Sami for short." It was perfect. In Askaran, Tar-el-sami meant dawn of a new day.

That was what she was and what she represented. Not just for Arrides, or Solonara, but for the whole of Askara.

The dawn of a new day.

The End.

Also by Victoria Sue

Love MPreg?

Check out these series and single title by Victoria Sue.

Standalone Novel

Daddy's Girl*

An Alpha who hates omegas. An omega who hates Alphas. Forced together by circumstances, both men are determined to see their arrangement through. Except the longer they stay together, neither of them is sure they want it to end.

Series

Sirius Wolves*

According to legend, when humankind is at its most desperate, the goddess Sirius will send three of the most powerful werewolf shifters ever created to save mankind. The alphas, Blaze, Conner and Darric, find their omega in Aden. They become true mates, fulfilling the ancient prophecy and forming Orion's Circle. Now, the battle against terrorist group The Winter Circle has begun.

Shifter Rescue*

911 for vulnerable shifters when there's no where else for them to run.

Unexpected Daddies

Daddy kink with heart and heat. No ABDL.

Heroes and Babies

Protective men find love while fighting to save a child. Contemporary suspense with heart-pounding action.

Guardians of Camelot

Hundreds of years ago, facing defeat, the witch Morgana sent monsters into the future to vanquish a humanity King Arthur wouldn't be able to save. The King might have won the battle, but now, centuries later, a few chosen men will have to fight the war. To battle an ancient evil, the greatest weapon each hero will have is each other.

Enhanced World

This series follows an enhanced H.E.R.O. team to provide the right mix of action and romance. This series is the perfect for fans of romance with a blend of military/law enforcement, urban fantasy and superheroes. As one reviewer put it, "This story was like S.W.A.T. meets X-men meets The Fantastic Four."

His First*

Omegaverse at it's finest! Set in the future, these novels pack in all the feels, while still wrapping up with a wonderfully sweet ending. Whether you've never tried MPREG or you're just looking for your next favorite Alpha/Omega pairing, check out the His First series.

Rainbow Key

Rainbow Key is an idyllic island retreat off the west coast of Florida. Think wedding destination, white sandy beaches, lurve... except at the moment Joshua is struggling to pay the electricity bill, they've no paying customers, and even if they did they can't afford the repairs from the devastating hurricane that struck three years ago. Then there's Matt who just got let out of prison, Charlie who ran away from home, and Ben, a famous model until a devastating house fire destroyed his face. Welcome to Rainbow Key — held together by love, family, and sticky tape.

Kingdom of Askara*

The Kingdom of Askara has been torn apart by conflict for centuries, where humans exist as subservient beings to their werewolf masters. Legend says it will only be able to heal itself when an Alpha King and a pure omega are mated and crowned together, but a pure omega hasn't been born in over a thousand years.

Innocents

A captivating historical duology set in Regency London. The Innocent Auction: It started with a plea for help and ended with forbidden love, the love between a Viscount and a stable-boy. An impossible love and a guarantee of the hangman's noose. The Innocent Betrayal: Two broken souls. One so damaged he thinks he doesn't deserve love, and one so convinced he would never find it he has stopped looking. Danger, lies, and espionage. The fate of hundreds of English soldier's lives depending on them to trust each other, to work together.

Pure

A madman has been kidnapping, torturing and murdering submissives. Join Callum, Joe and Damon as they race against the clock to stop the killings, while they each find love with a submissive. This trilogy of romantic thrillers is set against the backdrop of BDSM club Pure.

Hunter's Creek*

The Hunter's Creek novels will draw you in with action and keep you hooked until each satisfying HEA. This series won't disappoint fans of shifters, fated mates or MPREG.

*Stories contain MPREG

About Victoria Sue

Bullets and Babies

Victoria Sue has spent the last six years creating lots of stories, and sometimes other worlds, where boys can fall in love and lust with other boys. Not that she makes it easy for them and has often been accused of plotting many evil ways her guys have to struggle through to get their Happy Ever After.

These days, most of them have to dodge bullets, serial killers, and even kidnappers in between having contractions and concentrating on their breathing exercises.

After all, everyone knows that while making cute babies is fun, actually giving birth can sometimes be a little harder.

www.VictoriaSue.com
Facebook Group - Victoria Sue's Crew

Made in United States
Orlando, FL
14 April 2024